PEARLS OF ASIA

PEARLS OF ASIA

A LOVE STORY

⬤

LEE GEIGER

Preface

B ECAUSE I'VE BEEN blessed with the talent to write amusing Christmas letters, and so many people seem to enjoy The Marginal Prophet (marginalprophet.com), my online news-letter, I've been told many times I should write a book. I agreed, as penning a novel has always been one of my lifelong dreams. The problem was figuring out what to write about.

In the fall of 2000, I made my first visit to Asia SF, a wildly popular San Francisco restaurant staffed by "gender illusionists." The food and ambiance were addictive, and it quickly became one of my favorite "must go" places. Over the years I had the pleasure of getting to know the special "Ladies of Asia," and I always thought their stories would make a great book. However, I didn't think writing a biography or a series of short stories would be the right way to go. But a murder mystery, wrapped around a love story, might do the trick. I even came up with a catchy title: Pearls of Asia. It sounded pretty cool.

In May of 2005, I shared a dinner with Belle Yang, a highly regarded author and painter who was also a classmate of mine at Carmel High School in beautiful Carmel, CA. Belle had always encouraged me to become a writer, though I had no idea how to get started. Over penne pasta and red wine, I told Belle about a story I had brewing in the dark corners of my mind; a romantic mystery, revolving around a unique San Francisco restaurant, that contained elements of *Law and Order*, *The Crying Game*, *Sex and The City*, and *Cheers*. "You HAVE to write that story," she said.

One night in the summer of 2007, I stumbled into Asia SF after a Giant's baseball game and recognized authors Danielle Steele and Jackie Collins having dinner together. After downing four martinis in fifteen minutes, I summoned the courage to introduce myself and relay to these megastars of the publishing world my idea for a novel. "Darling, you HAVE to write that story," proclaimed Ms. Collins, who could not have been nicer.

On Thanksgiving 2009, at one o'clock in the morning, I found myself staring at my bedroom ceiling. A series of events over the prior days, weeks and months had been personally challenging, and sleep was difficult to come by. To distract myself, I thought about my story, when suddenly a possible ending popped into my head. I jumped out of bed and ran downstairs to my home office and wrote a five-page outline. Hours later, I typed the first word of my first novel.

What an incredible journey this has been.

ACKNOWLEDGMENTS

T HEY SAY IT takes a village to raise a child. Perhaps, but it takes a small army to write a book. I owe a round of drinks to the following:

To Belle Yang, my writing mentor, guru, spiritual advisor, and former classmate from the Carmel High School class of 1978. Belle threw down the gauntlet and challenged me to become a writer. In the process, she helped me find myself. Thank you, Belle. You saved me.

To Ivory Madison of **Redroom.com**, my first editor. Ivory taught me the concept of "The Hero's Journey." She also told me there are three phases to creating a successful book: writing, editing, and marketing. Each one is critical, and each one is difficult. She was right. Damn.

To Alan Rinzler, my second editor. Alan set the story on its proper course, and put in motion the tools for a possible series. Numerous people told me Alan was a legend in the publishing business. That was an understatement. What people didn't tell me was how much fun we'd have working together.

To those who were kind enough to volunteer their valuable time to reading my earlier drafts and delivering indispensable feedback; Scott Johnson, Susan Klein, Susan Morgan, Julianne Goldberg, Barbara Galligan, Angel Manaois, Carin Hawkins,

Sheila Krystal, Pat Moran, Kerry Lacy, Pam Eveleth, Ericka San Miguel, Kyle Bradbury, Jill Malley, Gerald Katz, Kimi Cole, and Victoria Parker. Yes, there really is a Victoria Parker.

To Cecilia Chung, who helped me to overcome the most painful episode of writer's block I encountered writing this book. A San Francisco-based human rights and HIV policy advocate, Cecilia is a leader who has the heart of a lion and the soul of a child.

To Katherine Patti, who spent countless hours painstakingly copyediting the manuscript not once, but twice. She also became the novel's cheerleader, encouraging me to aggressively pursue every avenue known to mankind to market *Pearl of Asia*. Katherine is more than a long-time friend. She is a godsend.

To Carole Galassi of **Creativemediaweb.com**, who designed **Pearlsofasia.net**, **Leegeiger.com**, and **Marginalprophet.com**. Technically, she's brilliant. Creatively, she's even better.

To Rich Lee at **Richleedraws.com**. Rich created the book's captivating cover, as well as the fun and imaginative graphics at **Pearlsofasia.net**. Rich is more than just a rabid Giants and Sharks fan. He is also very, very talented.

Finally, to the Ladies of Asia SF. Thank you for sharing your stories, your experiences, and your time. I hope you are as proud of this book as I am.

Disclaimer

This book is dedicated to Mom, whom I miss very much.

☙

CHAPTER ONE

Thursday, September 11, 2008 – 6:10 am

*"That's the news for tonight. I'm Michelle Osher. The 'Tonight
Show with Jay Leno' is next. Have a pleasant evening
San Francisco, and we'll see you tomorrow."*

KNTV Nightly News

THE WHITE WALLS AND bright lights all but blinded San
Francisco Homicide Inspector Mac Fleet. The polished
granite counters were spotless, and the sink hadn't seen
a dirty casserole dish since the Clinton Administration. The
gourmet kitchen was bigger than his first apartment, and it looked
as though it made more reservations than recipes. You could eat a
meal off the hardwood floor, although you'd have to set a place for
the dead body bleeding all over it.

Mac stepped around the corpse, making sure not to get any
blood on his shoes. His partner, Taylor Mayes, was kneeling next
to the deceased, writing in his notebook. "I was wondering when
you'd show up."

"Of course you were," said Mac, still rubbing the sleep out of his
eyes. Seventeen minutes earlier, he had been trying to get comfort-

able in his now too-short-for-him kid's bed, reclaimed since moving back in with his mother after the breakup of his marriage. "I had to crash through a wall of reporters to get here. What have we got?"

"A bloody mess is what we've got," said Mayes, who at forty-two was ten years older than Mac and often spoke to him like a naughty kid brother. Everyone above ground called Taylor Mayes by his last name, especially if they wanted to stay above ground. "Since you never watch anything except 'SportsCenter,' allow me introduce you to our victim. Her name is Michelle Osher, forty-nine years old, and the evening news anchor on KNTV. I've been watching her for years. She was like a female version of Anderson Cooper. Smart, tough, funny. Damn, what a pity. Did you know she was a Miss America back in the Eighties?"

"You're kidding, right? I was watching Big Bird back in the Eighties."

Mac knelt down next to Mayes and studied the body. Michelle Osher was wearing a navy blue business suit, though it's doubtful the fluffy pink bedroom slippers were part of her ensemble. Her hands and arms lacked any bruising, and there didn't appear to be any skin under her fingernails. Mac glanced over his shoulder at the undamaged front door. "Whoever killed her took her by surprise."

"It sure looks that way," said Mayes. "She has a single slash wound across the front of her neck. We haven't found a murder weapon, and the knife block on the kitchen counter is full. Based on her body temperature, CSI puts the time of death about five hours ago, between one and two o'clock in the morning."

"She must have just gotten home from work," opined Mac. He picked up her left hand. She was still wearing her diamond-encrusted Cartier watch, and the track lighting made the rock resting on her fourth finger sparkle like a disco ball. Robbery wasn't a motive.

"Her wedding ring is the size of a small house," said Mayes. "*PEOPLE* magazine had pictures of her and her husband buying it at Shreve and Company near Union Square."

"You read *PEOPLE* magazine?"

"I do when Pamela sends me to the grocery store."

"Another reason why my wife dumped me. Who does our victim send to the grocery store?"

"I keep forgetting you don't read anything other than the sports page. His name is Paul Osher. He owns half the apartment buildings in town. He's also a major venture capitalist who's bankrolled about a dozen companies in Silicon Valley. He could write a check and bailout General Motors."

"So where is he now?"

"Out of town; I already called his office. His voicemail said he'd be in Los Angeles all week, so I left a message to call back ASAP. I also left a message on his cell phone."

Mac looked up at Mayes and shook his head in amazement, astonished at the efficiency of his African American senior partner. "You're incredible, Mayes. Remind me to be like you when I grow up."

"You mean bald, black, and brilliant?"

Precinct Captain Steve Longley waddled into the kitchen. Mac's broad-shouldered and lanky six-foot-two swimmer's frame towered over his Napoleonic boss, yet both men looked like school boys next to Mayes, who played football in college and still maintained the physique of a heat-seeking linebacker.

"Who found the body?" Mac asked Longley.

"The live-in maid. She's waiting in the next room. She woke up at 5:00 a.m. and went into the kitchen to fix coffee like she does every morning. Found her boss dead on the floor. Hell of a way to start your day, don't you think?"

"Depends who my boss is."

"Don't start with me, Mac," replied Longley, whose sense of humor was even shorter than he was. "Now pay attention you two. See all those news trucks parked outside? Michelle Osher is the textbook example of a high profile victim: she had the best ratings in town, and her husband is filthy rich. And, if you'll pardon the expression, she was drop-dead gorgeous. After Dispatch alerted me, I phoned the Chief of Police, and we both agreed you two should have this one."

"Of course you did," said Mac. The twosome had collared several notable criminals since being paired together less than nine months ago after the Christmas Day shooting death of Mac's former partner.

A uniformed officer appeared in the kitchen. "Gentlemen, you're all needed in the living room. The Big Guy wants to see you."

The Big Guy meant Chief of Police David Stone. A thirty-year veteran of the force, Stone had a well-deserved reputation as a nimble politician. Mac and Stone shared a close bond. The first time they ever met, Stone presented Mac with a medal for graduating at the top of his class at the Police Academy. Mac looked up to Stone, like a second father. Mac's real father left the country over a decade ago and didn't leave a forwarding address.

The three shuffled around the kitchen floor's blood-soaked occupant and gathered in the living room. The contemporary artwork and oversized vases reminded Mac of the lobby of the historic Fairmont Hotel, located a scant single block down the street.

"Good morning, Chief. You wanted to see us?" asked Longley.

"Yes I did, Captain," insisted Stone, dressed in an expensive black suit and tie. He knew the cameras would be rolling. "I want to give you some background on this case. The press is going to be all over us like white on rice. Michelle Osher was beloved in this town, and it's no secret that Paul Osher has showered money like pixie dust on a lot of politicians."

"We'll do our best, sir," said Mac. "You know Mayes and I will put everything we've got into this one."

"I don't doubt that. As soon as I learned who the victim was, I told Captain Longley I wanted you two on this case. You guys did stellar work on the Larsen murders, and then you arrested that Russian wife slayer from Canada a few months ago."

"Thank you for the opportunity, sir," said Mac, his ocean blue eyes looking into Stone's. "We won't let you down."

"Of course you won't," replied Stone, parroting his favorite detective. "Because if you do, we'll all look bad, the police and city of San Francisco will lose face, and you two will be off homicide and back on narcotics busting crack dealers on Sixth Street."

CHAPTER TWO

Thursday, September 11, 2008 – 7:42 am

*"A body has been removed from a Nob Hill apartment building
located at the corner of Sacramento and Taylor, across from
Huntington Park. We don't have official confirmation, but it
is rumored to be that of Michelle Osher, the popular evening
anchor of KNTV Nightly News."*

KGO Radio

AFTER HOSTING A $10,000 a plate fundraiser at their home for President George Bush's reelection campaign in 2004, The New York Times described Paul and Michelle Osher as, "...not content with having a single luxury apartment on the penthouse floor. They had to own the entire floor. Their opulent six-bedroom palace, located two hundred feet above San Francisco's privileged Nob Hill, may appear excessive for a childless couple, but not to the Oshers. They view their private residence as the San Francisco equivalent of the Kennedy compound on Cape Cod: an appropriate stage for their generous activities – along with their equally generous egos."

The sun was rising as the detectives searched the six thousand square foot home. Mayes took a moment to admire the breathtaking views provided by the floor-to-ceiling windows: the Berkeley Hills to the east, Alcatraz Island to the north, and the morning sunshine radiating off the Golden Gate Bridge to the west. "Great God Almighty," marveled Mayes. "I've lived in the Bay Area my whole life, and if I could look at this view every day, I'd be thankful just to be alive."

"The only way we'd get to see a view like that every day," replied Mac, refusing to take a moment to glance outside, "is if we became window washers."

Mac Fleet loved being a detective, or as they are called in San Francisco, an inspector. His blue-collar father, who served up for his impressionable son a healthy dose of "Dirty Harry" movies, planted the seeds for what would become his passion. Jack Fleet and his son spent hours sitting on the couch, snacking on chips and soda, watching Clint Eastwood hunt down the bad guys and exact vigilante justice. To Mac, who possessed a curiosity worthy of the Smithsonian, every case was a puzzle, with evidence to discover, clues to follow, and unique characters to question. When he graduated ten years ago from San Jose State with a degree in Criminal Justice, he dreamed of making arrests and bringing Bay Area scum to justice. Wearing a badge was more than a job to Mac; it defined who he was as a man.

Taylor Mayes enjoyed a high-definition life on a 50-inch chest. Born with brains and a matching set of brawn, Mayes graduated magna cum laude with an English degree from UC Berkeley. In his spare time he crushed quarterbacks as an All-Pac Ten linebacker, until a knee injury dashed his dream of an NFL career. Despite being considered the brightest detective on the force, Mayes refused to take department exams or put in the hundreds of man-hours necessary to help him move up the ranks. He valued his free time, and Mayes preferred hanging around his Sunset District home with his very pregnant wife Pamela and their three-year-old twins, Buddy and Holly.

Chief Stone and Captain Longley had gone downstairs to address the growing throng of reporters assembled outside the exclusive art-deco building. Armed with their press cameras, boom mikes and satellite dishes, journalists representing media outlets from all over the world peppered the twosome with questions. The tall, distinguished and well-dressed Stone stood in stark contrast next to the rumpled and vertically challenged Longley. At this point the juiciest thing they could say was, "No comment."

Mac and Mayes combed through the apartment and confirmed no signs of a struggle or forcible entry. Jewelry, artwork and antiques were left untouched. It was time to talk to the maid.

Maria Madrigal, fifty-two years old, sat on the edge of a sofa holding a cigarette and staring out the window. Her hands shook in a shroud of blue smoke. No doubt she was in shock over discovering a dead body, but Mac wondered if she were frightened about something else.

"Ms. Madrigal, I'm Inspector Mac Fleet and this is my partner, Inspector Taylor Mayes. We know how upsetting this must be for you, but we need to ask you a few questions about what you saw and heard this morning. When did you last see Mrs. Osher alive?"

"I'm not in trouble, am I?" she asked with a heavy Mexican accent.

"No ma'am. We're with homicide, not immigration."

Maria breathed an audible sigh of relief and the color rushed back to her face. "Mrs. Osher came home from work, usual time. Close to midnight. She was very tired."

Mayes squatted down to Maria's eye level and sat on a coffee table to make her feel more at ease. Mayes had an instinct regarding when to use his massive physical presence to intimidate or encourage. "Ms. Madrigal, please tell us what you saw and heard last night."

Maria teared up. "I don't know," she said in a halting voice. "She...was still in the kitchen. I say goodnight...then go to my room and turn on the TV. Leno was almost over...but I was sleepy. I turn it off and go to bed."

"So the last time you saw her alive was around 12:30," confirmed Mac. Maria nodded. "Between the time you went to bed and the time you found her, did you hear anything at all during the night?"

"No," she said, composing herself. "There was a party on the floor right below. Very noisy. People shouting, loud music, so I wear earplugs. I'm sorry." Maria began to cry again, and she buried her face in a handkerchief. "Can I go to my room now?"

"A couple more questions," said Mac, who sensed the last thing Maria wanted to do was answer a couple more questions. "Do you know who was having the party?"

"Oh, that rude man. Mr. Grisham in 1901. He has parties all the time. He and Mr. Osher are friends."

"Speaking of Mr. Osher," said Mayes, standing up and returning to not-your-best-friend mode. "Do you know where he is?"

"Los Angeles. He left Monday. He goes there on business all the time. He is to come home tomorrow. Does he know what happened to Mrs. Osher?"

"We're trying to get in touch with him. One more question, Ms. Madrigal," said Mac, who stopped writing and looked at Maria as though the fate of the free world rested on her answer to his next question. "How would you describe the Osher's marriage?"

Maria wiped away her tears and blew her nose. Her eyes brightened, and a smile appeared on her face. "Wonderful," she said. "Mr. Osher loves her. He sends her flowers all the time."

"Thank you, Maria," said Mayes, handing her his business card. "Please call us if you can think of anything else."

Maria began walking to her room. Then, for no apparent reason, she dropped down on her hands and knees to peek under a chair. She then crawled along the carpeted living room floor and looked behind an armoire. She got up to walk into dining room, then dropped down onto her knees again, this time to look under a china cabinet. After several more "stop and drop" moments, she returned to ask the detectives a question.

"Excuse me, please," she said in a quiet voice. "Have you seen Misha? She is a little dog, a Teacup Yorkie. Mrs. Osher loved her. I not see her all morning."

It was the first mention of a family pet. Mac had noticed a fancy china dog dish and water bowl in the kitchen, but he didn't think to ask about the four-legged creature that went with them.

"We haven't seen her either," Mac answered while closing his notebook. "She may have run out of the apartment or is hiding somewhere. We'll keep an eye out and let you know if we find her." Feeling reassured, Maria turned and walked back to her room.

Mac stomped toward the plate-glass windows and looked down upon the phalanx of news trucks parked twenty floors below. "Goddammit," he grumbled, pounding his fist against a window frame. "How could I have missed that? I should have realized there was a missing pet. It's sloppy work on my part. No excuses."

"You know, I hate it when you do that," consoled Mayes. "Stop being so damn hard on yourself. We would have discovered the missing dog. Don't forget, there are two great detectives working on this case."

Mac ran his fingers through a full head of uncombed salt and pepper hair. The premature gray gave him a distinguished look for a man only thirty-two years old. His hair color wasn't surprising, since Mac was a world-class worrier and all-league second-guesser. He had even given himself an ulcer at the age of fourteen. Whether as a son, a husband, a student or detective, Mac was wired to feel he was never good enough; that he didn't deserve a seat at the table. He forever internalized his anger, his fears, and his self-doubts, and used them as fuel to drive his raging ambition. Every day was like an audition, and if he did all the right things, and made all the right moves, no one would discover he was the fraud he thought he was.

"At least we have an eyewitness," said Mac. "Too bad it has a tail. Since you know everything, Mayes, maybe you can explain to me what a Teacup Yorkie is."

"I wouldn't expect an alpha male like you to know what they are," replied Mayes, scratching a well-maintained midnight black goatee. "They're really tiny Yorkshire Terriers, so small they can fit into a tea cup, hence the name. They're what women like to call 'purse dogs.'"

"That's not a dog. Dogs are German Shepherds and Labrador Retrievers. A Teacup Yorkie sounds more like a rat."

"Well my ignorant friend, just so you know, some of those 'rats' cost thousands of dollars. Carrying one of those around can mean as much to a woman as having the right purse."

"Of course it does," replied Mac, who turned his head toward the kitchen and winced as he heard a disturbing sound. The finality of a body bag zipper still caused him to cringe.

∽

THE TWO INSPECTORS TOOK the stairs down to the nineteenth floor and found the Grisham's apartment at the end of the hallway. As they approached the double doors of unit 1901, Mac turned to his partner. "Mayes, you know how I feel about these cases where the wife is murdered. The husband has to be involved. That story about Paul Osher sending his wife flowers all the time? It's a dead giveaway of a cheating spouse. I mean, look at you. You're crazy about Pamela, but how often do you send her flowers? I know the maid said he was out of town, but I'm telling you, the sooner we get to Paul Osher, the sooner we'll solve this case."

"I hear you, Mac, but let's not get ahead of ourselves. And just so you know, I do send my wife flowers. Maybe if you had you wouldn't be sleeping under the same roof as your mother."

"Asshole."

"That's Mr. Asshole to you," quipped Mayes. He rang the doorbell. No answer. He knocked on the door. Still no answer. Mayes began pounding on the door like an angry jackhammer. The heavy footsteps of someone who wasn't expecting company approached the door.

They heard a dead bolt, then another one at floor level, and the door opened a crack. A rumpled, unhappy looking middle-aged man wearing pink paisley pajamas greeted them.

"Who the hell are you?" asked a belligerent Jim Grisham. He was short, about 5'2', and his breath reeked of sweet tobacco, the kind grown in the lush forests of Northern California. His baggy eyes were fighting a losing battle to stay open.

The inspectors flashed their badges. "I'm Inspector Mac Fleet and this is Inspector Taylor Mayes. We need to ask you a few questions. Are you Jim Grisham?"

"I was when I went to bed last night. What's this all about?"

"There was a homicide in your building, Mr. Grisham. Do you mind if we come in?"

"Homicide?" gasped Grisham, his face springing to life. "You mean someone died here last night? Jeez, I hope it wasn't one of my guests." Grisham opened the door to let Mac and Mayes squeeze by. Then he closed it and rebolted the locks. "Who was it?"

"Michelle Osher," said Mayes, emphasizing her last name to make sure he had Grisham's full attention. "The woman who lived upstairs. Did you know her?"

"Michele Osher? You can't be serious," exclaimed Grisham, the news opening his eyes made red from too many Happy Hits. "Of course I know her." Grisham's look of surprise soon turned to scorn. "Who didn't know Ms. Perfect? She made you feel fortunate to be in her presence whenever you saw her in the elevator. She called herself a reporter, but she was nothing more than a glorified newsreader. Wow, I can't believe she's dead. She was supposed to come to my party last night. She said her husband would be out of town and she'd try to make an appearance."

"Did she?" asked Mayes.

"Hell, no. I told my guests they'd get to meet the world famous Michelle Osher, but I knew she'd flake. She always did. I'm sorry she's dead, but I won't miss her. The woman was a first-class bitch."

"When did you last speak to this so called 'first-class bitch?'" asked Mayes.

Grisham raised his hands and began rubbing both sides of his head, as though the answer would pop out along with a genie. "Tuesday, I think. Yeah, that was it. Tuesday. I saw her right after lunch, around two o'clock. She was on her way to work."

Mayes asked if they could speak to Grisham's wife, but he shook his head. "Sonia drank too much Vitamin V last night. She's passed out in the guest room. She won't be waking up until next week."

"Vitamin V?" asked Mac.

"Vodka, genius."

Mac's pants pocket began vibrating from a text message sent to his cell phone. Paul Osher had arrived home.

"We're outta here, Mayes," declared Mac. "Mr. Grisham, we'll need a list of all the people who attended your party last night."

"No problem," answered Grisham, straining to unbolt the door. "I'll get you one as soon as I'm able." As Grisham started to close the door behind them, Mayes blocked it with one of his size fifteen shoes.

"You'll have it to us by the end of today," said the former line-backer, who looked like he would have enjoyed nothing more at that moment than to be penalized for a late hit, "or I'll return with a search warrant and check out what other 'vitamins' you keep in this place."

∽

MAC AND MAYES FOUND Paul Osher in his study, whispering into his cell phone. He was wearing an Armani suit that failed to hide his sack-of-laundry physique. Mac took a moment to notice the framed photos on the wall. One of Osher and President George Bush, and another of him with California Governor Arnold Schwarzenegger. Holding a special place on the wall was a picture of Osher, sitting on a sailboat with his arm around actress Sharon Stone. Her hand was on his knee.

"Gentlemen, would you mind waiting in the other room?" asked Osher, who then proceeded to talk on his phone as though he was making a Saturday morning tee time.

As soon as he laid eyes on him, Mac knew he wasn't going to like Paul Osher. Whether it was the way they dressed, the way they talked, or the way they moved, Mac had a sixth sense for jerks he knew would piss him off. Paul Osher was going to be one of those guys, even if he wasn't the husband of a murdered spouse. Mac's job was to make sure Osher never knew it.

"Okay gentlemen," Osher announced after making them cool their heels outside his door for fifteen minutes, "you can come in now. What can I do for you?"

The study's burnt-red mahogany walls and dark leather furniture spoke of power and wealth. The framed photos of politicians and movie stars shared wall space with wooden plaques that had gold letters engraved in black textured plates, proclaiming honors and accomplishments that meant nothing to Mac. Bookshelves displayed collections of Charles Dickens and Ernest Hemingway, umpteen golf trophies, and even a bronze bust of the man himself, Paul Osher. Mac thought it would look good wearing a Mickey Mouse hat, complete with ears.

"Mr. Osher, I'm Inspector Mac Fleet and this is my partner, Inspector Taylor Mayes. We're homicide detectives with the San Francisco Police Department. We've been assigned to investigate your wife's murder. We're very sorry for your loss."

"Gentlemen, please have a seat," replied Osher, sitting down on a sofa and sounding as though he was about to moderate a roundtable discussion on economic policy rather than discuss the murder of his wife. "You guys must be good. As soon as my close friend David Stone called me this morning, I told him I wanted his best men working on this case. I was in Los Angeles, and I ordered my private jet to fly me home."

"We appreciate that, sir," said Mac, taking pains to write the words "good friend," "ordered," and "private" in his notebook.

"Mr. Osher, we need to ask you a few questions. First of all, do you know anyone who would want to hurt your wife?"

"Well…you know we're a very prominent couple." Osher spoke in a deep, condescending tone, flipping his Hermes tie to cover a belt buckle yearning to be free. "I'm sure there are all kinds of people who want to destroy us. Just look at all the reporters standing outside. They wouldn't show up for just anybody. Besides, whoever killed Michelle may have been trying to kill me."

"Why would you say that, sir?" asked Mayes.

Osher reached for a humidor and pulled out a cigar. Mac recognized right away it was a Cohiba Esplendido. Before he got married, Mac enjoyed smoking an occasional cigar, and considered himself something of an aficionado, although Cohibas were beyond a detective's salary. His father gave him his first cigar on his thirteenth birthday, and then shared another after Mac lost his virginity. Jack Fleet was like that. He even gave Mac his first beer after he won a schoolyard brawl in the sixth grade.

"See these pictures and plaques on the wall?" said Osher, taking time to light his cigar. "You not only have to be smart to get those, but sometimes you also have to be a real prick."

A trait he had in abundance, thought Mac.

The detectives continued to question Osher about his slain wife: friends, family, and acquaintances. Osher claimed he didn't know anyone close to Michelle who would want to kill her. Mayes asked about her relationship with her co-workers, and Paul Osher said as far as he knew his wife got along with everybody and was the apple of her boss' eye. "Fortunately, I don't have to deal with crap like that," he added with a prideful smirk, "since I am the boss."

"Of course you are," said Mac, hoping Osher wouldn't pick up on his sarcasm. "Mr. Osher, besides you, the maid and your wife, does anyone else have access to your apartment?"

"The Grisham's have a key just in case we lock ourselves out. Why do you ask?"

"Just doing our job, sir."

It was time to ask "the question," the one that stood in the corner like an eight hundred pound gorilla. "Mr. Osher," began Mac, "how would you describe your relationship with your wife?"

Paul Osher gave Mac a contemptuous look while flicking away his cigar ash. "I know where you're going with this, Inspector. I'm aware that the husband is an obvious suspect. However, not a day goes by when our names are not in the headlines, so if Michelle and I were cheating on one another, you can bet the whole goddamn world would know about it." Osher took another long drag on his Cohiba. "The truth is, I loved my wife very much, and I haven't so much as looked at another woman since the day we were married."

There were two things Mac knew as a cop: when a suspect was lying, and when to conclude an interview. This was one of those times when both applied.

∽

MAC AND MAYES EXITED the building and marched past the bank of microphones and cameras.

"You like the husband?" asked Mayes.

"I always like the husband."

CHAPTER THREE

Thursday, September 11, 2008 – 4:00 pm

*"Chief of Police David Stone refused to comment on the identity
of the Nob Hill murder victim, rumored to be KNTV news
anchor Michelle Osher, once again giving credence to his
familiar nickname of "David Stone-Walling."*

KCBS Radio

MAC LIKED TO SAY if you're going to play baseball, be a Yankee. If you're going to play basketball, be a Laker. And if you're going to be a cop, work in the Tenderloin. The notorious San Francisco neighborhood bordered by Geary, Market, and Larkin streets offered up a troublesome dose of crime served with a strip club chaser, mixed in with a dash of poverty and enough seedy characters to fill a Dashiell Hammett novel. The police station at the corner of Jones and Eddy was more than just the place where cops collected a paycheck. It was destitution's address for Ground Zero.

Mac and Mayes were seated with Captain Longley in his office, which reflected the personality of its occupant: cheap, humorless and uninspiring. The detectives brought Longley up to speed while wolfing down a late lunch of cold pizza. They had spent a fruitless morning and afternoon canvassing the building's residents and the surrounding neighborhood, asking if they had observed anyone or anything unusual or suspicious. Nobody had seen a thing, though several did ask if there was a reward for the missing dog.

"We've ruled out robbery as a motive," said Mac between bites of jalapeno and garlic, "and whoever killed Michelle Osher was let into the apartment. We have no eyewitnesses and no murder weapon. The building's entrance does have a surveillance camera and we're getting a copy of the tape. An occupant, a Mr. Jim Grisham, was throwing a party one floor below the Osher's apartment, and we asked him to provide us with a guest list. You should have seen this guy, Captain. He looked worse than a Keith Richards mug shot. He also made it clear he didn't think a whole lot of Michelle Osher."

"That doesn't surprise me," said Longley. "Jim Grisham not only parties like a rock star, he's got the bank account of one as well. He also loves a fight, and he's one of the few Republicans in this town besides Paul Osher who isn't afraid to write a big check. When Michelle Osher changed her mind and went against her conservative brethren to support same-sex marriages, I'm sure it drew a line in the sand between them."

"There you go, Mac," joked Mayes, who also was a supporter of gay marriage. "If a right-winger like Michelle Osher can change her mind, maybe there's hope for you yet."

"Not in this lifetime," responded Mac, refusing to take the bait from his left-leaning partner. Though he had grown up in the Bay Area and considered himself something of a social liberal, Mac's support of gay rights stopped at the altar.

"Can we move on, please?" asked an exasperated Longley, who was never in the mood for political banter. "What else have you got?"

"We've also spoken to the victim's husband, Paul Osher, who claims he was in L.A. at the time of his wife's death. Of course, he says he loved his wife and has no idea who would want to hurt her. In fact, he believes the killer may have been trying to kill him."

"I'm sure you loved that line," said Longley, all too familiar with Mac's penchant for fingering the husband. "Be careful with Osher. He's tight with Stone and every other politician in this town."

"There's one more thing," said Mac. "Michelle Osher's dog is missing, although calling her a dog is an insult to the canine profession. She's a Teacup Yorkie, whose native habitat appears to be the inside of a purse. Her name is Misha, and she may have run out of the building during all the confusion. It's no big deal, but it's worth noting."

"Whatever. You guys aren't paid to be dogcatchers. Anything else?"

"It's just a thought, Captain, but I've got a theory on this case," chimed Mayes, who polished off half a pie. To the two hundred-fifty pound mass of muscle, consuming food was a sprint, not a marathon. Not to mention that Mayes thought jalapeño and garlic was the best California combination since Beach and Boy. "Based on what we know so far, whoever killed Michelle Osher realized news of her death would make headlines all over the world. My hunch is the murderer was sending a message."

Mac and Captain Longley nodded their heads in agreement. Mayes was right more often than he was wrong.

৩

MAC'S CELL PHONE HAD three text messages, all from his mother. The last one made him laugh. She attached a photo featuring the cover model from the last winter's *Sports Illustrated* swimsuit issue, saying in big, bold letters, "CALL ME!" Mac checked his watch. It was 1:30, which meant the stock market had been closed on the West Coast for a half hour. He pulled out his iPhone and tapped the entry for "Victoria Parker."

Victoria Parker was more than Mac's mother. She was his hero. Despite being old enough to carry an AARP card, she still bore a striking resemblance to her favorite singer, Stevie Nicks of Fleetwood Mac. When Jack Fleet abandoned his young family for a stripper with the I.Q. of a head of lettuce, Victoria Fleet was compelled to take a minimum wage job at a brokerage firm to support herself and her precocious adolescent. When she wasn't answering phones or getting her boss a pastrami on rye, she taught herself finance by listening to the parade of pundits shepherded daily on CNBC. Her charming personality, along with her penchant for wearing short skirts on casual Fridays, caught the attention of her branch manager, Henry Parker. After her first year-end review, Mr. Parker offered her a promotion to Trophy Wife.

After her second husband dropped dead at his desk from a heart attack, Victoria Parker decided to try her hand earning a living by day-trading stocks. She turned out to be a gifted trader with natural instincts and uncanny timing. Moreover, bored with watching soap operas after the stock market closed, she joined a fitness center and started pumping iron instead of chocolate. Armed with six-pack abs and the body fat of a carrot stick, the hours in the gym soon turned Victoria Parker into a Hall of Fame cougar.

"Mackey, where have you been? I've been thinking about you all morning. CNBC even interrupted their countdown of Lehman Brothers going to zero to break the news about Michelle Osher. I can't believe that poor woman is dead, though I never thought she was the sharpest knife in the drawer. I know, I know, bad choice of words. Did you get assigned the case?"

Mac sat at his desk and pulled out a drawer to use as a footrest. "I always told you, Mom. You may have raised an ugly child, but not a stupid one. Yes, I'm on the case."

"That's fabulous!" she shouted, causing Mac to pull the phone away from his ear. "I can't wait to celebrate. Listen Mackey, I've got to run to the gym or my personal trainer will make me wish I were never born. Not to mention I've got to fit into that lethal red cocktail dress I picked up last weekend at Saks. This handsome defense attorney invited me to dinner on his yacht tomorrow night, and I'm going to make sure he has no objections. Gotta go, Mackey. Love ya."

Mac hung up and laughed. His mother made him smile, but Victoria Parker made him laugh.

∾

A PILE OF SUBPOENAED phone records and bank statements sat atop Mac's forever-disorganized desk. Just pieces in a puzzle, he thought. It was late in the afternoon, and he and Mayes began the task of finding out as much as they could about Paul Osher.

"You're going to love this," said Mac after spending an hour poring over Paul Osher's phone records. "Over the past six months, these were his three most dialed numbers. Number three was to his wife, and most of those calls lasted less than two minutes."

"Maybe he was checking to see if she got the flowers," joked Mayes. Compared to Mac's desk, which resembled a landfill, Mayes's desk was better organized than West Point.

"Or maybe she wanted to talk to him as little as possible. Number two was to his office, and wait until you hear who was Numero Uno."

Mayes didn't have to answer. He knew right were Mac was going, which is where most men like to go when they start thinking below their belt.

"According to the phone company, her name is Sheyla Samonte, and she lives somewhere South of Market. I'm sure if we ask Osher about her he'll say she's his niece or some crap like that. I'm telling you, Mayes, this guy is bad news."

Mac was excited. He loved nailing a perp. He couldn't wait to call the number and speak to the woman who would send Paul Osher to a life of playing "drop the soap" at San Quentin. Harking back to his glory days as a high school swimmer, Mac felt like taking a victory lap.

He dialed the number and was immediately sent to voicemail. The voice was strong, confident, and sultry. "Hello, you've reach Sheyla..."

It was the sexiest voice he had ever heard.

"You alright over there, partner?" asked Mayes, noticing Mac's thousand-yard-stare.

"I just heard the voice of a goddess."

"You don't say? Tell you what, lover boy, since we need to move fast on this one, why don't you go over to her apartment and check her out while I stay here and track down Osher's alibi. You're better with the ladies than I am, anyway."

"Of course I am, Mr. Happily Married with Twins and One More Bun in the Oven."

୧୦

MAC RAN OUT OF the office and down to the department's underground garage. He still drove his first car, a restored Horizon Blue 1960 Chevrolet Kingswood Estate Cruiser that he called The Sub. The twenty-foot long land yacht, complete with miles of chrome and aluminum trim, had been given to him as a high school graduation present by his grandmother. The tuck and roll upholstery and push button radio said volumes about Mac and how he wanted to live his life; low key, under the radar, and cool. Class wasn't something you bought, he believed. You either had it, or you didn't.

What Mac had plenty of was charisma, and he rarely had a problem getting a lady's attention. Since crossing the finish line of puberty, women were drawn to Mac by his rugged good looks, boyish charm, and self-deprecating sense of humor. Mac liked to say his broad shoulders, blue eyes, and deep dimples were the few reminders he had of his father. And that was on those rare occasions when he would talk about his father. Mac had also mastered the fine art of conversation, and he made it a point to look into a woman's eyes while speaking to her. "Talk with your ears," Victoria

Parker always told him. "A girl likes it when you listen to what she has to say instead of staring at her chest."

Mac wanted to settle down, but he had no luck with his first marriage. Denise was charming and smart, and she had just become a Director at J.P. Morgan before she left him. He'd fallen hard for the perky blonde from San Diego, and they married after he graduated from the Police Academy. While Mac was searching for suspects, Denise earned an MBA from Stanford and pursued a career in investment banking. Both worked long hours and never had time for their spouse. On those rare occasions when they found themselves in the same room, Denise grew tired hearing Mac's stories of enforcing law and order, while Mac found her dissertations on how another mega-merger would reshape the global marketplace mind numbing and tedious.

After almost ten years of marriage, the big chill descended. The marriage took a turn for the worse on a Friday night last December, after Denise got her big promotion at JP Morgan. The company Christmas party was that evening, and she wanted to show off her brand new Lexus LS 460. Mac, however, wanted to stay low-key and arrive in The Sub. A nasty argument ensued, and Mac ended up staying at home. In fact, he went into the station and worked an extra shift.

When he got home at three o'clock in the morning, Mac found all her stuff cleaned out. Denise hadn't gone to the party, either. Every piece of furniture was gone, and torn photographs littered the floor. It was as if their marriage never existed. Denise just wanted to be done with him and gone

The way Mac saw it, as a husband, he was a failure.

∽

SHEYLA SAMONTE LIVED AT 229 Brannan Street, a chic thirty-story high-rise located in an up and coming neighborhood known as South Beach. Yuppies rollerbladed along the neighboring Embarcadero while sailboats and freighters cruised past. Cafes spilled onto the sidewalks as the sexy singles set dined on sushi and knocked back espressos.

Mac flashed his badge at the doorman, who told him a woman named Sheyla Samonte lived in apartment 2407. Mr. Doorman looked like one of those elderly rent-a-cops who retired from the police force and soon discovered that sitting at home and collecting a pension was overrated. Before catching the elevator, Mac asked him if there was anything special he should know about her.

Mr. Doorman got a faraway look and grinned so wide his eyes almost closed shut. "I don't know much about her, but every day she takes a walk down to the corner store, and a smile from her is the highlight of my day."

Mac stepped onto the twenty-fourth floor. As he walked down the ritzy taupe colored hallway, he realized the odd-numbered rooms, like Sheyla's, faced north and offered an unobstructed view of the Bay Bridge, which when lit up at night was nothing less than spectacular. Mac found his way to Sheyla's apartment, composed himself, and knocked on the door. He felt as nervous as a teenager on prom night.

He could hear the catlike steps of a woman. Mac tugged on his suit jacket and smoothed down his hair. This wasn't some serial rapist or drug lord. This was The Voice.

"Who is it?" she purred. The Voice sounded even better in person.

Mac had trouble getting the words to tumble out of his mouth. "Miss Samonte, I'm Inspector Mac Fleet of the San Francisco Police Department. I need to ask you a few questions about Paul Osher."

The awkward seconds of silence seemed like hours. An inch of pine separated them, but the longer he stood in the hallway, the more it seemed like miles.

"I'm sorry, but I'm afraid I don't know anyone by that name," she cooed.

"Miss Samonte, would you mind opening the door? I promise I won't take up much of your time."

"I'm so sorry, Inspector," she said. "But I just got out of the shower and I have to get dressed for work."

Mac's instinct was to say something biting and sarcastic, but a proper upbringing by his mother held him back. She was still The Voice, and she sounded so sincere and polite.

"Miss Samonte, I left several messages on your phone today. If you're not available to answer my questions right now, I'd appreciate it if you could call me back so we can set up a meeting. We need to talk."

"I'll do that, Inspector. I promise. I have to get ready now. Have a good evening."

As he strolled through the lobby, Mr. Doorman asked Mac if he had seen Sheyla. "No, I didn't. She said she had to get ready for work."

Mr. Doorman's face lit up, his eyes squinting so much his round face reminded Mac of a statue of Buddha. "Oh that's right. It's Thursday night, and she works as a waitress not too far from here. She waves at me from her Mercedes."

Mac reacted like he had just found a piece of a puzzle buried between the sofa cushions. "Wait a minute. Let me see if I've got this straight. She lives in this Trump Tower wanna-be, drives a Mercedes, and works as a waitress? She must get tipped in gold bars."

"I don't know how she does it either. She leaves for work around six o'clock."

Mac checked his watch. It was 5:30 pm.

He loved stakeouts.

❧

MAC HUNKERED IN THE Sub and stared at the entrance of the building's garage. It had already been quite the day. He needed a little quiet time for himself anyway. Not too long, however, otherwise the pit in his stomach would show up and start grinding away at his psyche. Again. Ever since the Twelve Days of Christmas, as Mac called it, when he lost both his wife and partner, the toxic brew of anger, resentment, and guilt woke up with him every morning. It joined him at every meal, and climbed into bed with him every night. Mac may have been lonely, but he was never alone.

After waiting almost an hour, Mac saw a late model silver Mercedes Benz leave the garage. "Waitress, my ass," Mac said to himself. "The only thing this gal waits on is a guy's wallet."

Mac slouched in The Sub and let her get a block ahead of him. He followed her for less than two miles before the Mercedes pulled over and parked on the east side of Ninth Street, across from a combination gas station and fast-food restaurant. He passed her and turned left onto Howard Street, where he found a shipyard-sized parking spot next to a discount furniture store.

Sheyla got out of her car wearing workout clothes and carrying a Louis Vuitton travel bag. Mac's ten years as a hard-bitten professional investigator told him three things about this potential murder suspect; she was Asian, she was tall, and she was hot. Sheyla disappeared through a doorway at the southeast corner of Ninth and Howard Street. Mac looked over and noticed a small sign on the side of the restaurant. For a guy who knew every trendy spot in town, this was one place he had never heard of.

The sign said *Pearls of Asia*.

CHAPTER FOUR

Thursday, September 11, 2008 - 9:00 pm

"Residents of this upper-class neighborhood are not used to seeing news vans, squad cars, and yellow crime scene tape while walking their dogs past freshly planted flowers and trimmed trees. South of Market, perhaps, but never Nob Hill."

Entertainment Tonight

THE SIGN OUTSIDE *Pearls of Asia* said in small letters "since 1998." Located at the corner of Ninth and Howard, in a neighborhood called South of Market, or SOMA for short, the restaurant was one block away from Folsom Street, where San Francisco's gay leather subculture thrived. Folsom was home for the notorious Folsom Street Fair, San Francisco's annual celebration of bondage, discipline, submission, and masochism. There isn't a Disney store anywhere in the neighborhood.

Mac watched an assortment of customers stream into the restaurant. They would first walk through a glass door, speak to a host, and then proceed past a curtain. A limo was parked in front, and six women wearing skimpy clothing and celebrating a bachelorette party tumbled out onto the street, each one already fortified with a healthy dose of liquid courage.

Mac wanted to go inside and check it out, but he wondered if he'd be out of place wearing a cheap suit and tie. "I'm going to stand out like a black crow in a bowl of milk," he said to himself. He got out and slammed the door of The Sub.

A slight Asian man wearing a black silk shirt, red tie, and tight black jeans greeted Mac at the door. His jet-black hair was tied in a ponytail, and his head was bobbing to the pulsating beat of the music. Mac pushed back the curtain and looked inside. Judging from the volume of voices and music, this wasn't just a restaurant. It was a party.

"Can I get a table?" asked Mac.

"I'm sorry sir," said Mr. Ponytail in a strong Japanese accent. "We only seat singles at the bar. Have you been dined with us before?"

"Nope. Never even heard of this place."

"You must live under a rock," said Mr. Ponytail, who seemed insulted. *Pearls of Asia* has been here for ten years. It has changed peoples' lives, if not their sex."

Mac didn't know what to make of Mr. Ponytail's last statement, so he chose to ignore it. He was escorted to the bar and given a seat at the very end, right next to what appeared to be the stage. "If you don't mind me saying, sir, you are a very good looking man. I just gave you the best seat in the house. Try not to get molested."

Mac had never seen a place like this. The restaurant consisted of a single, windowless room that had just enough space for the hundred or so diners. The room was divided in two, with bar tables, chairs, and a long bench and upholstered red leather backrest on one side, and dining tables on the other. A forty-foot U-shaped bar dominated the room; one half for serving customers, the other half raised slightly higher and covered in red rubberized vinyl to make it look like a catwalk. The high ceiling was painted black and adorned with spotlights, and several Asian-influenced papier-mâché chandeliers hung from the ceiling. One wall was accented in lime green paint and massive stalks of bamboo set at dramatic angles, while two others featured color morphing shoji screen walls that changed from pink to blue to gold. The room was more than just sexy and intimate. It was sensuous.

The scene was wild. Mac noticed every type and flavor of free-wheeling humanity you'd expect to find in San Francisco; lesbian couples holding hands; a table of gay men laughing and giving each other high-fives; a group of straight looking financial types in dark suits hoisting martinis in every color of the rainbow; a gaggle of middle-aged women getting sloshed and silly; an older couple, licking away at ice cream cones, wearing khaki hiking shorts and talking in what sounded like Swedish. And there was the table of bachelorettes, already toasting each other with a round of tequila shots. Everyone seemed to be having an outrageously good time.

Above all else, what caught Mac's eye were three stunning Asian women serving drinks and taking orders. They wore full stage makeup and five-inch heels that didn't slow down their mad dashes around the room one bit. One wore a tight-fitting, strapless amber tube dress, while another had on an off the shoulder, tiger-striped mini-dress. They were chatting up the crowd and appeared to be flirting with every man or woman they saw.

Mac ordered a beer. Laid out on the glossy wood bar in front of him were red and white napkins and flame-colored chop-sticks folded together in an origami-style sculpture. Mac smiled as he scanned the red leather bound menu, featuring dishes best described as Cal-Asian cuisine, with delicious sounding cocktails named after exotic women: Diamond's Daiquiri, Nadia's Navel, and Reyna's Love Potion. There was even a three-course combina-tion special called a Ménage a Trois. You had to love a place like this.

Across the room a man made eye contact with Mac. It was Jackson, another officer from his precinct, out of uniform and sitting with a woman who looked like an anthropology student doing research, including the notepad. Mac remembered him from his days at the Police Academy.

Thirty minutes had passed and Mac still hadn't seen Sheyla. He asked the bicep bulging bartender wearing a tight black t-shirt and spiked hair where she was.

"Oh, you mean Kimora," he answered. "Sheyla's her real name, but when she's working here, she calls herself Kimora. She came in late today. She's downstairs getting ready. She's the star of the next show, the featured dancer, so she'll be going on second. Ashley leads off, and she'll be onstage in a minute or so. I'd put on a seatbelt if I were you."

The three Asian waitresses walked up and gathered behind Mac. Though they were speaking Tagalog, the native tongue of the Philippines, Mac could tell they were sizing him up like a prized steer at a cattle auction. *"Ang mga mata, sarap gumising sa tabi n'ya?"* (Can you imagine waking up to those blue eyes?) *"Ang sarap halikan nga mga labing yan."* (I would love to kiss those lips.) *"Ano ka ba? Dedma ang mga mata at labi; sight mo ang mga kamay...ang lalaki!"* (What's up with you? Forget the eyes and lips; check out those hands...they're huge!) They must have liked his suit.

Mr. Ponytail sat a young couple next to Mac. The girlfriend had brought her boyfriend to *Pearls of Asia* for his birthday. Mac made small talk and wished him a happy birthday by buying a round of drinks. Mac soon realized he was having too good a time. He was still on the job, and though he wanted to be cool, he first needed to be a cop.

Without warning, the music died and the lights dimmed. The rhythm of "Umbrella" by Rihanna began to play, and the table of drunken bachelorettes shrieked in delight. A single spotlight came on, and standing like a statue in the middle of the bar was Ashley, an Asian woman with legs that soared to her neck. Her dirty blonde hair flowed down to her waist, and it was straighter than half the men in the room. She was wearing a black leather dress, fishnet stockings, and red stiletto heels. She carried an umbrella as a prop. Topping it off was a gold sequined bowler. Mac closed his menu and placed it back on the bar. There were times to think about food. This wasn't one of them.

Ashley's Ferrari red lips moved in synch with the lyrics, and her tiptoeing spins, razor-sharp movements, and hair tossing turns soon had the room in a frenzy. She was having fun without being freaky, sexy without being tawdry. The place was rocking.

Then Ashley stopped, brought her hands to her chest, and ripped off her dress. The audience gasped at first, and then like a massive wave hitting the beach, followed it up with a thunderous roar. In less time than it took to flip a light switch, the energy in the room went from festive to fierce.

Ashley tossed her dress at a table of men lusting for leather. Wearing a lacy black bra, red patent leather shorts, and a smile that could halt an armada, Ashley placed her hands on her hips and lifted her head high, and like a Parisian model, held the provocative pose for the scores of flashes from cameras and smart phones. Armed with a pair of voluptuous breasts, much too perfect to be found in nature, Ashley turned and strutted toward Mac.

Standing above him and grinding her hips, Ashley fell to her knees, threw back her hair, and gave Mac an up close and personal tour of her flawless décolletage. With lights flashing all around him, Mac rose from his chair, only to have Ashley use her umbrella to shove him back into submission. So much for being cool.

The song came to an end, and the crowd rose to its feet for a standing ovation. As Ashley walked away, Mac was left with two thoughts. Where did she get that firm ass? And what was up, literally and figuratively, with that feeling in the nether region of his pants?

"Who is that girl?" shouted the girlfriend to nobody in particular. "Is she new? What an incredible dancer. She is so…damn… sexy!"

"Her name is Ashley," the bartender yelled over the din. "She's only been here a couple of weeks. I think she's going to be one of the best dancers we've ever had."

Soon the noise died down and an expectant hush came over the room. The notes of Bonnie Raitt's haunting "Let's Give Them Something To Talk About" began to play, and from the darkness strolled the second performer, the much-anticipated "Kimora."

Wearing a shiny blue cocktail dress that featured a never-ending slit, and a black feather boa that framed her cleavage, Kimora's beauty sucked the oxygen right out of the room. She had the chiseled cheekbones of a model, the lithe body of a runner, and the presence of a beauty queen. She had a major in glamour, with a minor in charisma.

Unlike Ashley, who bounced along the stage like a ball, Sheyla moved with the grace of a swan, mesmerizing the audience with an air of sophistication and class. Camera lights flashed all around, like a crowd of tourists taking pictures of the Mona Lisa. Mac stood straight up and stared. He was captivated, infatuated, and more awestruck than if he'd just seen Joe Montana.

The mood in the room became downright reverential. "That's the one I told you about," Mac overheard the girlfriend say to her boyfriend, "Would you ever imagine?"

Kimora danced like a spoiled Siamese cat: graceful, elegant, and sensual. She turned and slinked her way toward Mac. As the song neared its climax, she dangled the boa in front of him, dropped down to her knees, and wrapped the feathery rope around his neck. She then pulled Mac's head next to hers, placed her lips on his, and gave Mac a deep, wet, and passionate kiss on his mouth. Instead of pulling away, Mac closed his eyes, arched his neck, and held the kiss for what seemed like forever. Hers were the softest lips he had ever felt.

The audience erupted in pandemonium. Kimora rose to her feet, gave Mac a flirtatious wink, and strolled off the stage.

The lights returned and the house music boomed. Mac sat back down on his chair, his mind on sensory overload. The young couple laughed, and the boyfriend gave Mac a fist pump.

"So how do you like sitting in the Hot Seat?" asked the girlfriend. "The girls do that to everyone who sits there."

"Incredible...fantastic." Mac was speechless, which happened about as often as a San Francisco snowfall.

"It is, isn't it?" enthused the girlfriend. "And you would never know, would you?"

Regaining his composure, Mac took a healthy swig of his beer and asked with a quizzical look, "Know what?"

"The girls, " she said, looking at him as though he was the last person to get the punch line of a joke. "They're transsexuals. All these girls are male underneath."

Mac's mind went blank, and the color ran from his face. It was as though someone had just hit the control-alt-delete function of his brain.

The young woman gave Mac a concerned look, wondering if he was okay. "You can't say you didn't know. Everyone knows the waitresses at *Pearls of Asia* are transsexuals, or as they like to call themselves, 'gender illusionists.' Like the hottest girl here, Kimora, who just gave you that amazing kiss."

Mac's head began to reboot. Sheyla Samonte was a transsexual? A man dressed as a woman? She was Paul Osher's mistress? And she, or he, just kissed him?

Mac reached for his wallet, threw the bartender some bills, and bolted for the door.

CHAPTER FIVE

Friday, September 12, 2008 - 8:00 am

*"The San Francisco Police Department has announced that
Michelle Osher, the award-winning broadcaster and former
Miss America 1985, whose body was found in her penthouse
apartment on Nob Hill Thursday morning, was murdered.
Few details are known at this time. According to San Francisco
Police Chief Daniel Stone, 'Finding the people responsible for the
death of Michelle Osher is this department's highest priority.'"*

The San Francisco Chronicle

MAC LAY ON TOP of his bed, still wearing yesterday's
suit. His tongue bore the brunt of a midnight cigar,
which lasted longer than the bottle of wine. His alarm
went off over an hour ago, and he was nursing more than a bad
hangover. The image of Sheyla Samonte, her lips pressed against
his, was etched in his mind. Whoever she was, or whatever she was,
no one had ever kissed him like that before.

Struggling to upgrade to vertical from horizontal, Mac
undressed and dragged himself to the bathroom. After making a
pit stop to disgorge the poisons that had turned his stomach into

a cesspool, Mac headed for the shower. This one would go into extra innings.

Sitting cross-legged on the tile floor, Mac let the water cascade over his head like a waterfall. This daybreak deluge, however, wasn't accompanied by his normal routine of bright lights and the morning KNBR sports report blaring from the shower radio. This morning the bathroom was dark. Unlit. As pitch black as a raven's feather. Not a single glow from a nightlight or a crack in the door. This was Mac's way of making sense of a nonsensical world: sitting on his butt, surrounded by the song of a shower, baptized by hot water and darkness. The bathroom blackout provided a still and blank canvas to help him find the answers. Where was his father? How did he lose the race? Why would a mother murder her child? Only those closest to Mac knew of his unusual method of meditating. Denise knew, but she tolerated his habit by ignoring it. His mother knew, and she understood it was the reason why her thirty-two year old son, whom she hadn't seen cry in over twenty years, wanted to move back in with her. After losing both his partner and wife in the course of two weeks, Mac didn't want to be alone, and unlike the apartment he shared with Denise, the bathroom he had as a child didn't have a window.

Sitting in the murky obscurity, his mouth tasting like a greasy back alley puddle, Mac tried to make sense of what happened at the corner of Ninth and Howard. What was a 'gender illusionist?' How does a man make himself look like that? And why did admiring The Body that Ashley Built get him so aroused last night? Or now?

Get a grip, Mac thought to himself. Get your mind back in the game, back on the case. But first get some coffee.

ↂ

MAC CLIMBED THE STAIRS toward the kitchen. His mother lived in a five-story townhouse on Grand View Avenue in Noe Valley that she inherited from her late husband. There were two bedrooms, a kitchen, a living room, a dining room, and a two-car garage, and the rooms were stacked one on top of the other like layers on a wedding cake. Mac and his mother moved into this working-class neighborhood when he was six years old, after she divorced Mac's father and got remarried a week later to Henry Parker. Five years later, Henry Parker walked into work, sat down at his desk, and minutes later died of a heart attack. He left Victoria Parker the townhouse, no debts, and a small pile of cash, which she used to transform herself from a retired soccer mom to Wall Street's version of Tyra Banks.

With a mug of coffee in one hand and a cup of green tea in the other, Mac skipped the private elevator and walked up two flights of stairs to the dining room, which his mother had converted into an office after Mac moved back home. Unshowered, her chestnut hair piled carelessly on top of her head, and wearing her every day trader's uniform of flannel pajamas with matching slippers, Victoria Parker was speaking into a wireless headset while listening to CNBC and scanning four computer screens. This was a woman who took multi-tasking to a new level.

"Listen Dustin, I don't care if the float on Lehman Brothers is skinnier than Paris Hilton. They're going broke faster than Nicholas Cage. If you can borrow enough stock so my short position gets north of a hundred thousand shares, I'll treat you and your latest boy toy to another crazy night at Badlands. Now get to work."

"Badlands?" Mac asked while placing her tea in front of her. "What's my mother doing hanging out at a gay nightclub in the Castro with her stockbroker?"

"Having more fun than I care to tell you about. Now talk to me about this case. It sounds exciting, like the San Francisco version of O.J. Simpson."

"You got that right. A former Miss America is murdered, her wealthy husband has a mistress, and it turns out she works at a place called *Pearls of Asia*, where every waitress has the same plumbing as me. Even Hollywood couldn't make this stuff up."

"She works at *Pearls of Asia?*" she cackled. "You've got to be kidding...I love that place! My girlfriends and I had a Cougar Committee party there a few months ago. The food is great, the drinks are ferocious, and the girls are jaw-dropping gorgeous. Have you ever been there?"

"Not until last night. It's not exactly a sports bar."

"Mackey, you need to get out more often. For my money it's the best restaurant in the city for just plain fun. What did you think of it?"

"I had a good time, at least I did until one of those make believe 'girls' decided to give me a good night kiss smack on the lips."

Victoria Parker put her hands over her mouth and burst into a howl of laughter. "Well that explains the empty wine bottle I discovered this morning."

Mac could feel his face flush, although he wasn't sure if it was from anger or embarrassment. "It's not funny, Mom. Another guy from the precinct saw it happen. I'm sure by noon it will be all over the office."

Victoria Parker removed her headset and turned CNBC to mute, which she never liked to do. As far as she was concerned, CNBC provided the best analysis on Wall Street. If every talking head they paraded before the cameras said to "sell," then she knew it was time to buy. In the case of Lehman Brothers, she knew the biggest player in the mortgage-backed securities market was in a fatal death-spiral when her illegal alien manicurist from Guadalajara scored a zero-down mortgage on a half-million dollar home. She needed more documentation to cross the border than she did to buy a house.

"First of all, that girl who kissed you last night is more of a woman than that cold-blooded bitch you called a wife. Denise did everything she could to be more like a man so she could get a bigger bonus check. Those girls at *Pearls of Asia*, on the other hand, spend every waking moment of their lives trying to be the best woman they can be. Have you ever noticed how they glide when they walk, or how they gracefully arch their neck when they flip their hair? It's amazing how truly feminine they can be. You shouldn't be embarrassed because she placed her lips on yours. You should be proud. She has good taste."

Mac shook his head. "'Proud' is not the word I'd use, Mom. 'Confused' is more like it."

Victoria Parker gave her computer screens a passing glance, just to make sure the financial world hadn't come to an end. At least not until she rounded out her position in Lehman Brothers.

"Here's something else you should think about before you pass judgment on these women. You think it takes guts to be a cop? Or to fling money from one side of the globe to the other? Imagine for a moment how much courage it takes to change your sex. To explain to your parents why you want to go from George to Georgette, or to tell your boss that from now on you'll be wearing Bebe instead of Brooks Brothers? I couldn't do it, you couldn't do it, and I know for a fact that sorry excuse for femininity named Denise Fleet couldn't do it."

Mac's watch said he was already late, and that he'd better get his tail into work or face the dreaded Wrath of Mayes. His natural curiosity, however, was getting the best of him.

"Okay, Mom. Fess up. How do you know so much about trannies?"

"Show some respect, will you Mackey? A 'tranny' sounds like something that needs replacing on my Toyota. The girls at *Pearls of Asia* are transsexuals. And speaking of respect, do you have any idea what those girls go through? It costs money, and plenty of it, for them to transition from one sex to the other. Hell, I bet you didn't know my accountant is a transsexual."

Mac leaped out of his dining room chair. "Hold it right there. You can't be serious. Andrea Connors? The same woman who sat at this table last Thanksgiving with her husband Max and heard me say that her body defied the laws of gravity? Damn, I can't believe it. I had no idea."

"Of course you didn't," said Victoria, mocking her son. "Andrea likes to say that she's the best white woman from Nebraska $150,000 can buy. She cashed in her 401-K and got her face feminized, her boobs implanted, and unlike those girls at *Pearls of Asia,* had a vagina installed for good measure. She's as much a woman as I am, although not quite as shy and sensitive."

"That's a hell of a story. Does her husband know?"

"Of course he knows. He could care less, too. He's crazy about her."

Mac took a final sip from his cup. How remembered what it was like to be crazy about a girl.

⌒

MAC STROLLED INTO THE precinct to find Mayes examining the list of party guests faxed over by Jim Grisham. Thirty people were invited to the party, including ten men who came by themselves, along with ten couples. There were a few notables on the list, including businessmen, politicians, and even the proprietor of a North Beach strip club. What Mayes found interesting were two additional names scribbled in ink at the bottom of the list. Whereas the computer printout had the names, addresses and phone numbers of the invitees, these two were lumped together as "tall blonde from LA" and "skinny brunette in a black dress."

"Did your mother forget to wake you up?" asked Mayes, looking at his watch. Mayes was a stickler for punctuality, a habit Mac was still getting used to. Mac and his former partner, Larry Kelso, had worked together for years, and were so close they could finish each other's sentences. Mac enjoyed working with Mayes, and the two enjoyed a playful banter, but the true bond that was necessary for two detectives to completely trust one another was still in its formative stages.

"Osher's alibi check out?" asked Mac, signaling to Mayes that his focus was laser sharp despite the late start. Mayes told him that three witnesses corroborated Osher's story that he indeed was in Los Angeles at the time of the murder.

"What about you, Romeo? Did you come up with anything on Paul Osher's girlfriend?"

"I did, Mr. Mom. It turns out that Miss Sheyla Samonte lives in a swanky high-rise apartment in South Beach that our combined paychecks couldn't afford. I went to her place, but she played coy and wouldn't open the door. I did recognize that marvelous voice of hers though, and she's definitely the one from Osher's phone records. That woman could make a fortune starting her own 1-900 number."

"And I'm sure you'd sign up for a platinum membership. Did you ask her if she knew Paul Osher?"

"I did. She claims she doesn't know him, but we both know a mistress isn't wired to tell the truth. I also found out she's a waitress at a restaurant South of Market, so I waited around the corner and watched her drive away in a six-figure Mercedes. It's called *Pearls of Asia*. Ever hear of it?"

"Yes I have. It's somewhere over in SOMA; one of those Asian fusion places. The food is supposed to be good. They have some kind of cabaret show, too. Pamela and I have been meaning to go there."

"What else do you know about it?" asked Mac, doing his best to feign indifference.

Mayes placed a finger on his lip and paused. "Oh yeah, and all the waitresses are transsexuals, men to women type of thing. Supposed to be a heck of a show. So what else did she say?"

Mac wasn't sure what to say next, or even how to say it. If he were talking to Larry Kelso, the words would spill out like a broken oil well, because Larry was single and rolled with the punches. Mayes, on the other hand, layered with the responsibilities of a mortgage, wife and children, was wound tighter than the nuts on a new bridge. How would he react to Mac being kissed by a man?

More importantly, how would he react to Mac being kissed by a potential murder suspect during an investigation?

Mac shuffled some papers and decided telling the truth was the way to go. "Nothing. I never got to ask her any questions. But she did give me a big kiss on the lips, on stage, with the whole place watching."

Mayes laughed out loud. "You'll be okay on this one, partner. I don't think she's your type of girl."

"You got that right," agreed Mac, nodding his head. "Do you realize what this means? Osher calls Sheyla Samonte numerous times a day. We're assuming she's his mistress, and it turns out she's a transsexual. Is this far out or what?"

"Not in San Francisco," replied Mayes, the drab fluorescent bulbs reflecting off his black bald head. "Help me out, Mac. You run with this part of the investigation. It's late night work, and I can't afford to spend too much time away from my pregnant wife and kids. Otherwise, I'll need the name of your divorce attorney."

"Not to worry, partner. I got your back. Besides, 'Divorce for Dummies' was written for dopes like me, not upstanding rocks of Gibraltar like you. Now let's start digging into this pile of bank and credit card statements. I heard Osher wasn't too thrilled to let us get these."

౿

THE OSHER'S FINANCIAL STATEMENTS reflected the lifestyle of a rich couple with expensive hobbies; money flowed out as fast as it flowed in. The couple maintained a joint checking account, but the average balance was less than $1,000. Meanwhile, an individual account for Michelle Osher had an average balance of $75,000. The former beauty queen was spending almost $10,000 a month at stores like Nordstrom, Barneys, Saks, and Bloomingdales.

"How many clothes does a woman need to have in her closet?" asked Mac to no one in particular. "I've never understood why some women consider shopping an Olympic sport."

"And you wonder why your wife left you," chuckled Mayes.

Mac began perusing over Paul Osher's financial records, admitting right away what he was hoping to find. "You know what I always say, Mayes. Just follow the money. We're going to prove this guy has a mistress or two on the payroll. Michelle Osher was too busy working or shopping to pay any attention to him. Then again, if I were married to him, I wouldn't want to screw him either."

"Something else to consider," said Mayes, looking up from his desk with a pair of reading glasses perched on the tip of his nose. "Perhaps she found out her husband had a thing for this alternative lifestyle and decided for reasons of her own to let him indulge his fantasy. Not every couple lives like Pamela and me."

"Is that why you keep farm animals in the backyard?"

"You got something against sheep?"

Mac dug deeper. Paul Osher would make large deposits every month into his personal account and then, like clockwork, had daily five hundred dollar withdrawals. Over half of them were from an ATM machine located at 120 Brannan Street, one block from Sheyla Samonte's apartment, inside the corner store Mr. Doorman said she visited everyday. Mac crunched the numbers, and Osher's mistress was on the payroll earning an annual salary of almost $200,000. Tax-free. "Damn Mayes, at these prices I'd be Osher's mistress."

"I bet you look good in high heels," quipped Mayes. "Besides, we both know you'd do it for half the price."

Osher's credit card statements were as thick as a small phone book: meals, hotels, flights, flowers, taxis, and online gifts. Besides going to Los Angeles several times a month, Osher also took frequent trips to Las Vegas, Pebble Beach, and Cabo San Lucas. "This guy spends money like he's got a terminal disease," said Mac.

Mayes asked to look at a credit card bill and began matching up travel receipts with a calendar. "Check this out. Most of these trips are during the week, not weekends. I watched Michelle Osher give the news almost every night, and she was here in San Francisco."

"Zippy the Monkey could figure this out," said Mac, handing another credit card statement to Mayes. "Cash, trips, spas, jewelry. We need to see Osher. Today. We're going to nail this guy to the wall."

Mac's cell phone rang. The medical examiner was ready to see them.

CHAPTER SIX

Friday, September 12, 2008 - 1:00 pm

"Unconfirmed reports indicate Michelle Osher's throat was slashed and her head nearly decapitated."

Fox News

ASSISTANT MEDICAL EXAMINER HIROSHI Kitano, M.D., a short Japanese man who had worked in the San Francisco Medical Office for over twenty years, met the detectives in the morgue operating room, a windowless enclosure that smelled of rubbing alcohol and pork fried rice. Next to them on an operating table lay the body of Michelle Osher, covered by a blue hospital sheet. Kitano pulled it back to reveal her face and neck.

Mac tried not to wince. What had once been an aging but still attractive beauty queen was now a slab of dead meat with a cavernous gaping void where most of her neck had once been. What he could see was white, twisted, and distorted.

"It's not rocket science," said Kitano. "Her throat was slashed, and then she fell to the floor and bled out. The murder weapon appears to be a fixed-blade knife, about four inches in length."

Mac heaved a heavy sigh and gave Kitano a look like a teen-ager being asked where he's going on a Saturday night. "You called us down here for that? You could have told us that in a two-minute phone call. C'mon Chief, you know better than to waste our time."

"Not so fast," said Kitano, whom Mac nicknamed "Chief" after Kitano came to a Halloween party dressed as Sitting Bull. Asian Indians, Mac articulated after too many Red Bulls and vodka, are as oxymoronic as giant shrimp. Or San Francisco republicans. "Take a closer look at that wound. Her right carotid artery is sliced all the way through, while the left wasn't touched. Also, notice how the wound has an upward trajectory to it?"

"I see it," answered Mac. "What does it mean?"

"If a person gets their throat slashed by someone standing in front of them, the wound is straight across or has a downward tra-jectory. The upward motion to cause this wound indicates that the victim's killer slashed her throat while standing behind her, using one arm to hold the victim around the shoulders and the other to cut her throat. It also means that the murderer was taller than Michelle Osher, who was 5'8". The depth of the cut would indi-cate the murderer cut her throat from right to left, which means Michelle Osher was held across the shoulders with a right arm and slashed with the left hand. Solve for 'X' gentlemen, and your mur-derer is six-feet or taller and left-handed."

Mac and Mayes looked at each other, smiled, and shook their heads in amazement. Kitano was good. "Great job, Chief," pro-nounced Mac. "Keep up the good work and maybe they'll put you on full-time. What about the murder weapon?"

Kitano led the detectives to a corner of the morgue, away from the x-rays of smashed skulls and bottles of formaldehyde. Resting on top of a table were three distinct switchblades. "Since you guys are still relatively new to homicide, I thought I'd give you a lesson in Switchblade 101."

"Why a switchblade? Didn't you say it was a fixed-blade knife? What about a regular carving knife?" Mayes asked.

"Based on the length and depth of the wound, I'm certain this in no standard kitchen knife," lectured Kitano. "Listen and learn, Grasshopper. There are three types of so-called switchblades." Kitano picked up a black handled knife with a silver knob on its spine. "This is an automatic spring blade. It has a button, or trigger, or some kind of mechanism within the handle itself to fire the knife open." Kitano pushed the silver trigger. Snap. The blade shot out.

"I carried one of those growing up as a kid," said Mayes.

"Of course you did," replied Mac. "You used it to sharpen your pencils."

Kitano picked up another switchblade which had the top of the knife partially exposed. "This next one is a spring assisted knife. Notice there is no button in the handle. A thumb stud connected at the base of the blade trips the knife open. By legal definition it's not classified as a switchblade because there is no button or trigger to open it."

"That's like saying a rifle is not legally a handgun, yet both achieve the same objective," said Mayes.

"Now pay close attention, because I believe this type of knife is your murder weapon." Kitano picked up a silver knife, and with a flick of the wrist a blade seemed to appear out of thin air. No buttons or thumb studs, just a move a Ninja warrior would appreciate.

"This is a Balisong switchblade, also known as a butterfly knife. They're handmade in the Philippines and are illegal to carry in many countries and states, including California. It's a folding pocketknife with two handles counter-rotating around this centerpiece called a tang. There are no springs or buttons, so it too is not considered a switchblade, even though it really is. When a well-made Balisong switchblade is opened and the two handles are locked together like this, it is as strong and reliable as any fixed blade knife."

"What makes you think this type of knife is our murder weapon?" asked Mac.

Kitano walked back toward the body of Michelle Osher. "Look at that wound. The killer almost cut her head off. A simple switchblade or spring-assisted knife couldn't do that. So unless the killer brought along a butcher knife, the Balisong switchblade is your murder weapon."

"Chief, can I see that knife?" asked Mac. He closed the blade and turned it around in his hands. "Will you look how small and light this thing is? You could carry it around in your pocket and no one would ever notice."

"Or in a purse," said Mayes.

❧

MAC NAVIGATED THE SUB in the direction of the Financial District toward Paul Osher's office. Mayes sat quiet, deep in thought, which was rare for him. He liked to banter, whether it was discussing the intricacies of the case or bragging about his Twin Terrors, as he liked to call his children.

"Penny for your thoughts?" Mac asked while turning left from Folsom Street onto Fremont.

"I was just thinking about Michelle Osher," replied Mayes in a quiet voice. "She wasn't just murdered. She was slaughtered. Did you see how deep the wound was on her neck? Use a gun and it's murder, but use a knife and it's personal. Remember what I said yesterday, that whoever did this wanted to make a statement? This was not some cold-blooded killing, Mac. She was murdered in a passionate rage."

Mac waited for the light to change before crossing Market Street. "You know who gets passionate about killing a spouse? The other spouse."

"Or the other woman," replied Mayes.

❧

PAUL OSHER'S OFFICE WAS on the thirtieth floor of One Embarcadero, one of the premier office buildings in San Francisco. After making

Mac and Mayes wait for twenty minutes, a perky blonde bimbo secretary ushered them into a corner office the size of the SFPD's entire homicide and narcotics bullpens combined.

"Good afternoon, Inspectors," welcomed Osher, who remained seated at his desk without bothering to smile or shake their hands. The view of San Francisco Bay behind him was stunning, extending from the Golden Gate Bridge all the way past Angel Island, with a tiny hundred white sailboats in between. Standing next to Osher was his lawyer, Ray Woodson, who glared at the detectives without saying a word. Woodson, a tall, thin man who fancied himself more of a Mafia consigliore than a mere lawyer, was dressed in white slacks and a white blazer and some kind of Italian loafers with tassels that Mac could never afford. Or ever want to.

"Mr. Osher, we've checked your alibi and verified that you were in Los Angeles at the time of the murder," said Mac. "You also told us you loved your wife, and you've been faithful to her since the day you were married. Do you still stand by that statement?"

Lawyer Woodson decided to make his presence felt. "What does that have to do with the case? He doesn't have to answer that."

"I'll be happy to answer that," responded Osher. He reached for a cigar humidor on his enormous glass desk and pulled out a Montecristo 2. Mac wondered if Osher smoked cigars because he liked them or because he mistakenly thought they made him look taller. "Yes, I stand by that statement. Why do you ask?"

Mac looked down at his notes and paused before asking his next question, giving Osher the impression he was having difficulty putting the pieces together. This was Mac's mode of operation. He never went into an interview without knowing exactly what he was looking for.

"Well, Mr. Osher, can you help me out here? We're trying to understand the large deposits and daily cash withdrawals from your bank account." He pulled out bank statements with numerous transactions highlighted in yellow. "Can you tell us what's going on here?"

Osher put on his reading glasses and looked over the statements. He handed them over to Lawyer Woodson.

"You have a subpoena from a judge to get these from the bank, I assume?" asked Lawyer Woodson, trying to justify his thousand-dollar an hour fee.

"Of course we did," replied Mayes. "Do you think Wells Fargo would have handed them over without one?"

Lawyer Woodson glanced at them, nodded, and handed them back to Osher. "You don't have to answer any questions about this, Paul. This isn't a court of law and you're not under oath."

"I'm fine with this," said Osher. He took a draw on his forty-dollar cigar. "I always like to carry cash on me. I use it as walking-around money for tips, wagers, and cab fares, that kind of stuff. I'm also a very generous man, Inspector. I'm sure I have the best-paid shoe shine guy in San Francisco."

Mayes presented credit card receipts and asked about the frequent trips in and out of the country. Osher glanced at Lawyer Woodson, who nodded his head. "My job requires me to travel, and taking side trips to Vegas or Mexico helps me to relax. You guys got something against laying in the sun, gambling, and playing a little golf?"

Lawyer Woodson had heard enough. "Okay, he's answered your questions. This interview is over. Unless you have any evidence that Mr. Osher was involved in his wife's murder, then I suggest you come back with a grand jury indictment. I can assure you that Mr. Osher was not involved, and that he will help you in any way he can once you identify a suspect."

Mac and Mayes said their goodbyes, but not before Mac noticed a picture of Osher swinging a golf club. He had just teed off on the 18th hole at Pebble Beach, one of the most famous golf holes in the world. Mac had been fortunate to play the famous oceanside course once in his life, and he could still remember every shot he hit on every hole.

"That's the 18th hole at Pebble Beach, isn't it Mr. Osher?" asked Mac.

"Why, yes it is. That picture was taken at last year's AT&T Pro-Am tournament. The gentleman watching the flight of my ball is the other amateur in our foursome, Maury Povich, the famous talk show host. He's a great guy and an outstanding golfer. Have you played there?"

"Yes, I have. Once. I can't help but notice that you're aiming at the sand trap to the right of the tree in the middle of the fairway. Weren't you afraid your ball was going to fly that bunker and land out-of-bounds in some mega-millionaire's backyard?"

"Not at all," said Osher, sounding like he was about to give Mac a golf lesson. "Look at where my hands are when I finish my swing. You can tell I play a strong fade off the tee."

"Of course you do, Mr. Osher. How foolish of me." The detectives thanked Osher and Lawyer Woodson for their time and departed.

The elevator doors closed. Mac and Mayes stood in silence, alone in their thoughts. As the elevator approached the parking garage, Mayes, who had never picked up a golf club in his life, asked Mac what the last conversation was all about.

"Sorry, Mayes. I forgot you're too manly to play golf. Anyway, a 'strong fade' is another way of saying he slices the ball."

"So what does that mean?"

"It means he sucks at golf."

"So what does that mean?" repeated Mayes, his patience falling faster than the elevator.

"It means he hits the ball from right to left."

"Am I going to have to beat the answer out of you? I'm going to ask you one more time, Mac. What the hell does it mean and what does it have to do with the case?"

"It means he's left-handed."

The elevators doors opened to the garage. "Damn, you're good," said Mayes.

"Of course I am."

❧

MAC DROPPED MAYS OFF at his home located at the corner of
Moraga and 28ᵗʰ street, across from the Sunset Recreation Center
tennis courts where Mayes liked to work on his backhand. Buddy
and Holly sprinted out the front door and wrapped their tiny
bodies around their super-sized father. Pamela walked outside,
welcomed her husband home, and waved to Mac as he drove away.

Partnering with Mayes was a hundred and eighty degrees from
working with Larry Kelso. Mac and Larry had been like two college fraternity brothers. They worked hard when they had to, and
played even harder when they didn't. Forty-eight hour shifts had
not been uncommon, and neither were spontaneous trips to Reno.
Kelso had been more than just Mac's partner. He had been his best
friend. And he still was.

Mac peered into The Sub's rear view mirror. Mayes looked
like Gulliver fighting off the Lilliputians. The kids had their gar-
gantuan dad pinned to the ground and were tickling him while
Pamela caught the action on a video camera. Daddy's suit was getting dirty, and no one cared.

Mac never had a brother or sister. Despite being told often by
his mother that he was a bundle of joy and the love of her life, Mac
grew up blaming himself for the lack of a sibling. Maybe he was
such a difficult child his parents couldn't bear the thought of having
another. Why else, he figured, would his father abandon his five-year
old son for a life with Miss Lap Dance?

The way Mac saw it, as a child, he was a failure.

❧

SHEYLA NEVER CALLED MAC as promised. He tried calling her
several times, none of them successful, so he decided to take
another shot at finding her at work. After guiding The Sub back

to *Pearls of Asia,* Mr. Ponytail recognized him and ushered Mac past the throng of table seekers.

He'd been there for an hour nursing a Pellegrino, and there still was no sign of Sheyla. A waitress on the floor appeared to be in charge, so Mac decided to ask her about Sheyla Samonte's whereabouts. "Excuse me, Miss, can I ask you a question?"

"Yes, I'll go home with you tonight,"

"That wasn't going to be my question."

"Okay, my name is Reyna, and my phone number is…"

Reyna was tall like the other girls, but a bit stockier, a touch older, and not quite as attractive. She was wearing a black dress and a heavy dose of makeup that failed to hide a nasty scar above her left eye. Mac was more likely to share a foxhole with her than a bed.

"Not that either. I was wondering if you could help me. Do you know someone who works here named Sheyla Samonte?"

"Yes, but when she's here she's better known as Kimora, Sheyla's evil twin sister. Kimora's our most popular girl. The customers call her human Viagra."

"And she's a 'gender illusionist' like yourself?"

"Of course she is, silly," she answered while at the same time getting her picture taken. "All the ladies who work here are transsexuals. We're Women 2.0…special girls with a little something extra. That's what makes us, as well as this place, so unique."

"Trust me, I get it. Is she working tonight?"

The restaurant was packed, and Reyna was being bumped and shoved like a pinball in the tight aisle. A hand reached out from the crowd and grabbed her breast. She didn't seem to mind. "No. Sheyla doesn't work on Fridays, but she'll be here tomorrow night."

"Damn," said Mac, the expression on his face doing a poor job of hiding his disappointment. "Do you know where I can find her? It's important that I talk to her."

"It's not my turn to watch her," replied Reyna. "But I'd be more than happy to sleep with…I mean…talk to you. What would you like to know?"

"How well do you know Sheyla?"

Reyna had no idea who Mac was, but this was a woman who never passed on the opportunity to chat up a handsome man. She described how Sheyla, whom she had known while growing up in the Philippines, showed up at the doorstep of her small Mission District home ten years ago after moving to San Francisco from Thailand. Out of money and out of work, Reyna let Sheyla stay with her. She even helped Sheyla get a job selling makeup at Macy's. They were good roommates and each other's best friend, but Reyna had asked Sheyla to move out of her house two years ago after Reyna and her boyfriend decided to live together. "A gal's got to have her priorities," she said.

Mac asked Reyna what she did for a living, when she wasn't slinging cocktails and flirting with strange men. Or women. "I oversee the Transgender Advocacy Program at a local health clinic. Our budget is over a million dollars. I may not be as pretty as some of these young pop tarts running around here in their underwear, but I've got three things they don't have: a good job, a home that I own, and a wonderfully supportive boyfriend who wakes up with me every morning. Otherwise I'll beat the crap out of him."

"It sounds like you're a big deal in this town."

"I am. I have the mayor's private number on my speed dial."

"For business or pleasure?"

"Depends if his wife's around. Anyway, last year he appointed me to a special commission on transgender rights. The way I see it, one of my job descriptions is to be a role model. Too many girls in the trans community 'think they're all that' and measure themselves by what kind of shoes they wear, or which designer purse they carry. And whenever they meet a quality guy, they use them to pay their bills or promote themselves. I feel it's my responsibility to make these girls wake up and realize there's more to life than makeup and men. Although I'm not sure what."

Mac took an immediate liking to Reyna. Her plus-size personality made it easy to forget her plus-size body.

A passerby shoved Reyna in the back, and she used it as an opportunity to wedge herself between Mac's legs. "You know," she whispered into his ear, "if you take real good care of me, I can get you Sheyla's phone number."

Mac fought the urge to tell Reyna he already had that information. Plus he didn't want to give her the wrong impression. "Thanks, but I don't think so. I'm sort of out of my comfort zone here."

"Honey, you have no idea what you're missing," she demurred. "Men who start dating TS's rarely go back to GG's. Just ask my boyfriend."

"Are we talking about girls or movie ratings?"

"I love first-timers," declared Reyna, speaking louder so those around her could hear. "Pay attention, because we're going to have a quiz later. A 'TS' means someone who is a transsexual. 'GG' stands for 'genetic girl,' also known as one of those nasty bitches you straight guys chase around the Marina."

"Okay, Reyna, you hooked me. What is so special about dating a TS?"

"I'd love to show you," she said, peering over his shoulder, "but there's a line to the bathroom."

A bar manager called for Reyna's attention. "Well Mr. Who-ever-you-are, nothing would make me happier than to climb onto your lap and chat some more with you, but I need to get ready for the Blowout Show. I do want to tell you one last thing that I like to say to all of my customers; a GG is good, a TS is better, but a PG is the best!'"

"Now I'm confused. What is a 'PG?'"

"A PG is a Pearl Girl. You see, there are a lot of TS's in San Francisco, but just like the movies, only the best girls ever get a PG rating."

Mac shook his head in mock confusion. "How about a 'TMFA?'" he asked.

"What's that?"

"Too Many Fucking Acronyms."

෴

NO STRANGER TO A microphone, Reyna stepped onto the stage. "Okay people," she announced, "Everyone should order another round and get ready for the Blowout Show. It's time to fill up those nooks and crannies, and remember to tip the cooks and trannies." For the next fifteen minutes, three girls stepped onstage and entertained the audience with a feast of sky-high heels, almost-there outfits, and provocative dance moves. At the end of each number, tables of customers feeling buzzed and brave would shout out the names of their captivating servers: Diamond, Nadia, and Ashley.

Reyna stood on the middle of the runway and spotlighted diners who were celebrating birthdays, anniversaries, and for tonight at least, divorces. She asked tourists where they were from, then followed up by saying, "Thank you for coming to San Francisco, where men are men, and so are the women."

Reyna singled out the waitresses, each of whom stood on stage in the slinkiest of attire. "Ladies and gentlemen, it is now my pleasure to introduce to you the very special 'Pearls of Asia.'"

She led off with Diamond, who had more curves than Lombard Street. "You see before you this alluring, vivacious, and irresistible lady. Her name is Diamond, because she shines brighter than anyone else. Most of you must be wondering 'is she, or isn't she?' Well, let me assure you, she is NOT a vegetarian." The room erupted in laughter.

Next up was Nadia, a skinny brunette who had the best legs of the bunch. "A lot of you wonder what we do when we're not trying to seduce you. Well this very special lady is a software engineer by day and a vixen by night. Her specialty is turning your software... into hardware." The revelers whistled and screamed. "For a small consultation fee, of course."

Last was Ashley, the newbie who danced the night before. "This statuesque blonde just turned twenty one, and she's new to our horny harem. We like to call her 'gifted,' if you know what I mean. Her dancing is amazing, but you know what's even more amazing? Her Jimmy Choos are a size twelve." The crowd went nuts, and Ashley received the loudest applause of the night.

Reyna had one more announcement to make. "Ladies and Gentlemen, not only does *Pearls of Asia* offer a feast for your eyes and well as your tummies, there is also a dance club downstairs, where the room gets hot, the women get hotter, and the drinks are as stiff as a wedding night prick."

The lights came back up, but Mac had seen enough. It had been a very long day.

As he headed out a side door that lead onto Howard Street, he saw Nadia and Ashley outside sharing a cigarette. "Have a good night, ladies," he said as he strolled toward Eighth Street.

"I would if you'd take me home with you," suggested Ashley.

Mac turned and smiled. The ladies from *Pearls of Asia* must have been on their school's varsity flirt team. And they weren't shy about speaking in Tagalog around him. *"Dyos ko day hihimudin ko ang buong katawan nyan.* (I'll lick his whole body.) *"At ang puwit...winner!"* (Now that's what I call a great ass!)

"You like the suit?" Mac asked, clueless.

"The suit looks good on you, babe," said Nadia, taking a long drag from the cigarette, "but I'd rather see you naked and handcuffed to my bed. If I didn't have to do a web cam show tonight, I'd put a leash on you and put you in the back seat of my car."

"Of course you would."

Ashley and Nadia waved as Mac drove south on Howard Street toward Ninth. It was a very cute scene, two attractive women, one a tall blonde and the other a skinny brunette, running into the street to say goodnight.

A tall blonde. A skinny brunette.

"No way."

CHAPTER SEVEN

Saturday, September 13, 2008 - 7:30 am

"Michelle Osher's body was discovered by the couple's live-in maid, Maria Madrigal. An anonymous tipster has informed the Examiner that, according to immigration records, Miss Madrigal entered the United States from Mexico seven years ago on a work visa. U.S. law requires her to annually renew her visa, but she failed to do so. Efforts to reach Ms. Madrigal have been unsuccessful, and she is rumored to have left the country."

The San Francisco Examiner

"THEY'LL CRUCIFY THE GUY," deplored Mac. His feet propped on his desk, Mac was speculating with Mayes on the mass media's reaction upon learning the true identity of Paul Osher's alleged mistress. "Whether he killed his wife or not, there'll be nothing left of him but a few scraps of decomposed arrogance."

"I don't know why you're so surprised," said Mayes, already on his third cup of coffee. "It's not like the world hasn't seen this kind of relationship before. Ever hear of a play called 'M. Butterfly?'"

"Who hasn't, Mr. Magna Cum Laude English Major? Mac picked up a Rubik's Cube on his desk and tried to solve it for the millionth time in his life. He had yet to be successful. "Didn't the 49ers use that play to score the winning touchdown in the Super Bowl?"

"At least those guys are scoring instead of living at home with their mother," quipped Mayes. "M. Butterfly is a Broadway play, inspired by the opera 'Madame Butterfly' by Giaccomo Puccini in 1904. The modern update is based on a true story, and the main character, a French diplomat, falls in love with a beautiful Chinese opera singer who is a man masquerading as a woman. At first he doesn't know it, and then it doesn't matter to him, he doesn't care, and he's happy with her forever after. It's a wonderful love story. You should see it if you ever get the chance. I think you'd like it, and you might learn something."

Mac was intelligent, but rare was the opportunity when he could teach his cerebral partner a thing or two. "Speaking of learning something, smart guy, I've been doing some homework this morning. Do you know why they call the place where Sheyla Samonte works *Pearls of Asia?*"

"No I don't," replied Mayes, relishing the moment. "Do tell."

"You see, the girls who work there are like pearls," Mac explained, putting down the Rubik's Cube that looked more unsolved than when he had picked it up. "Very early in their lives they have the sense they're not who they should be. It's like they're trapped in a shell. Over the course of time they get braver and braver and the shell starts to crack open. Then one day, the shell opens up, exposing a pearl. Then the real self comes out and the pearl gets polished to a beautiful radiance. Since all of the girls who work there are Asian, they call the place *Pearls of Asia.*"

Mayes was impressed. It was the first time in months he'd seen that twinkle in Mac's eyes, a spark that disappeared along with his best friend and his wedding ring.

"Okay, Mac, that's very interesting. Now here's a question for you. Is someone born transgender, or do they become transgender?"

Mac's voice pitched to another level, and his hands became as animated as a puppeteer's. "I'll take a stab at it, partner, no pun intended. I think they're born that way, just like you were born to read books and I was born to chase bad guys. In fact, my mom and I were talking about this yesterday, and she pointed out how much courage it takes for someone to transition from one sex to the other. You put everything at risk: your job, your family, and your friends. It's more than just being gay and coming out of the closet. You have to expose yourself everyday, to everybody, while you evolve from A to B. It takes courage for you and me to put our lives on the line every day, but imagine the guts it takes to say to the world, 'You all may not be comfortable with what I'm doing here, but I have to do this.'"

"Well Oprah, you've convinced me. By the way, did San Jose State offer a class in Gender Studies? They did over at Cal, and I got an 'A.' Now shut up and grab your coat. In ten minutes, Longley expects us to be in Chief Stone's office for a briefing."

ஃ

NINE AND A HALF minutes later, the detectives found Chief of Police David Stone sitting behind a desk as vast as an aircraft carrier. His chair was placed beneath a large portrait of Thomas Cahill, not only because his name was on the building, but also because Stone and Cahill shared an affinity for strong Irish whisky. And even stronger Irish women.

"Where do we stand on the Michelle Osher case, gentlemen?" barked Stone. "The media's farther up my ass than a botched colonoscopy. Please tell me after forty-eight hours you're closing in on suspect."

"Sir, the medical examiner's report indicates that based on the depth of the wound, the murder weapon was a Balisong switchblade," said Mayes, who didn't enjoy as close a relationship with

Stone as his partner. "They're handmade in the Philippines and illegal to carry in California. So far we haven't been able to find it. The report also said the angle of the wound suggests the killer was left-handed, and at least six feet tall."

"Great. So far you've described my gardener," growled Stone. "What else?"

"We've checked the financial and phone records of both Paul and Michelle Osher," interjected Mac. "Other than spending money faster than my soon-to-be ex-wife, Michelle Osher's records are fine. Paul Osher is another story. His spending patterns and phone calls are consistent with someone having an affair. He denies it, of course, but we believe we've identified a...um...woman...who could be his mistress."

Stone's face turned redder than a poison ivy rash. "I was afraid of this. Paul Osher has always had a hard time keeping it in his pants. Who is she, and have you been in contact with this 'maybe mistress' yet?"

Mac squirmed in his seat, knowing the next words out of his mouth might set off Stone's famous temper. "When Mayes and I interviewed him, Osher claimed he had never been unfaithful to his wife. However, the woman he appears to have been contacting several times a week is named Sheyla Samonte. She works as a waitress, but somehow she manages to afford a late-model Mercedes and live in an expensive luxury apartment in South Beach. We haven't interviewed her yet, but we know where she works."

"Are you going to tell me or do I have to hear it from the press?" yelled Stone, his impatience growing by the second.

Mac fought the urge to duck, cover and roll. "Yes sir. I can tell you she works at a restaurant called *Pearls of Asia*, located at..."

Too late. Mount Stone had erupted. "*Pearls of Asia?*" he shouted, recognizing the name. "Are you telling me that one of the richest, most powerful men in this city is dating one of those goddamn transvestites?"

Mac sat up in his chair and cleared his throat before continuing. "Sir, you can infer that. We've made a couple attempts to talk to her, but so far without success."

"Holy shit," said Stone, his face now redder than a sunburned farmer. "What a nightmare. Paul Osher can have any woman in the world he wants for a mistress, and he picks a damn crossdresser. You think you know a guy. I had no idea he was gay."

"Actually, she's a transsexual, sir, not a transvestite or a cross-dresser," said Mayes, who never missed a lecture during his Gender Studies class. "Also, Paul Osher's not gay, per se, and..."

"Shut up," screamed Stone, annoyed with Mayes' attempt to educate him on the sexual labels of the rich and famous. "I don't give a damn who or what any of these assholes screw. I just want to know if we have any viable suspects and when we plan to make an arrest."

"Yes sir," responded Mayes, wisely deciding not to engage the Chief in a debate on social policy. "One more thing, sir. The Oshers kept a very small dog in the apartment, a Teacup Yorkie, and she hasn't been seen since the murder. We also need to find out what happened to Maria Madrigal, the Osher's maid. Reading about her disappearance in the Examiner was the first we heard about it."

"How does it affect the case?" asked Stone.

Mac had been wondering the same thing since reading the headline with his morning coffee. At that moment two pieces of the puzzle came together. "It's only important if Paul Osher is lying about being in Los Angeles. Osher could have bought himself an alibi in L.A., and the maid may have seen or heard him that morning in the apartment."

"Alright, gentleman, I've heard enough. Remember, this is a very delicate case. Paul Osher is a major figure in this town. If this business about a tranny mistress were to leak to the press, it could destroy him. So be careful. Now get out there and arrest somebody. Now!"

∽

MAC AND MAYES SPENT the afternoon huddled in a not-dark-enough screen room in the SFPD's cold and dank basement, watching surveillance tapes from the Osher's apartment building on the night of the murder. They were joined by a wide-eyed and much more alert Jim Grisham.

"That's Mike Rogers and his wife, April," said Grisham. "She's his third wife, actually. Mike owns an Internet security company. He likes to tell people that his company has made several people millionaires, including his two ex-wives."

According to the list submitted by Jim Grisham, thirty people were invited to his Wednesday night soiree, and two women later showed up uninvited. He had names for everyone except the two late arrivals: the mysterious "tall blonde from LA" and the "skinny brunette." Twelve partygoers lived in the building and were already interviewed and ruled out. That left eighteen guests who needed to be accounted for walking into and out of the building, along with the two party crashers.

"Okay, I recognize that couple," said Grisham. "That's Meredith Foxx, the writer, and her boyfriend Jay. You talk about an interesting couple. She stays at home and makes a fortune writing lousy books that sell like hot cakes, while he slums around town looking for places to play his guitar. I want to be him when I grow up."

The quality of the tape was grainy and fair at best, and the camera angle above the building's entrance shot mainly the top of people's heads, so it was impossible to see them as more than pixilated fuzz balls. After watching two hours of tape, the detectives counted eighteen party guests arriving between nine and ten o'clock. Mac fast-forwarded the tape to a few minutes before midnight. Two well-dressed women were seen walking into the building together. "Mr. Grisham, do you recognize these women?"

Grisham moved closer to the screen, squinted his yes, and nodded his head. "Yep. Those are the two girls who came late to the party. I don't know who they are, but they were there. I saw them come in, but I never got a chance to talk to them."

"Are they the women classified on your list as the 'skinny brunette' and 'tall blonde'?"

"They are. Too bad you can't see their faces. I remember they were both Asian, and they were both hotter than a summer in New Orleans. Too bad I didn't get their names. Do me this one courtesy, would you please? Can you let me know if you find out who they are? I want to make sure they come to my next party."

"Of course we will," sassed Mac, who had no intention of following through on Grisham's request.

Twenty people were seen leaving between midnight and four o'clock in the morning, most of whom were too intoxicated to walk, much less drive. The mysterious "tall blonde" left by herself at 1:30am, and the "skinny brunette" was seen walking arm and arm with a man around 2:00am. After watching almost seven hours of tape, the detectives sent Grisham on his way.

"I think our killer has to be one of the two women who showed up at midnight," said Mac, rubbing his strained eyes after staring at a projection screen for most of the day. "What if Sheyla Samonte was one of them? Maybe she and one of her gal pals from *Pearls of Asia* showed up and blended in so they could slip upstairs and kill Michelle Osher? Think about it, Mayes. Slap a pair of heels on any one of them and now they're all over six-feet tall. What if it was Paul Osher who put them up to it, so he could get rid of his boring, sexless wife and spend his time and money playing around with Sheyla?"

Mayes thought about it for a minute. "An interesting idea. It would confirm my theory that the 'other woman' committed the crime, and your premise that the husband was involved. But we have to prove it. Where's the knife? Were there any eyewitnesses? What about the other people on the tape? And why the hell hasn't Sheyla Samonte called you back?"

"I have my suspicions. Sheyla's working tonight at *Pearls of Asia*. I'll go there and see what I can find out."

"You do that, Romeo. In the meantime, I'm going to find a judge and get a search warrant. If those two women were at

Grisham's party, then we have enough probable cause to search his apartment."

❧

THE LONG LINE BUNCHED at the front door and snaked into the darkness of Ninth Street, so Mac decided to sneak through the side door adjacent to Howard Street. To his left was a stairway that led down to the restaurant's nightclub and the girls' dressing room. Directly in front of him was the kitchen, and a chef the size of a small house was barking orders in Spanish to a half-dozen cook's assistants. The air was hot, the music loud, and the customers were laughing and shouting. To the veterans of *Pearls of Asia,* it was just another eleven o'clock on a Saturday night. To rookies like Mac, it was Mardi Gras.

Every seat at the bar was taken, so Mac squeezed himself into a corner near the stairway. The sensation of someone grabbing a handful of his ass interrupted Mac's careful analysis of the scene.

"Hi handsome. Welcome to *Pearls of Asia,*" flirted an Asian woman sporting high heels, long painted nails, and porn-star-wanna-be makeup. "I see you're empty handed."

"That makes one of us," responded Mac.

She was young, a twenty-something, and she was a monument to artifice and excess. Her painted pink lips matched her painted red dress, which matched her painted green heels, and her painted black hair. Her eyelashes were false, but they were more natural than her breasts. A long necklace adorned with a cheap gold plated "D" protruded from her chest and was as inconspicuous as a Las Vegas volcano. She looked like a drug store mannequin, but to the hundred or so diners suddenly fluent in Martini, she was inviting, enticing and sexy.

"Can I get you something?" she asked.

"I'd love a beer, if you don't mind?"

"Why would I mind? I just met my next boyfriend." She walked to the bar and returned with a beer. She handed it to him with one hand, and used the other to pull him close to her botox-enhanced lips. "I'm Diamond," she whispered, "and you'll never forget me."

Diamond was summoned to the stage to perform, and she climbed a step stool onto the runway. The Latin melody "Ain't It Funny" by Jennifer Lopez soared over the room, and Diamond began dancing across the bar, shaking her hips like a broken washing machine. Her hands tried to tell a story, but the message got lost in translation. Diamond flirted with a woman sitting in the 'hot seat,' who laughed so hard she spilled her drink between Diamond's Twin Peaks. The almost-too-painful-to-watch number thankfully closed to muted applause. As Diamond descended the stage she walked past Mac and grabbed the front of his shirt. "Don't you dare go anywhere," she insisted. "I'm taking you home tonight in a doggy bag."

Mac grabbed an empty seat at the bar. For a change of pace he ordered one of the colorful martinis named after the waitresses at *Pearls of Asia*. He tried a Kimora Cocktail, a blend of gin, rum, orange juice and Cointreau. Mac took a sip, and knew right away what it tasted like: another.

A gentle tap on his shoulder interrupted a second sip. He turned around expecting to go Round Two with Diamond, but instead he saw a face and heard a voice that took his breath away.

"Hello there. I'm Kimora."

Wide-eyed and slack-jawed, Mac had the look of a stunned boxer. Kimora was wearing a red lacy chiffon cocktail dress, the kind of outfit that could cause a man to forget his name.

"Nice to meet you, Kimora, or should I call you Sheyla?" replied Mac, recovering quickly. "I'm Inspector Mac Fleet from the San Francisco Police Department. You may recall I showed up at your apartment on Thursday afternoon, but later that night you indulged me with a kiss. Why haven't you returned any of my calls?"

"Oh dear. I'm so sorry. So many people call me," said The Voice, her words caressing his ears like a cashmere ski cap. "I was so disappointed when you left Thursday night. I hope I didn't scare you off."

"Not at all. Complete strangers walk up and kiss me all the time."

"You're cute," commented Sheyla, with a flirtatious chuckle that was as charming as her voice. "You weren't by chance here last night, were you? Reyna called this morning to tell me a handsome man was looking for me. Make my night and tell me she was talking about you."

"Yes I was, Miss Samonte. We need to talk as soon as possible. Like right now."

"'Miss Samonte,' is it? My, aren't we being formal. I have to take care of a couple of tables, first. Be a good boy and I'll be back in two shakes of a girl's tail."

Mac watched Sheyla walk away, her hips swaying like a lazy palm tree on a Caribbean island. There was something different about her. The waitresses at *Pearls of Asia* all wore outfits skimpier than Saran Wrap. Sheyla, however, looked like she bought hers at Gucci, while the others shopped at Goodwill. Sheyla must have been putting the Paul Osher gift cards to good use.

"So tell me your name," yakked Diamond, her return as discrete as a blow to the head. After learning Mac's name, she decided his lap looked more comfortable than the empty barstool next to him. "I love your hair, Mac," she said, combing his silver and black locks with her fingers made sticky from spilling too many drinks. "Did you miss me?" Before he could tell Diamond he missed her as much as the measles, she made an unusual request. "Give me your phone."

"Why would I do that?"

"Because if you don't, I'll pull down your pants and we'll see who's bigger."

Mac handed her his cell phone, and Diamond punched her phone number into his contact list. She then dialed herself up, and now she had Mac's number. The staff at *Pearls of Asia* had a name for this charade; Mac had just been "diamonded."

"By the way," she said as she handed Mac his phone. "I saw you talking to Kimora. You may think she's pretty and all that, but you should know she's just a fucking whore. And she gets clocked everywhere she goes."

"Clocked?" asked Mac. "Is there a radar gun in here?"

"'Getting clocked' is when someone calls you out as a tranny. You know, like when Sheyla walks into a bar and some guy yells, 'That's a man.' It happens to girls like her all the time, but never to me. I always pass."

"You're killing me, Diamond. 'Always pass?' Even Joe Montana didn't always pass."

"I like you, Mac. Are you this funny when you're lying on your back? 'Pass' means you look like a woman, like I do. You should see how many guys try to pick me up at the grocery store when I'm not wearing makeup. It's so annoying. Don't you think I'm stunning?"

"Like a Taser gun," answered Mac, pushing Diamond off his lap like a sack of potatoes.

A short Mexican food runner came up and told Diamond an over-served woman at one of her tables wanted a 'Blowjob Shot.'

"I love this place," chortled Mac. "You need to take a vocabulary test before you walk in here. What's 'Blowjob Shot?'"

Diamond placed her bulging bosoms under Mac's chin and shoved a shot glass in between her overinflated mammary glands. "You see, I fill this glass full of booze, place it between my breasts, and a customer pays for the privilege of fishing it out with their mouth. Doesn't it look like fun? We can do it all night at my place if you want." Before running off to perform her unique job skill, Diamond reached between Mac's legs and gave him a not-so subtle squeeze to his groin. "Oh Mac, you ARE happy to see me, aren't you? Wait here and Dr. Diamond will take care of this as soon as I get back."

Sheyla witnessed the entire episode from across the room while entering drink orders into a cash register. As they were about to pass one another, Diamond addressed Sheyla in Tagalog. *"Akin s'ya maghanap ka ng iba!"* (He's mine, look for someone else!) Whatever words of wisdom Diamond tried to impart, Sheyla looked straight ahead and ignored her. To most of the girls at *Pearls of Asia*, Diamond's antics were like a comedian's tired jokes; she needed some new material.

Sheyla glided over to Mac's chair and said in a song that could stop a train, "I'm back. I'm sorry, Mac. I hope you'll forgive me for not returning your calls."

"Miss Samonte, if I wanted to, I could haul you down to the precinct right now and throw your pretty little ass in jail for obstructing an investigation."

Sheyla's tone went from velvet to sandpaper. "I've got news for you, Inspector. We both know you're full of shit. I know the difference between obstructing an investigation and not returning a phone call. Trust me, I've dated enough lawyers to pass the bar exam."

She was right, and Mac knew it. In no time Sheyla returned to her charming self. "So tell me, handsome, what were you and Miss Silicon City talking about?"

"Diamond was giving me a vocabulary lesson. She claims you get 'clocked' all the time."

Sheyla shook her head like a disappointed mother. "She says I get clocked all the time? Who is she kidding? Diamond gets clocked so often she should be doing Rolex commercials."

Mac took delight at Sheyla's zinger. "She also says guys hit on her even when she's not wearing a ton of makeup."

"Diamond not wear makeup?" responded Sheyla, shocked by such an assertion. "She'd rather be blind than leave her house without wearing false eyelashes. Trust me, Mac, that girl wakes up in the morning wearing makeup. She has too. Diamond never met a mirror she didn't like."

"What's with the heavy metal charm around her neck?"

Sheyla sighed. "She tells customers the 'D' on her necklace stands for 'Diamond,' but we girls all know better. It stands for 'Diva.'"

Mac let out a boisterous laugh. He always appreciated a woman with a sense of humor, especially if it could keep up with his own. "Listen Miss Samonte, I do need to ask you a few questions. Is there someplace we can talk?"

"First off, please call me Sheyla. And second, I don't have time to talk tonight. But I know what you want from me. You see, besides having a lot of lawyers on my speed dial, I'm also a *Law and Order* junkie. You asked me if I knew Paul Osher. Well, I'm not going to lie to you. I do, and I know you've got the records to prove it. You also want to know where I was the night his wife was killed. All I can tell you is that I was home alone, and no, I can't prove it. But it's the truth. If you want to know anything else, then you can either drag me out of here in handcuffs kicking and screaming, or take me out for brunch tomorrow. Your choice."

Mac thought he had heard every threat in the book. Being blackmailed with a date was a new one.

"First of all, Miss Samonte, I don't address murder suspects by their first name. And I certainly don't take them out to brunch. It's not what anyone would call proper police procedure."

"Oh, so I'm a murder suspect, am I? Sounds exciting. I guess I'll have to just have to put that on my Facebook page." Sheyla slid her arm around Mac's shoulder. "C'mon, Inspector. It'll be fun. Don't get your boxers in a wad."

"How can you tell I'm wearing boxers?"

"Oh, please," she said, aiming her eyes at Mac's .45 caliber erection. "Tell you what. I'll buy. Plus I promise to tell you everything you want to know about Paul Osher and me. By the time we finish dessert, you'll be calling me 'Sheyla.' That's my deal. Take it or leave it." Sheyla leaned over and kissed Mac on the cheek, glancing in Diamond's direction to make sure the D-cupped diva was watching. She was, and the look on her face could have melted dry ice. Like a dog peeing on a bush, Sheyla was marking her territory.

Mac did the math. What was Sheyla hiding from him? What secrets would she spill about Paul Osher? What was that perfume she was wearing?

"What time shall I meet you?"

CHAPTER EIGHT

Sunday, September 14, 2008 - 11:15 am

"Paul Osher, multi-millionaire businessman and husband of murdered KNTV anchorwoman Michelle Osher, said in a statement issued by his attorney that, 'He learned about his wife's death while on business in Los Angeles, and he is devastated and vows to cooperate fully with the police to help find her killer.'"

The Wall Street Journal

MAYES TORE THROUGH JIM Grisham's medicine cabinet like a bear hunting for ants. He found over a dozen prescriptions made out for either Jim or Sonia Grisham, and Mayes bagged and tagged a pill from each bottle and sent it off to the crime lab for analysis. He still hadn't found what he was looking for: a reason to suspect anyone who attended Jim Grisham's Thursday night soirée.

It was 11:15 on a beautiful sunny Sunday morning. Grisham hadn't been expecting visitors, but Mayes had a schedule to keep. Just one hour earlier, Mayes knocked on the door of a junior assistant district attorney, who took the advice of a large black man pacing in his living room and woke up a judge to issue a search warrant. At that hour of the morning, figured Mayes, size did matter.

"What do you do for a living, Mr. Grisham?" asked Mayes.

"I'm an attorney," Grisham managed to say between yawns. "And you better find what you're looking for and get the hell out of here."

"We'll leave when we're finished, Mr. Grisham," said Mac, rubbing his latex-gloved hand along the top of a living room bookshelf. "Speaking of which, Paul Osher told us you have a key to his apartment. Would you mind showing it to us, please?"

Grisham walked over to a table underneath a large mirror hanging in the entryway. He pulled open a drawer and fished his hand among its contents. "That's strange," he said. "It's always in here. If my wife were home she'd know where it is."

"Mrs. Grisham isn't here?" asked Mac. "Where is she?"

"She's in New York. She left a couple days ago. Friday, to be exact. She said she wanted to visit her college roommate and do some shopping."

"But you said she was wasted and wouldn't wake up for a week." said Mayes. "Why the quick exit?"

"How the hell should I know? Maybe Bergdorf's was having a sale," barked Grisham.

"Is this her?" asked Mac, holding a faded picture of a much younger Jim Grisham and a woman in a wedding gown. Mac at first thought the picture was a joke, because the bride was at least six inches taller than the groom despite his platform shoes. She had a Farrah Fawcett-inspired hairdo, while Grisham had long hair and wore bell-bottom blue jeans.

"Yes, back when Sonia was eighteen. That was from our wedding day."

"Of course it was," said Mac, who was thrilled he wasn't around during the Seventies. Watergate and disco made people do things they would later come to regret. "When was the last time you saw her, Mr. Grisham?"

"Sometime after midnight, I think. She said she had to excuse herself from the, uh.... festivities, because she had too much to drink and wasn't feeling well. She said she was going to sleep in our guest room because she didn't want to risk puking all over me in bed."

"How considerate of her," opined Mayes, rolling his eyes. "And she never once mentioned to you that she was flying across the country the next day? What do we look like, Mr. Grisham? Dumb and Dumber?"

"She's an adult, for crying out loud. Sonia does whatever the hell she wants. Now are you guys almost done?"

"Not even close," stated Mac. "Mr. Grisham, you uttered some less than flattering remarks about Michelle Osher to us after you learned of her murder. Our captain told us you and she didn't see eye-to-eye on a few subjects, specifically the issue of gay marriage. Is that the real reason why you called her a 'first-class bitch?'"

Grisham spent the next several seconds tying and retying his bathrobe, like a boxer preparing for a fight. "I know what you want to hear, Inspector. You want me to say 'yes' so you can suspect I had some kind of beef with her, and that maybe somehow our political differences gave me a motive to kill her. Well you just swung and missed. The truth is Michelle and I agreed on most issues, just not when it comes to same-sex partners tying the knot. Michelle believed extending marriage benefits to gay couples would increase the number of child adoptions, since God doesn't allow gay couples to make babies. It was only after an hour-long debate on the topic over a bottle of '97 Joseph Phelps that Michelle told me she was adopted. After that, I respected her opinion because she had some skin in the game. I would never admit this in public, but she changed my mind and now I'm a supporter of same-sex marriages. So I had no political beef with her. I just didn't like her, that's all. Last time I checked, that wasn't a crime."

Mac stopped what he was doing and scratched his salt and pepper locks. "Wow. I never thought about the issue that way.

How come you never made that argument, Mayes? You're the brilliant thinker."

"The truth is I never looked at it that way, either. Maybe because Pamela and I have two kids and I've still got plenty of bullets left in my pistol, if you get my drift."

An hour into the search and Mac and Mayes had found nothing. As they were about to leave, Mac peered into a large porcelain vase near the front entryway. Lying at the bottom was a Fairmont Hotel room key card. Strange, because the Fairmont Hotel was just a block away. Mac turned the heavy vase over and out fell dozens of Fairmont Hotel key cards.

"Check this out, Mayes." Mac picked up the cards, and about half had pictures of the newly restored lobby on the front. "Some of these were used during the past nine months. They just finished remodeling the hotel last winter. Do you know anything about these cards, Mr. Grisham?"

"I've never seen those cards in my life," professed Grisham. "I swear, I have no idea how they got there."

Mayes took a card and pointed at the magnetic strip on the back. "You see these strips, Mr. Grisham? Each one of these is labeled with a date and room number. No doubt each one has a story to tell. For all we know they may lead us to our killer. I sure hope you're not lying to us."

"When did you say your wife was returning?" asked Mac.

"I didn't say and I don't know," protested Grisham.

Mayes glared a hole through the back of Grisham's skull. "Find out."

᠎᠎᠎

MAC AND MAYES MADE their way up one flight of stairs to Paul Osher's apartment. They had requested another meeting to confirm his relationship with Sheyla Samonte. Lawyer Woodson greeted them at the door. The taciturn, blank-faced attorney led Mac and Mayes into the living room. Paul Osher sat in a brown leather easy chair, wearing a pair of red silk pajama shorts and a blue robe. Osher's worn body had more miles on it than the Space Shuttle.

Mayes led off by asking about Misha, the couple's missing dog. Osher claimed he didn't know where the dog was, nor did he care. As far as he was concerned, the dog belonged to his wife.

"I hated that rat," proclaimed Osher. "Michelle's the one who wanted a dog. She thought getting her picture taken while walking Misha through the neighborhood would make her look more...I don't know...stylish. We couldn't have any kids, so that mutt was her substitute. What does that four-figure fur ball have to do with the case anyway?"

"We don't know, Mr. Osher," answered Mac, who wondered why, after Grisham's revelation about Michelle Osher, the couple didn't consider adoption. "But every piece of the puzzle always fits somewhere."

Osher rose up and fetched yet another cigar, this time an H. Upmann Magnum 46 " That's wonderful, Inspector Fleet. Maybe the dog murdered my wife. Now can we get this over with, please? My favorite caddy is waiting for me at the San Francisco Golf Club."

"Sure thing, Mr. Osher," continued Mac. "Where is your maid, Maria Madrigal?"

"You mean my former maid. She packed up all her crap and took off yesterday. Good riddance as far as I'm concerned. And I can testify she told us she had a green card, if anyone gives a damn."

"We don't care about that," retorted Mac. "What we do care about, Mr. Osher, is if she knew something you didn't want us to know about."

The silence in the room was deafening. Lawyer Woodson decided to earn his fee by venturing into the void. "What are you implying, Inspector?"

"Nothing," replied Mac, looking at Paul Osher. Osher stared back at Mac, blowing smoke into the air. Like two kids engaged in a schoolyard stare-down contest, neither one would back down.

Mac finally had to lower his eyes to check his notepad. He may have lost this battle, but he was about to win the war.

"Mr. Osher, there is one last topic we need to discuss with you. Your phone records point to a woman you've been calling quite a bit...uh...wait, here it is...Sheyla Samonte. Can you explain this, sir?"

Osher gave a long pull on his cigar. "No, Inspector, I can't."

"You can't or you won't," countered Mac. "Let's say we cut the crap, Mr. Osher. By this time tomorrow we'll have records of any text messages you sent to her as well. So do yourself a favor and stop bullshitting us."

Osher heaved a heavy sigh and threw a anxious look toward Lawyer Woodson, who nodded his head. The detectives had uncovered a piece of the puzzle Osher hadn't wanted them to find.

"I'm not thrilled to admit this, but my lawyer says I should be completely honest with you. I've got nothing to hide."

"A great policy to live by, Mr. Osher. And thank you for such good advice, Mr. Woodworth."

"Woodson," the attorney snapped.

"Of course you are."

Osher cleared his throat and took a quick puff. "Yes, I've been uh.... been involved... with Sheyla Samonte for a long time now. I'm not the first man to have a relationship outside my marriage. Its one of the perks of being rich."

"Did she know you were married?" asked Mayes.

"I thought you were supposed to be the smart one," needled Osher, chafing at Mayes question. "Of course she knew. Women like Sheyla prefer to date men who are married."

"Do you provide for her?" continued Mayes.

"You mean do I pay for her to be my girlfriend? She lives in one of my apartment buildings, for God's sake. What do you think?"

"What about the daily ATM transactions?" asked Mac. "Is that her meal money?"

"It is if she's having champagne and caviar every day." Osher stood up and started pacing around the room. "I'm not sure what she uses the money for, and I don't care. Just so long as she's available when I want to see her, and smart enough to leave when I don't."

Osher also confessed to taking Sheyla with him to such exotic ports of call as Maui and Cabo San Lucas, and countless trips to Las Vegas. Besides first class airfare and four-star accommodations, Osher would also give Sheyla his black American Express card so she could shop 'til she dropped.

"Did you make her any promises, Mr. Osher, like you would divorce your wife and marry her?" asked Mayes.

"Of course not. Women like Sheyla know who they are and what they want. Once a mistress gets married, she knows there's another job opening."

Osher walked over and gazed out toward Alcatraz Island. His eyes began to take on a dream-like quality. "You know, if you ever saw her, you would wish you were me."

"Is that right, Mr. Osher?" challenged Mac. "Enlighten me as to why I'd want to be like you."

"Because she's gorgeous as hell. She's the most exciting woman I've ever met. I get a woody just thinking about her."

Osher may have had money, but as far as Mac was concerned, he was broke when it came to class. It was time to lay his cards on the table.

"Well, Mr. Osher, I'm going to let you in on a little secret." Mac walked over to the window, and spoke in a near whisper to Osher. "We've already been in contact with Miss Samonte. We got her address from your phone records, and I've been to her apartment. I've also seen where she works when she's not working on you. I'm sure you wouldn't want the press to find out that when your mistress isn't employed as your personal piece of arm candy, she's a "gender illusionist" at *Pearls of Asia*."

Osher's face turned whiter than the walls in his living room. The secret he hoped to keep buried forever had just been unearthed.

The world learning he had a mistress didn't bother him, while the world learning she was a pre-operative transsexual scared him to death. He wanted to speak, but the words just wouldn't come out. "So you know?" he finally uttered.

"Know what, Mr. Osher?"

"You know she's a little...different."

"We know that she works at a restaurant called *Pearls of Asia* if that's what you mean."

"Then you know what I'm trying to say." Osher began to shake and needed to sit down. Lawyer Woodson went to the liquor cabinet and opened a bottle of scotch. Even at a thousand bucks an hour, what his client needed at that moment was a bartender more than a lawyer.

"Do you think she would have any reason to kill your wife?" asked Mayes

"None, whatsoever. She's on the gravy train, for Christ's sake. She's living a fantasy life. Why would she risk giving it up? She had nothing to gain by killing Michelle."

Mac checked his watch. It was 12:30, and they needed to go. They were scheduled to meet Sheyla in thirty minutes.

As Mac and Mayes headed for the door, a visibly upset Paul Osher rose from his chair to cut them off. "Detectives, please, please. Do me this one favor. Try to keep our little secret out of the press. Information like this could be devastating. It could ruin me. I beg you."

Paul Osher wasn't the first suspect Mac had in the hot seat. But Osher was so stressed out, Mac could actually hear him sweat.

❧

"MAYES HERE. YES....YES...alright Captain. We'll be right there."

"What's going on?" Mac asked as The Sub approached the Embarcadero.

"A freighter from the Philippines arrived at the Port of Oakland Friday night. During inspection by customs agents, a box containing a dozen Balisong switchblades was found. Longley wants us to drive to Oakland and find out as much as we can about the shipment. We won't find our murder weapon, but we may find out who's dealing the contraband. We can't begin to connect the dots until we have dots to connect. Not to mention Longley needs to see some progress on this case. Stone's all over his ass. I told him we'd get there ASAP."

Mac sat in silence while navigating The Sub. They were just minutes away from the Oakland-San Francisco Bay Bridge. Once they got on the lower deck of the aging double-decker span, their fate for the rest of the day would be sealed.

"What about our meeting with Sheyla?"

CHAPTER NINE

Sunday, September 14, 2008 - 1:00 pm

"A memorial service will be held on Tuesday, September 16th,
at the Cathedral of the Blessed Sacrament in Sacramento, CA,
Michelle Osher's hometown. Thousands are expected to attend,
and celebrities, politicians, and fans flying in from all over the
world are scrambling to find hotel rooms."

PEOPLE

MAC'S STOMACH WAS DOING cartwheels. It was already 1:15, and Sheyla was nowhere in sight. His badly-in-need-of-resoling black Florsheims had already paced a dozen laps around the elegant atrium of the Rincon Center, it's massive skylight roof signaling the burn off of the morning fog. Hundreds of hungry diners waited in line to spend a week's wages at Yank Sing, famous for having the best dim sum in San Francisco. Carts loaded with bronze-skinned Peking Duck, lamb dumplings and flying fish eggs maneuvered through the aisles of white-clothed tables, many topped off with bottles of champagne. Mac always wanted to try the place. Too bad he couldn't afford it.

His cell phone bleated. It was The Voice. "Hello, handsome. How are you?"

"'Where are you?' is more appropriate," answered Mac, not even trying to hide his frustration. "You better not be standing me up, Miss Samonte. Otherwise, I will have you arrested."

"Calm down, cutie. I'm just running a little late. I operate on Filipina time. Is your partner with you?"

"No. He got called away. It's just me and five hundred other people waiting in line for an egg roll. How soon can you be here?"

The atrium's waterfall masked the seconds of silence. "Tell you what. I've got another place in mind. You're just a few minutes from my place. Come pick me up. I'll meet you downstairs in five minutes." Then she hung up.

Two and a half minutes later, The Sub was moored in front of Sheyla's apartment in South Beach. While waiting in the lobby, Mac could feel his breathing pick up, and his right hand started to reach for the handcuffs hanging from his back pocket. His frustration had reached a boiling point. If Sheyla Samonte didn't show up in thirty seconds, he was going upstairs to arrest her.

At the last possible moment, the elevator doors parted. What Mac saw next was a daydream straight from the pages of Vogue. It was Sheyla, wearing an off-the-shoulder white linen sundress, which she had decided looked better without a bra. Her white Chanel watch and matching handbag worked well with her gold hoop earrings. Strands of long, silky brown hair framed a pair of Gucci sunglasses that hid her eyes, but not her smile, which said she was happy to see him.

Her heels made her nearly as tall as Mac, and she used them to walk straight up and kiss him on his lips. He tried to pull away, but she grabbed the front of his jacket and pulled him close to her, kissing him like a girlfriend who hadn't seen her man in months. As hard as it was for Mac to believe, this kiss tasted even better than their first. Mac glanced around, and sure enough, there was a surveillance camera above the lobby door entrance. So much for public discretion.

As soon as they started walking back to The Sub, her arm locked in his, Mac knew he was toast. They had been together less than sixty seconds, and Sheyla had already taken control. Always a gentleman, Mac opened her car door. As he walked around to the driver's side, he laughed at himself. He would never have done that for another man.

"Okay Miss Samonte. Where are we going?"

"Can we just drive around for awhile?" she asked excitedly. "I love this car! It's so cool. What kind is it?"

"It's a Chevy Kingswood Estate Cruiser, built during the Eisenhower Administration. It's got almost 300,000 miles of charm on it, and it has the turning radius of a small European country. I call it 'The Sub.'"

"Mmmm…really? Does that mean I get to go down on your periscope?"

In less than twenty-four hours, Mac had learned two things about Sheyla that he liked. She had a wicked sense of humor, and she adored his car. Both were big pluses in his book. His soon to be ex-wife was just the opposite; Denise had all the witticism of a mothball, and she had wanted The Sub to be decommissioned and turned into scrap.

"How about we do this, Miss Samonte? You tell me where to go, and I'll take the scenic route."

"That sounds wonderful. I know the perfect spot, too. The Grand Café at the Hotel Monaco. It'll be fun because one of my best friends works there. It's on the corner of Geary and Taylor, across the street from the Clift Hotel. And please, you would sound so much sexier if you called me Sheyla."

"I could call you Kimora. That's a sexy name."

"Oh, please. Kimora is a performer who works at *Pearls of Asia*. She's my alter ego, a cartoon character. I want you to know Sheyla. She's much more interesting."

"Of course she is," he said while flashing her his patented deep-dimpled smile. "By the way, you look very nice today."

"Why thank you, Mac. I wanted to look good for you. I've been dying to wear these Kate Spade pumps that I bought last week at Bloomingdales."

The last thing Mac was looking at were her shoes. Sheyla's dress was hitched up slightly, exposing a pair of legs a mile long. Instead of facing forward and looking straight ahead, Sheyla shifted her body toward him. Mac spoke fluent body language, and hers said she was excited to be in his company.

"Mac, do you mind if I ask you a question? Why did you become a cop?"

"I'm the one who is supposed to be asking the questions, Miss Samonte. The short answer is I like to solve puzzles."

"Really? Is that what I am to you, a puzzle?" said The Voice with a flirtatious smirk. "If that's the case, you're going to have a lot of fun putting my pieces together."

∽

THE GRAND OPERA STYLE architecture of the Hotel Monaco's ballroom blended with the art deco windows and glass ceiling fixtures, giving The Grand Café an elegance befitting its location at the heart of San Francisco's Theater District. The room had a European turn of the century style and made one feel as though they had stepped into a restaurant in Prague. Mac had never been to The Grand Café. He had also never been to Prague.

After being seated, an angelic Asian waitress approached their table, and Sheyla jumped out of her seat to offer a hug. "Nicole! It's so good to see you."

Nicole was pretty and petite, and she had a warm smile. She looked to be in her mid-thirties, and her body was as fit and trim as an athlete's.

"Mac, this is my dear friend Nicole. Nicole, meet my newest heartthrob, Mac Fleet. He's a detective. Can you believe it?"

"Girlfriend, nothing you do surprises me. It's nice to meet you, Mr. Mac."

"It's nice to meet you, Nicole. Miss Samonte insisted we come here."

"That's because we have such huge portions, and Sheyla always eats like it's her last meal." Nicole's voice had a sexy touch of a French accent. "You are one handsome man, Mr. Mac. Later on I'll ask Sheyla what she did to win your favor. You should know, by the way, that she's my role model. Anyways, what can I get for you Mr. Mac?"

Mac asked for a simple glass of water, while Sheyla ordered a Bloody Mary. Mac couldn't help but smile. Sheyla apparently didn't mess around when it came to enjoying a Sunday Brunch.

"How do you know Nicole?" asked Mac.

"When I came to America ten years ago, the first job I got was selling makeup at Macy's in Union Square. Nicole worked at the counter next to me. Isn't she amazing to look at? She's so shy and self-conscious. She has no idea how beautiful she is. She's a trans woman also, but you would never know it, would you?"

Mac shook his head in disbelief. "Are you kidding me? Not in two million years. She's gorgeous."

"I'm so lucky to have Nicole in my life. It's rare to find a true friend in the San Francisco TS community, especially among the Filipinas. Everything is a competition, particularly when it comes to looks. The prettier you are, the more jealous and hateful the girls get. I mean, just look at Diamond. She was a sweet little gay boy when she graduated high school and began her transition. Two years later she started to blossom, but so did her attitude. She told anyone who would listen to her that she was the prettiest girl in town. I don't know, maybe she's insecure because she was an only child, or that she was born in the States. She started alienating everyone in the Filipina trans community who cared about her. I mean, don't you think it's better we support one another instead of ripping each other to shreds? Diamond's a beautiful girl, but she's just so annoying and spiteful; it's impossible to like her. She's turned into a narcissistic bitch who cares only about herself. All she does is talk about how pretty she is while backstabbing her friends and gossiping about people she doesn't know. I swear, Mac, she's evil."

"Don't sugar coat it, Miss Samonte. Tell me how you really feel," joked Mac.

"You know how TS is supposed to be short for 'transsexual?' In Diamond's case it means 'tropical storm.' Whenever she gets a hormone shot, she's so paranoid and neurotic we upgrade her to a hurricane."

Mac laughed out loud. Sheyla's wit was quick and biting. Just like his. "Anyway, I don't want to waste our time together talking about that tramp." Sheyla slid her chair closer to Mac. She kissed him on the cheek, and then nibbled on his ear. Her hand managed to find Mac's knee while they looked over the menu. This was not going to be a typical interrogation.

Nicole brought over their drinks. "You must be someone special, Mr. Mac. My friend is positively glowing this morning."

"It must be the sun."

"Isn't he funny?" remarked Sheyla. "I just love his sense of humor." Sheyla and Nicole spoke to each other in Tagalog and laughed. *"Pogi n'ya no?"* ("Isn't he gorgeous?") *"OO! Meron ba s'yang mga kaibigan?"* ("Yes! Does he have any friends?") Mac had no clue what they were saying. For all he knew, they could have been planning to cut his throat and dump his body in the bay.

Mac ordered a simple western omelet, while Sheyla asked for eggs benedict...and a side of bacon...and sourdough toast...and blueberry crepes...with hash browns. And don't forget the orange juice.

"Did you just get a tip on a famine?" Mac asked. "Most of the girls I know eat like birds."

"Not me, Mac. I live for today. Remember all those women on the Titanic who passed on the dessert tray? Besides, being on a date with a hot looking man always gives me an appetite."

"You just don't stop, do you Miss Samonte? What makes you think this is a date?"

"Because I'm here with you, and I don't spend my precious time with just anybody."

Mac needed to get down to business. Police business. He removed Sheyla's hand from his knee and slid her chair back to where it belonged. "Tell me about Paul Osher. How did you meet him?"

Sheyla's smile vanished from her face. It was clear discussing Paul Osher was not one of her favorite topics. "Nadia told me about Paul Osher two years ago. He later came to *Pearls of Asia* with a couple of businessmen, gave me his business card, and asked me to call him. I've been seeing him ever since."

"Did you know he had money?"

"The first thing you need to know about Nadia is that she only pays attention to men with money. Besides, I can tell a lot about a man by his choice of shoes and watches. The night I met Paul he was wearing a pair of black leather wingtips from John Lobb and a Patek Philippe watch. Paul wants the entire world to know he's rich."

Mac was wearing a cheap department store Timex, and his shoes were still in need of their annual shine. "I guess you can tell I'm broke."

She again slid her chair closer to Mac. "Honey, I'll let you in on a little secret. I've been broke and I've been poor, and I can tell the difference. One is temporary while the other is permanent. Besides, it's obvious you're more down to earth; there's no pretense with you. You're a real man, Mac Fleet. Not to mention easy on the eyes." Shela leaned over and tried to kiss him again. This time Mac was able to pull away before she made contact.

"Okay, Miss Samonte. Back to Paul Osher. Did you know he was married?"

"Of course I knew. Nadia told me. I'm okay with that. With someone like Paul, I'm not looking for love."

"What are you looking for?"

"Security," she said before taking a healthy belt from her drink. "The last thing I want from Paul is love. I want him to take care of me financially, to give me the freedom to do anything I want. Every time Paul comes over to my place, I turn on my stereo and blast Tina Turner's 'You Better Be Good To Me' to remind him why he's there."

"And what is he looking for?"

Sheyla polished off the rest of her Bloody Mary and signaled to Nicole she was ready for another. "A fantasy. Paul Osher is the poster boy of tranny chasers. He's into the whole super glamorous, hyper-femininity thing we girls are famous for. Whenever I see him, he expects me to look like I just stepped out of a Parisian fashion show. He wants me to be sexy, seductive, and stylish. He gets off on the fact that I spend more time deciding what shoes to wear than his wife does investing her 401(k)."

"Do you think Michelle Osher knew about you two?"

"To be honest, I never gave it a thought. Michelle was Paul's problem to deal with, not mine. He claimed she didn't want to have sex with him, but I didn't believe him for a second. Part of Paul's fantasy is to be consumed sexually, to have done to him what he's done to women his whole life. At some point he decided he wanted to suck his own dick, and when he figured out he couldn't, he started looking for girls like me. Where is my damn drink?"

"Okay Miss Samonte. Why you then? How come Paul Osher has made you his favorite charity?"

"You mean besides being beautiful and brilliant? I'm not sure. Maybe it's because I can suck George Washington off a quarter."

Nicole brought over their food and the afternoon's second Bloody Mary, and once again she and Sheyla shared a few words in Tagalog. *"Naka do mo naba s'ya?"* ("Have you slept with him yet?") *"Wiz, pero malapit na."* ("Not yet, but I will.") These intimate private conversations they were having in Tagalog were starting to get on Mac's nerves.

Mac noticed a sapphire ring on Sheyla's right hand. "That's a beautiful ring, Miss Samonte. Where did you get it?"

"It was a gift from my mother. She gave it to me when I was young. She was the only person who believed in me when I decided to transition. I wouldn't be who I am without her."

"That's impressive," said Mac, his natural curiosity piquing between bites of peppers and cheese. "I was wondering how supportive a family would be about their son becoming a daughter. Do you mind telling me what happened?"

"Not at all. My parents named me Stanford. Stanford Samonte; a good boy's name, after my mother's brother. But my older sister and some of her girlfriends knew I was different, and they would let me wear their clothes and put on makeup when no one was looking. One of my sister's friends was Reyna, whom you met the other night. One time she saw me dressed up, so she decided to enter me in a local transsexual beauty pageant. She did my makeup, gave me one of her gowns, and took me to the pageant."

"A transsexual beauty contest?" questioned Mac. "You mean there is such a thing?"

"Yes, and I won! I was crowned Queen of Cebu, one of the most prestigious titles in all the Philippines. I had just turned sixteen years old, and it was the happiest moment of my life. It was a real turning point for me."

"That's incredible," marveled Mac, amazed by Sheyla's story. "What happened after that?"

"I went home that night to the little grimy two-room apartment we all lived in; my mother and father, my sister and me. I felt so good. I took a big chance and didn't change my clothes or try to hide who I was any more. As I stood there in my wig and fancy dress, wearing lipstick and mascara, I announced that from that moment on I was going to live my life as a woman."

"That must have been quite a shock to your parents."

"You have no idea. My mother was speechless, but my father was infuriated. He stood up enraged and screamed at me, 'Look at you. You're a disgrace. You have brought shame to our family.'" Sheyla's eyes began to glisten, and a tear started rolling down her cheek.

"I'm so sorry," said Mac. "That must have been terrible."

"Those were the last words my father ever said to me," she said, as she dabbed a napkin beneath her eye. "My mom came to me a week later and gave me what little savings she had, along with this sapphire ring. Then I caught a plane and moved to Thailand...but that's another story for another time."

Sheyla opened a compact from her purse to check her makeup. "Oh dear, I look like hell. Excuse me while I run off to the ladies room, and if you see Nicole, ask her to bring me a Mimosa."

While Sheyla went to powder her nose, Mac recalled the last words his father ever said to him. "I wouldn't miss it for the world," announced Jack Fleet, upon hearing from his only son that he would be receiving a special commendation medal from Chief of Police David Stone after graduating at the top of his class at the Police Academy.

One week later, at the graduation ceremony, Jack Fleet was a no-show. Chief Stone, cognizant of the raw emotions of his number-one recruit, treated Mac Fleet and his mother to a celebratory dinner. The next day, Mac showed up at his father's apartment in North Beach, only to learn that just days earlier he had sold all his personal belongings and fled the country. Jack Fleet never told anyone why he left, or where he was going.

Sheyla returned ten minutes later, sparkling with fresh mascara and lipstick. Her Mimosa was already waiting for her.

"Tell me, Miss Samonte, how did you pick the name Sheyla?"

"Believe it or not, it was Reyna who first called me Sheyla," she said after taking a sip from her champagne and orange juice concoction. "I had chosen the name Sheila– S-H-E-I-L-A– which in Latin means 'blind.' I had this noble idea that I wanted to be judged by my actions, not by my looks. How silly of me. Anyway,

Reyna thought I should try to be different, so I changed it to S-H-E-Y-L-A."

"Reyna helped pick out your name?"

"She did. Don't you think it fits me?"

"Like a tight sweater," he answered. Mac needed to get the conversation back on business. "Miss Samonte, I know Paul Osher has been very generous with you. We have his bank and credit card statements, so we know how much you're receiving each month. Are those your terms or his?"

Sheyla took a moment to polish off her eggs benedict before sliding over the plate of blueberry crepes. Mac added up the calories in his head and wondered how she could eat like a defensive lineman and still maintain a figure worthy of a swimsuit model.

"I've never asked him for anything, but we have an understanding."

"An understanding? That's quite the understatement. He's paying you a king's ransom."

Sheyla picked up her napkin and wiped a bit of syrup from the side of her mouth. She turned her lips to Mac's ear, while at the same time placing her hand on his lap, close to his happy zone. "You have to remember something, Mac. I'm a special girl, and I'm worth it."

Sheyla once again placed a kiss on Mac's cheek, only this time he didn't pull away. Mac had never been around a woman so bold, who used her femininity to such an advantage. Sheyla's energy was exhilarating, and she possessed an aura about her that was unlike any woman he had ever met. Mac paused a moment to admire her; Sheyla was all woman, and an amazing one at that. She had beauty, style and class. Sheyla caught him staring at her and flashed a smile that said, 'Yes.'

Mac decided it was time to pop the big question, the ostensible reason for this out of the ordinary encounter. "Miss Samonte, where were you Thursday morning, say between one and two o'clock in the morning?"

"I already told you. I was at home, all by my lonesome I'm afraid."

"And of course no one can verify that?"

"Not unless you want to ask my cat. Besides, why would I want to kill Paul's wife? He gave me everything I could want. Why would I jeopardize that?"

"Maybe you wanted more. Maybe you wanted to marry him and live in that palace of his."

Sheyla leaned back in her chair and laughed so hard she spilled a few drops of Mimosa on her legs. "You're joking, right? Paul already lets me live rent-free in one of his beautiful apartments. And he would never marry me. How long do you think it would take before the whole world learned he married a woman who worked at *Pearls of Asia*? He may have guts when it comes to business, but Paul would never be brave enough to marry a trans woman. Very few men do."

"Would you marry him if he ever got the nerve to ask you?"

"Hell no! I'd rather stick pins in my eyes."

Nicole came over to clear the table. "My goodness, Sheyla. As usual, you managed to eat everything on your plate. What will this do to your fabulous figure? I think you and this gorgeous hunk of maleness need to have a few hours of raging sex to burn off some calories."

"We're not there yet," she purred while handing Nicole her credit card to take care of the bill. "This is our first date. He's been quite the gentleman."

"Your first date! How exciting. Have you had 'The Conversation' yet?"

"Not yet." Sheyla began running her fingers through Mac's hair. Women had a habit of doing that to him. He didn't mind.

"What is 'The Conversation?'" asked Mac.

"Well, Mr. Mac," answered Nicole, "it's the discussion we special girls have when a man gets interested in us. He asks all sorts of questions, you know, 'TG 101' kind of stuff: why, when, how come? We call it 'The Conversation' because you have to have it if you want to keep seeing each other. I've even thought of handing out a list of FAQ's just to save time."

"I'm saving that for our next date," said Sheyla, having just put on fresh lipstick.

"Next date?" remarked Mac, taken by surprise. "I don't think so, Miss Samonte."

"Yes, Mac. There WILL be a next date. You know you want to learn more about me; to find more pieces to my puzzle." She flirted by flipping her long hair over her shoulder. "Plus, I want to wear something naughty and dazzle you while I'm telling you all about myself."

Mac wondered what a 'next date' with Sheyla would be like. Even the sight of her putting on lipstick was sensual. Sheyla was exotic and stunning, no doubt, but now Mac noticed the softness of the skin on her sun-kissed shoulders, and her lovely brown eyes, so bright, alluring and mischievous. He became aware of the gentle curves of her breasts, and legs that seemed to go on forever. Her rich brown hair, so soft and luxurious. Her kissable lips, the ones that were smiling at him, were nothing less than a work of art.

As they were about to leave the restaurant, Mac heard a woman call out his name. He turned and recognized Melanie, a female patrol officer from his precinct, and her husband. Mac handed Sheyla the keys to The Sub and told her he'd meet her outside.

"Mac, what a surprise to see you," said Melanie. "Who's the hot date? She's a knockout!"

"You should know me by now, Melanie. She's just a friend."

"Oh shut up. I'm sure she's more than a friend. Don't worry, Mac. It'll be our little secret." Mac made small talk, and then sprinted to The Sub, praying he had dodged a bullet.

∽

While driving Sheyla back to her apartment, Mac thought about what his mother had told him earlier, how the courage it took to transition from one sex to the other not only deserved, but also demanded, his respect. He also thought about Sheyla and the stories she told about her journey. He wanted to ask her one last question.

"Miss Samonte, were you ever scared about being a transsexual? Wouldn't it have been safer just to stay 'normal?'"

Sheyla stared out the window, enjoying the buzz of a three-cocktail feast with a handsome man on a beautiful September afternoon. "Being a transsexual doesn't scare me, but being 'normal' does."

Mac rode the rest of the way in silence.

∽

MAC ESCORTED SHEYLA TO the lobby door. Mr. Doorman recognized him and gave a discrete "thumbs up" signal. Mac wasn't sure how they were supposed to say goodbye. Though they had covered a lot of ground, Mac didn't know how, or if, he would see her again.

As he was about to open the door for her, Sheyla turned toward him, wrapped her arms around his neck, and gave him a steamy kiss. It was so good, he asked for an encore. Mac could feel his shorts tighten. Again.

"So do I get to see you tomorrow night?" she asked.

This was a dangerous question. Sheyla was still a person of interest in the case. Her alibi was shaky at best, and the smart thing for Mac to do was to just say no. Besides, they had already been caught out in public together, and he couldn't risk letting that happen again. And, though he enjoyed her company, it didn't change the fact that Sheyla wasn't his type of girl.

"How about Tuesday?" he said, throwing every logical thought he just had out the window.

"I work that night, but I'll be done by eleven.

"I'll see you then."

CHAPTER TEN

Monday, September 15, 2008 - 1:45 am

*"Reclusive billionaire Scott M. Johnson is offering $1,000,000
for the missing Teacup Yorkie belonging to murdered
anchorwoman Michelle Osher. Johnson once offered a similar
reward for the bloody glove worn by O.J. Simpson.*

*"In other news, Lehman Brothers, the revered investment bank
which began business as a Montgomery, Alabama grocery store
in 1844, plans to file for bankruptcy protection later today."*

CNBC

MAC'S BACK WAS AGAINST the wall, next to the door, listening for sounds from the third floor flat. Customs agents at the Port of Oakland had provided Mayes the name and address of a man who received a case of illegally imported Balisong switchblades buried beneath some fresh mangos from the Philippines. San Francisco SWAT team members took positions inside the hallways and near the exits of the fleabag hotel located near the corner of Sixth and Mission.

His silver .45 caliber Glock 21 pistol drawn, Mac adjusted his flak jacket one more time. Mayes, on the other side of the door, did the same. Mac reached around with his right hand and pounded on the door. "Police! Open up!" Nothing. He shouted one more time, and then heard what sounded like a window opening. Mayes motioned for Mac to break down the door.

A young Filipino man in filthy jockey shorts was forcing open a window, trying to flee onto the fire escape. "Stop right there," shouted Mac, running across the room. The poor half-naked sap was climbing out the window when Mac grabbed him by the leg and pulled him back inside. Then he took a swing at Mac, who dodged the punch and hit him back as hard as he could, straight into his midsection. Falling to his knees, a rib or two broken, his breath sounded like air being released from a balloon.

Mayes came over and applied the cuffs. "Fernando Mateo, you're under arrest for attempting to distribute illegal Balisong knives in California."

༄

AS HE STEPPED OUTSIDE the hotel, Mac, still rubbing the soreness from his right hand, took a moment to be by himself and looked straight up into the sky.

"That one's for you, partner," he said in a quiet breath.

Less than nine months earlier, on a rainy Christmas Day, Mac and Larry Kelso responded to this same hotel after a report of a fight between two men devoid of Christmas cheer. As they were getting out of The Sub to investigate, Larry told Mac to wait in the car, to drink his coffee, and to sober up. Denise was gone, so Mac was spending the holidays decking the halls with bottles of Jack Daniels. "Besides," said Kelso, "I'm sure it's routine. Just a couple of guys down on their luck who got stiffed by Santa Claus. I'll handle it, partner."

Less than one minute later, Mac heard a shot. Kelso was dead. The way Mac saw it, as a partner, he was a failure.

ご

BACK AT THE STATION, two hours of interrogation had yielded nothing. Fernando Mateo claimed he was just the drop and would have received two hundred dollars when he delivered the knives. He could also keep the mangos. Police records showed Fernando Mateo had been arrested fourteen times for petty theft, resulting in two deportations back to the Philippines. A search of his apartment didn't turn up anything. At this point, it still wasn't clear who Fernando Mateo was working with, and he wasn't about to give it up.

"We can book him," said Mayes, "but my guess is this guy is telling the truth and was nothing more than a courier for whoever was taking delivery of the knives. Who picks them up and sells them after that? We need to find out."

"A couple days at county jail should do the trick," said Mac, nursing his right hand with an ice pack.

"Perhaps, but right now I think Chief Stone is going to be less than thrilled with us. Here it is five days after the murder, and we don't have squat to show for it. No murder weapon, no eyewitnesses, and no real suspects. I'm telling you, Mac, Stone's going to make us wish we were never born."

"I'm glad you were born, Mayes," said Mac, "because when you're around, I don't have to look things up on Wikipedia."

ご

"ONE OF THE BENEFITS of being a celebrity is everyone takes your picture." Mayes was surfing the Internet looking for pictures of Misha, Michelle Osher's tiny dog. Reports from all over the city poured in with sightings of mutts in all shapes and sizes, but none were pint-sized Teacup Yorkies.

Mayes held a magnifying glass over some photos he had printed off. "Mac, take a look at this picture. See that shiny spot inside her ear? This dog is wearing a diamond earring stud.

A damn diamond earring. Can you believe that? Like the rich don't have anything better to do with their money. You can hardly see it, but it's there."

"Great. So we're looking for a piece of evidence the size of a tennis ball, wearing a diamond earring, that has four legs and can outrun both of us. I don't know about you, but I think our best chance of finding this dog is to put its picture on a milk carton."

"Laugh now," said Mayes, "but when we find Misha, we'll find our killer."

"You mean IF we find Misha. Mayes, for all we know that little rodent may be dead, lying in the middle of a road somewhere. And you've still got to convince me why someone would knock off Michelle Osher and take her dog."

"All I'm saying is it's not a coincidence that the dog is missing. Do you remember seeing any bloody paw prints at the crime scene? Whoever killed Michelle Osher took the dog as soon as she hit the floor. I'm telling you, Mac. That dog is still alive."

"Great. The suspense of waiting for the ransom call is killing me."

∽

BACK AT THE WASTE dump masquerading as his desk, Mac began looking over the report Mayes produced about the Grisham guest list. After leaving the Port of Oakland, Mayes had managed to track down a couple of guests from Grisham's party who remembered the two mystery women. The "skinny brunette" was a woman in her mid-thirties who went by the name of Monique, while the "tall blonde from L.A." was a much younger woman who called herself Savannah. Both were Asian.

"Savannah and Monique," laughed Mac. "They don't sound like the girls next door. Maybe we should stop by the Gold Club and see what the strippers are up to."

The Grisham guests said the mysterious twosome was seen entering the party together around midnight, but no one recalled seeing them leave. Mayes' notes made reference to the surveillance tapes that showed the blonde named Savannah leaving by herself around 1:30 a.m., while the brunette known as Monique was seen leaving with a man a half-hour later.

"Good work, partner," said Mac. "It might not win you a Pulitzer, but it's good enough for government work. Do you think our killer could be one, or both, of these women?"

"What do you think of this theory?" asked Mayes. "The girl who left the party alone, Savannah as she called herself, could have been in Grisham's apartment just long enough to make her presence felt, gone upstairs, killed Michelle Osher, and then escaped before anyone could notice. CSI said the murder took place between one and two in the morning, so the timeline of her coming and going fits with the time of the murder.

"I like your theory, Mayes. Besides, I don't think Sheyla Samonte is our killer."

"Why is that? How do you know she's not one of the two women on the surveillance tape?"

Mac had been dreading this question all day. He and Mayes had planned to meet up with Sheyla at Yank Sing, ask a few questions about her relationship with Paul Osher, and then get on with their investigation. He knew he'd experience the dreaded 'Wrath of Mayes' if he told him he'd gone out to lunch with a potential murder suspect. Mac decided to tell Mayes the truth. He just didn't want to tell him the whole truth.

"I did get in touch with her as we planned, only she told me to meet her at a restaurant where she was having lunch with a friend. She told me she knew Osher, admitted having an affair with him, and that he was paying her a boatload of money to be his girlfriend. On the night of the murder, however, she still claims she was alone in her apartment."

"Do you believe her?"

"I do, Mayes. I do. There doesn't appear to be any way to corroborate her alibi, but I believe she's telling me the truth. Paul

Osher was paying her a fortune. Why would she want to screw that up?"

"She's having an affair with a married man, Mac. That makes her a professional liar."

"Mayes, under most circumstances I would agree with you. But my gut feeling is Sheyla Samonte just doesn't seem like the type of person who would kill anyone."

Mayes glared at his partner. His gut told him something else.

∽

DESPITE SPORTING A SUIT and tie, Mac considered himself underdressed. He felt that way every time he stepped into The Fairmont, the granddaddy of Nob Hill's elite cadre of ritzy hotels. The lobby's vaulted ceilings, Corinthian columns, and spectacular spiral staircase presented an aura of grandeur and sophistication. The last thing this classy century-old landmark needed was a couple of stressed-out cops loitering at the front desk asking questions.

"Just tell us when she used those keys," asked Mac, rubbing the tired out of his eyes. The detectives had already confirmed Sonia Grisham's fingerprints were on the hotel key cards found inside a vase at her and Jim Grisham's apartment.

"Hmmm…Here's something interesting," said the attentive and well dressed front desk clerk. "The reservations were always on a Tuesday, and always for room 1601. That's one of our balcony suites overlooking the city's skyline."

"Why would Sonia Grisham want to keep renting a hotel room just one block from her apartment?" Mac asked Mayes.

"Excuse me, sir," interrupted Mr. Front Desk, "but the name you just mentioned, Sonia Grisham, is not the one on these reservations. According to our records, the person who reserved these rooms has been reserving the same room every Tuesday for the last three years."

"You've got to be kidding," said Mayes, the strain of a long day disappearing from his face. "Who reserved the room?"

"Am I allowed to give you that information?" asked Mr. Front Desk, who was younger than the scotch being consumed in the hotel's renowned Tonga Room and Hurricane Bar. After being assured by Mac that there was no such thing as hotel/hotel guest confidentiality, Mr. Front Desk gave it up. "Wow, this name sounds familiar. I think I may have read it in the paper. Are you sure I can tell you this?"

"You've got five seconds, genius."

"Okay, okay. It's Michelle Osher."

༄

MAC CALLED IT A day and slumped home. He was beyond exhausted. He had been working on the Michelle Osher case non-stop for five days. He arrived home just in time to catch up with his mother, who was dressed to kill and in high spirits for a Monday night.

"What's with the excitement, Mom? Did the stock market crash or something?"

"What rock have you been under?" replied Victoria Parker, dressed like a star in The Trader Wears Prada. "Didn't you hear the news? Lehman Brothers filed for bankruptcy today. This is going to make the collapse of Bear Stearns look like a piano recital. Pardon the expression, Mackey, but I made a killing today. I'm taking a bunch of my girlfriends to Bix. Are you man enough to join us?"

"I'm beat, Mom, and the last thing I need is to go out and chaperone the Cougar Committee. We'll have our own private celebration when capitalism collapses and there's anarchy in the streets."

"You just wait, Mackey. It's going to get a lot worse before it gets better. Remember what I told you? Snowballs roll downhill faster at the bottom than they do at the top, and this mortgage mess we're in is the Mother-of-all-Snowballs. How's the Michelle Osher case coming along?"

Mac took off his shoes and crashed onto a sofa. "Nothing is coming together yet, but I did have a lunch date with Paul Osher's mistress, Sheyla Samonte. You were right, Mom. Those women don't have it easy. Her story was both heart wrenching and inspiring. I have a lot of respect for what those girls go through. By the way, how was your date last week with Mr. Yacht Owner?"

"Oh my Lord! It was the date from hell. He wore Old Spice, which reminded me of your father. So I stabbed him in the eye."

Victoria Parker grabbed her Dior purse and wished her son a pleasant evening.

CHAPTER ELEVEN

Monday, September 15, 2008 - 9:00 pm

"James E. Grisham, a partner at the prestigious law firm of Goddard and Goddard, held a Republican Party fundraiser at his apartment, located one floor below Paul and Michelle Osher's, on the night of September 10th, which ended just hours before her murder."

The New York Times

MAC TRIED TO WATCH television, but nothing grabbed him. He cracked open a book, *The Red Harvest,* one of his favorites, and read the same page seven times before he flung it across the room. He couldn't concentrate on anything.

He decided to do the one thing he knew would interest him; he called Sheyla. As usual, he got her voicemail. She must have left for work. Frustrated, Mac grabbed his keys and guided The Sub to *Pearls of Asia.*

There wasn't as much action on a Monday night, and Mac was able to score a small table by himself. The energy was still high, thanks to a table full of casually dressed women sharing several bottles of champagne. Upon closer inspection, Mac noticed they were the same group of gals he saw tumble out of a limo Thursday night celebrating a bachelorette party, only this time they all wore t-shirts that said "Hurray for Linda's Divorce." These girls knew how to party.

Diamond sprinted in her sky-high stilettos to greet Mac. Flies don't go to road kill that fast, he mused. "I knew you'd want to see me again" she gushed with a beaming smile.

"Actually, I heard it was Ladies Night, but my dresses are still at the dry cleaners."

"You are so funny. Hey, I heard you went out with Sheyla yesterday. Did you remember to disinfect?"

Diamond's comment hit Mac like a bucket of ice water. He wanted any contact with Sheyla to stay off the radar screen. "Ah...I just needed to ask her some questions. Is she here?"

"Not tonight. She's probably getting her nose fixed again. The last seven or eight haven't worked out so well for her." Diamond took a load off her heels and placed her ample derrière on the bar stool next to him. She sat so close Mac could pick up the scent of her perfume, which smelled like Eau de Unleaded. Diamond was wearing a tight latex dress that had the Budweiser beer logo silk-screened across the front of it, making her look like a walking billboard, albeit with dimensions of 38-24-36. "Anyway sweetie, now that you've had the rest, it's time you have the best."

"Is that right?" responded Mac, pushing Diamond's chair away from his. Her perfume was making his eyeballs sweat.

"Look at my lips, baby. They don't call me 'Diamond Head' for nothing. Besides, Sheyla's already got a sugar daddy. She goes out with that jerk that's been in the news a lot, Paul Osher. Sheyla may be a slut, but he's nothing but a disgusting tranny chaser. They're made for each other. The only reason the girls even acknowledge his pathetic existence is because he throws gobs of money at them."

Mac's seat wasn't even warm, and already Diamond was dropping more bombs than a B-52. "Are you telling me you know Paul Osher?"

"Who doesn't? He used to come here all the time until that piece of Filipina ghetto trash put a leash on him. I used to go out with Paul, but having sex with him was as fun as plucking my eyebrows. A suppository is bigger than his dick. He still keeps asking me out, but I always blow him off." Diamond wrapped her arm around Mac's shoulder. "I'd never blow you off, Mac. Unless, of course, you asked me to."

"As tempting as that sounds, Diamond, I'll have to take a rain check. Your dress is making me thirsty. Could I get a beer please?"

"Nothing would please me more, except maybe biting your ass. But I'm not your server tonight. You can't see her because she's with a customer in the bathroom. Nadia always does that when she wants a bigger tip. Let me get her for you." Diamond stuck two fingers into her mouth and belted out a whistle that would have made a football coach proud.

"Are you always this charming?" asked Mac, half interested in her answer.

"I am, especially when I'm on my knees. By the way, if you think I look good now, wait until you see me next week. I'm leaving after work with my girlfriend Anna and driving to Tijuana. We're going to pick up some hormones and go to a pumping party."

"A pumping party? Sounds like a convention of tire technicians."

Diamond took a step back and placed her hands on her hips. "How do you think I got this fabulous figure? You see, we cross the border, meet up with some doctor guy, and he pumps silicone into our hips. I might even get some in my cheeks this time. It's fast, easy and cheap."

Mac was incredulous. "It's also dangerous. Why would you want to put crap like that in your body?"

Diamond waved her hand up and down her body like a game show model. "Because I want to be flawless…"

Mac shook his head in disgust. "Of course you do."

The too-busy-to-be-bothered waitress appeared at his table. "Mac, allow me to introduce you to the second most beautiful woman working here tonight. Say hello to Nadia. She just got back from New York, where her unique services were required this weekend."

Mac recognized her right away as the skinny brunette from the Friday night cigarette break. "Nice to meet you, Nadia. You're the webcam mistress. That must have been a quick trip."

"This stock market crash is creating a lot of stress, babe. I spent my weekend with a Murderers' Row of Wall Street CEO's," she announced while nuzzling up against him. "So you're the famous Mac Fleet. Wow, babe, I'm impressed. Sheyla's told me so much about you. She has such good taste in men. Too bad Diamond still measures a man by how many tattoos he has."

"At least my men aren't collecting Social Security," retorted Diamond before tending to another table.

"Can I get you anything, babe?" Nadia addressed every man, woman, or child she met as 'babe.'

"A beer would be nice, that is if you didn't already know that. It's amazing how fast news travels in this place."

"There aren't many secrets among the ladies at *Pearls of Asia*, babe. We call it TG-TV. It comes with the territory. I'll be right back."

Nadia's hair was a lighter brown than the first time he saw her, and much fuller as well. She also didn't have breast implants, which made her stand out from the other full-figured waitresses. She was thin, small-boned, and attractive, but her features seemed edgier than the other girls. She wore a skin-tight tube dress with leopard spots that bore the outlines of a barely-there thong, which was wrapped around an ultra-firm ass that must have spent hours on a Stairmaster.

A familiar voice caught Mac's ear. "Well, look who we have here. Are you stalking me?" It was Reyna. Her black hair, black dress, black nylons and black shoes reminded Mac of a Mafia godfather.

"I'm afraid I'm not man enough for you, Reyna. By the way, we've never been formally introduced, I'm..."

"Mac Fleet," she interrupted, catching him off-guard. "I know. You went out with my former roommie yesterday. I hear you're also a submarine commander. You know what they say about men; the more expensive their car, the smaller their penis. You must fold yours in half. Anyway, Sheyla's quite smitten with you, and she's excited about your date tomorrow night. Which reminds me...why are you here?"

"I heard the ribs were good."

"Honey, the ribs may be good, but the breasts are better. Speaking of breasts, or the lack thereof, what do you think of Nadia? She's not like the rest of us."

"How so?"

"Let's just say Nadia is into role playing, and being a woman is just one of her favorite roles. Nadia is a girl of many...talents. That's why she doesn't take hormones."

"That's the second time tonight I've heard about hormones. Is it that time of the month or something?"

Reyna laughed out loud. "Honey, it's a good thing you're a hung like a fire hose, because for a cop you sure are naïve. Girls like us take estrogen hormones to get our bodies used to the idea of being female, like softening our skin and promoting breast growth. They take care of things a scalpel and electrolysis won't. Unfortunately, they can also make you go from an angelic princess to a blazing bitch in less than sixty seconds. You have to be careful, though. If you abuse them, they can turn your liver into a weapon of mass destruction."

"That's interesting, because Diamond just told me she's going to Mexico tonight to buy some hormones and get her hips pumped full of silicone."

Reyna sighed and shrugged her shoulders. "I swear, sometimes I think Diamond's dumber than a box of hair. She's having a D.U.I. right now."

Mac flashed a double-dimpled grin at Reyna. "You girls and your lingo. I can't understand a word when you speak Tagalog, and I can barely keep up when you speak English. What's a D.U.I.?"

"'Dramatically Under the Influence.' Diamond got another hormone shot today. I do worry about that girl. Nothing is more important to her than chasing this mythical dream of becoming 'flawless.'" Reyna used her fingers to mimic quotation marks. "She takes an injection once a week when she should be taking them once a month. Another side effect is what it does to your sex drive. Too many hormones in a girl's body can make her libido as limp as an overdone linguine noodle. What remains of Diamond's penis isn't even worthy of the name."

Mac was sitting on the edge of his chair, hanging on every word. "This is amazing, Reyna. Listening to you is better than watching the Discovery Channel."

"Oh wait. There's more. We girls have an unofficial rule at *Pearls of Asia*. You must wear heels at least as tall as your...how shall I say this... 'equipment'. That's why most of us wear these skyscraping stilettos you men are so fond of. But in Diamond's case, she takes so many hormones she could get away with wearing flats."

Mac howled in laughter. This was the kind of chatter he'd expect to hear in the precinct locker room. "So what does this have to do with Nadia? Why doesn't she take hormones?"

"Because...well...let's just say it's bad for business. In Nadia's case, if she could find nine-inch pumps in her size, she'd wear them."

Nadia presented Mac his beer before she playfully sat down on Reyna's lap. Seizing the moment, Reyna asked Mac a question. "Mac, do you know what a transvestite is?"

Mac shook his head.

"An ugly transsexual."

∾

THE LIGHTS DIMMED, AND Mac recognized the song that soon rocked the room; "Bitch," the signature tune by Meredith Brooks.

Denise used to play it all the time back at their apartment in the Marina. Victoria Parker would later refer to it as "The Denise Fleet National Anthem."

The statuesque girl in the middle of the stage was Ashley. She was wearing white hot pants, a wide white belt, and white thigh-high boots over a pair of legs so long and firm they could easily become a man's best friend. Ashley danced like a Broadway showgirl, and the audience reacted as though they'd be willing to pay her a premium to have her walk all over them. As the last note played, Ashley jumped up high in the air, extended her legs, and pulled off a leg split worthy of a perfect score from an Olympic gymnastics judge. The audience rose to its feet and roared its approval. Mac was awestruck. It was the second time he had seen Ashley dance, and both times she had walked off to a standing ovation.

When the lights returned, Nadia was standing next to Mac holding two shots of whiskey. "Babe, I figured you would need one of these after watching her perform, so I brought one for each of us. Isn't Ashley sexy? Normally I don't think blonde hair works on Filipinas, but it does on her."

"Ashley should come with a warning label," said Mac while knocking back his shot.

" You know what we say around here, babe? If good girls are sugar and spice, then Ashley is vodka and ice."

Like every other customer at *Pearls of Asia,* Mac was still in awe of Ashley. "I thought only a genetic girl could pull off doing the splits. What is she like in real life?"

"Ashley is quite the story, babe. Three years ago she was known as Mark Ashley, and he got kicked out of Beverly Hills High School for dealing ecstacy on campus. After he got his G.E.D., he shocked his parents and volunteered for the Army. That incredible pair of legs survived a year in Afghanistan searching for land mines. He looked fabulous in camouflage, and soon the guys in his platoon started to read the fine print in their 'don't ask, don't tell' manuals. After he got discharged by both the Army and his parents, he decided to become Ashley Marks."

"Are you joking?" proclaimed Mac. "That girl used to be a guy in the military? What a story. How did you find her?"

"Six months ago I took a client…I mean a 'friend'…to a gay nightclub in West Hollywood. Ashley was one of the featured dancers. She had just started to transition, but it was clear she was going to be gorgeous. I mean, look at those lips, babe. She could suck start a Harley motorcycle. Anyway, this friend of mine became super infatuated with her, so I got to know her and became their matchmaker. He bought her those breasts as a birthday present."

"Wait a second," said Mac. "You mean to tell me some guy gave Ashley breast implants for her birthday?"

"Not for *her* birthday, babe. His."

Mac asked Nadia for another beer. She strutted across the room as though she owned the place; fearless and confident in her own skin. Nadia knew exactly who she was, and she didn't give a damn if anyone didn't approve.

"Nadia, do you mind if I ask you a personal question?" asked Mac upon her return.

"I don't give freebies, babe. Not even for good looking cops."

"No, no. I'm not going there. But I'm curious. Where do you girls hide it?"

"Hide what, babe?" Nadia flashed a knowing smile. She knew full well what he was talking about.

"You know. IT. How do you girls keep it from bulging through your panties or suddenly slipping out."

"Babe, it's called the power of duct tape. There's enough of it in the dressing room to supply a hardware store. And it comes in all kinds of shapes and colors to match our outfits. Now let me ask you a question, babe. Is it true you're sleeping with Sheyla?"

Mac squirmed in his chair and thought for a moment before answering. He never discussed details of a case with anyone outside the department, but what bothered him more was the nature of her question. He had seen Sheyla just once, yet the girls at *Pearls of Asia* seemed to think they were already an item. They gossiped more than a sewing circle. "I'm not dating her, if that's what you're asking."

"Babe, you two had lunch together yesterday at The Grand Café, and you're investigating the murder of her sugar daddy's wife. In some countries, that's the same as saying 'til death do you part."

"Is nothing sacred in this place? So you know about Sheyla and Paul Osher?"

Nadia sat down on the bar stool next to Mac, taking a load off her Roberto Cavallis. "Are you kidding, babe? I'm the one who introduced them after Sheyla started working here two years ago. Paul has been coming to *Pearls of Asia* since the place opened. He likes to bring his customers here. He figures they've been to every fancy French or Italian place in the city, but they seldom remember where they went the next day. But bring them once to *Pearls of Asia,* where the food is fabulous and the scenery is sexy, and they'll never forget it. It's good business, babe, and if there one thing I know," she said, now whispering into Mac's ear, "it's business."

"How well do you know Paul Osher?"

"That friend of mine I told you about? The one I took to that gay nightclub in West Hollywood? That was Paul."

"Time out, Nadia. You first called him a 'client.' Did you two date each other?"

"Babe, I'm not the kind of girl who likes to kiss and tell. Let's just say that I date a lot of men. My dick is like a glue stick; once a man gets hold of it, it's impossible to let go. To be honest, I know a lot of cops too, including some whose names you'd be surprised to hear. Very surprised."

Mac couldn't tell if Nadia was telling the truth or just trying to get a reaction. He was familiar with transvestite prostitutes who made a living walking the streets of the Tenderloin, but none of them came close to looking as natural or being as well-spoken as

Nadia. Who on the force, he wondered, would be interested in a girl like her?

"Back to Paul Osher," said Mac. "Why would you introduce him to Sheyla and then later introduce him to Ashley?"

Nadia gave a hearty laugh. "Babe, you're too funny. For the money, of course. Paul Osher has never met a tranny he didn't like. Whenever I introduce him to a new girl, he pays me a very generous finder's fee. For a while it was the perfect arrangement: Sheyla in Northern California and Ashley in Southern California. And babe, you should see the woman he has in New York!"

"I don't understand. Why would Ashley move up to San Francisco? Wasn't Osher taking care of her in Los Angeles like he takes care of Sheyla up here?"

"Not even close, babe. Ashley was living in a Studio City dump with cockroaches for roommates. Sheyla's been around the block a few times. She knows what a man wants from her and she's going to make them pay top dollar to get it. Ashley is young and foolish and still believes in this ridiculous concept called love. Paul would throw her a bone every now and then when he went to L.A, and he even bought her a Louis Vuitton purse, which in our world is like a badge of honor. Ashley claims she moved to San Francisco to work at *Pearls of Asia*, but my guess is she did it to be closer to Paul. Big mistake, babe. Big mistake. Paul prefers his women cosmopolitan and sophisticated like Sheyla, not raw and naive like Ashley."

Mac's mind began working in overdrive. Osher had dated Sheyla, Diamond, Ashley and Nadia: the *Pearls of Asia* version of the Grand Slam. "So what is Osher doing now that Sheyla and Ashley both live in the same zip code?"

"I have no idea, babe. It's Paul's problem, not mine. Although I was curious to see how he'd handle a wife and two girlfriends in the same city. Talk about your high-maintenance women. Juggling chainsaws might have been easier."

"So would getting rid of one woman," alleged Mac. He looked across the room and saw Ashley heading outside with a cigarette and a lighter. If he didn't know any better, he'd think she was just another...tall blonde from Los Angeles. He took another look at Nadia...a skinny brunette.

"Nadia, I've got one more question. The other night I asked you and Ashley where you were on Thursday morning between the hours of one and two, and you both gave me answers that could fertilize Golden Gate Park. We looked at surveillance tapes from Paul Osher's building and saw two women matching your descriptions entering and leaving that night. There was a party on the nineteenth floor, and people who were there said two women crashed it; a tall blonde named Savannah, and a skinny brunette named Monique. Are you two the girls on the tape?"

The house music was loud enough to enjoy, but quiet enough to talk. The color of the walls morphed from amber to purple. Reyna was delivering a round of rainbow colored martinis, and Diamond was writing her phone number on a man's business card. Nadia flipped her expensive faux hair over her shoulder before clearing the table.

"Of course we are."

CHAPTER TWELVE

Tuesday, September 16, 2008 - 6:45 am

*"President George Bush sent Mark Leavitt, Secretary of Health
and Human Services, to represent him at Michelle Osher's
funeral. Hank Paulson, Secretary of the Treasury, had planned
to attend, but the ongoing crisis roiling the financial markets
required his presence in New York."*

The Washington Post

"YOU'RE UP EARLY," said a pajama-clad Victoria Parker to her wider-than-awake son. She had returned home after the morning newspaper was delivered and never bothered going to bed. Besides, CNBC's rendition of "Apocalypse Now" was playing. The global financial meltdown was like a car crash; difficult to watch, but you couldn't look away. Victoria Parker's short positions were paying off, and for today at least, her favorite color was red. "What's going on with the Michelle Osher case?"

"I think we caught a break," said Mac, cinching a tie that matched his shirt for a change. "I stopped by *Pearls of Asia* last night and learned that two women we saw on a surveillance tape the night of Michelle Osher's murder happened to work there.

I also discovered that Paul Osher has turned the restaurant into his own personal dating site. Every girl who works there has him on their speed dial, not just Sheyla Samonte. I'm telling you Mom, whoever did the wiring on this guy needs to get his license revoked. Now all I have to do is look for a motive. Why would any of these women want to kill Michelle Osher?"

"Maybe for her shoe collection," chimed Victoria Parker, her eyes glued to a computer screen flashing stock prices screaming for mercy.

"I'm going to pretend I didn't hear that."

"Oh, lighten up Mackey. By the way, did you know Michelle Osher's funeral is this afternoon in Sacramento?"

"I did, and I'm planning on being there. Mayes and I like to attend the funerals of the victims of our cases. The perpetrator may decide to show up, pretending to be mourning or observing the fruits of his crime. Not to mention we might find out something important about their relationships, who's talking to whom, that kind of thing. That's how we cracked the Larsen case. I've still got to work things out with Mayes, though. The services won't end until late in the afternoon, and the traffic coming back to San Francisco is going to be brutal. His wife is expecting their third rug rat any day now, so he's leaving the late night work to me."

"I wish I could go," lamented Victoria Parker. "Her funeral is going to be the social event of the season. Everyone who wants their face in the news is going to be there. Last night the gals and I ran into a few politically connected gentlemen who are heading to Sacramento for the funeral. These handsome men bought our dinner at Bix, and then they rented one of those super-stretch Hummer limos to take us to Spruce for dessert. You know, the place with those incredible sugarcoated beignets dipped in chocolate? After eating a few of those and drinking enough Chateau d'Quem to bankrupt Goldman Sachs, I was ready to give our cute limo driver a hummer."

"Mom, I love you, but do me a favor," pleaded Mac, aghast at Victoria Parker's last statement. "Try to remember I'm still your son and not a member of the Cougar Committee. Where on earth do you get all this energy at your age?"

"Mackey, like I always tell you. I'm only as strong as the coffee I drink and the hairspray I use. Now let me get back to the markets. Japan hasn't seen this much red since Godzilla went thirteen rounds with Tokyo."

∽

MAC WAS AT HIS desk by seven o'clock, which made him the second member of his two-man team to show up for work. "Where have you been, kid?" inquired Mayes. "I've been waiting for hours."

"More like ninety seconds. You're still out of breath."

"What a good detective you are. You'll go far some day."

"Of course I will. So what do you think the connection is between Michelle Osher renting a suite at The Fairmont and Sonia Grisham having a collection of room keys?"

"I don't know," said Mayes. "One person who could tell us is dead, and the other is out of town. I looked at these hotel bills, and all I see are room service charges for two and the occasional movie rental. We'll have to ask their husbands what their wives were up to. I can bet you they weren't throwing Tupperware parties."

Mac sat down in his chair and reached over and picked up his Rubik's Cube. "Mayes, I think I've got something. I was at *Pearls of Asia* last night, and we may have caught a break."

"Let's hear it."

"Longley's in his office. Let's go in there so I can tell you both at the same time."

Mac's cell phone suddenly demanded his attention. It was Sheyla. Mac told Mayes he'd meet him in Longley's office.

"What are you doing calling me at this hour of the morning?" asked Mac, dispensing with any notion of wishing Sheyla a pleasant good morning.

"Thinking of you, of course," answered The Voice, in fine form for such an early hour. "I can't wait to see you tonight. Listen, I've got some good news. I switched nights with Ashley. Can we get together earlier, say around seven o'clock? I've already picked out the perfect dress. I promise, you won't be disappointed."

There was no way he could meet her by seven. The earliest he'd be back from Sacramento and ready to see her would be nine o'clock at best. "Can't do it. How about nine o'clock?"

"This isn't a negotiation," asserted Sheyla, who wasn't going to take 'no' for an answer. "Besides, I've already planned out my day. This morning I'm going to my favorite spa to get a massage, manicure and pedicure, and then after lunch I've got an appointment with my Maiden Lane stylist to get my hair cut and colored. By that time I'll just have a few hours to get ready for you. I'm going to look fabulous tonight; so don't make me wait one minute longer than seven o'clock. Have a good day, Inspector Fleet." She blew Mac a kiss before hanging up on him.

"Dammit," yelled Mac, fighting the urge to throw the phone across the room. Sheyla had made plans for a full-blown date, complete with all the expectations. Mac had to figure out a Plan B, which included changing his plans to ride shotgun with Mayes to Sacramento. He walked toward Longley's office spinning his Rubik's Cube even faster.

༄

THE SUNRISE HAD JUST kissed San Francisco good morning, and already the precinct's compact commander was in a foul mood. "You better have something for me," barked Longley.

"I do," said Mac. "I went to *Pearls of Asia* last night and found out the two women who crashed Jim Grisham's party were two waitresses who work there named Nadia and Ashley, and Paul Osher has a direct connection to both of them."

That's great work, partner," Mayes chimed in, "and I can confirm you're onto something. I was rechecking Osher's phone records, and there are dozens of calls between Osher and someone by the name of Damian Puti, including one call just an hour before the murder. I pulled Puti's phone records, and I saw a steady flow of calls between his phone and *Pearls of Asia.* To put the cherry on top, Osher's bank records show two $10,000 checks made out to Puti, one six months ago, and another last Friday, the day after Michelle Osher's murder."

"Wait a second," paused Mac. "Last night Nadia told me Osher pays her a 'finders fee' if she hooks him up with women. She also said she introduced him to Ashley six months ago. Ten grand is a pretty steep price for her to pimp girls for him. Osher's got to be paying Nadia off for something else, for some other 'service' she's providing. We've got to find out what those checks are for."

"Damian Puti? That name sounds familiar," mused Longley, his morning frown tinged by a worried look of worry. "What do we know about him?"

"I did a Google search and learned he's some kind of software consultant," answered Mayes, handing Mac and Longley a recent photo of Damian Puti he scanned from the Internet.

Longley looked at the picture for a nano-second before throwing it down on his desk, while Mac took a long, hard look. Minus the expensive wig, mascara and fake eyelashes, he recognized the ultra-thin Asian gentleman in the picture. "I never would have believed it," he said. "That's the one they call Nadia at *Pearls of Asia.* Damian Puti is Nadia. Incredible. You would never think she, or he, is anything but a woman."

"I also pulled his credit information," continued Mayes, "and it looks like he owns his own company and travels all over the world. He's wicked smart too. He graduated summa cum laude from M.I.T. thirty years ago."

"Wait a second," contested Mac. "That would make him, I mean her, over fifty years old. She doesn't look a day over thirty-five."

"That's because Asian women always look at least ten years younger than their actual age," interjected Longley.

The two detectives gawked at their rotund boss, shocked that he knew anything more extraneous than the police compliance manual. Something must have been in the air, because Longley's mood during the last sixty seconds had turned from irritable to intoxicated. "Excuse me?" asked Mayes.

"I just know these things," rendered Longley, signaling he wanted to get back to the case rather than discuss any other knowledge he possessed regarding Asian woman.

Mac became more animated and seemed to be spinning the Rubik's Cube at light speed. "One thing we're missing in this case is motive. What if Paul Osher paid Nadia, or Damian Puti, twenty grand to kill his wife? We know she called him on the night of the murder. He was conveniently out of town, and she's seen leaving the building after Michelle Osher was killed."

Mayes didn't quite share the same enthusiasm as his partner. "I don't know, Mac. I think a mistress always has a motive. I'm sticking with my theory that Michelle Osher was killed in a moment of passion. A murder for hire is more calculated and cold-blooded, like a bullet to the back of the head. A 'no fuss, no muss' type of thing."

It was rare for the two partners to disagree. "You and I are usually on the same page, Mac," continued Mayes, "but this time we're looking at the same picture and seeing two different things. Let's get on the road and talk about it on our way to Sacramento."

Mac's mind began oscillating faster than the Rubik's cube. He came up with a Plan B, except "B" stood for bullshit. "Mayes, something's come up. That was my mom on the phone, and she's come down with something. Headaches, fever, sore muscles. She needs me to take her to see her doctor this afternoon. Do you mind taking the trip yourself?"

Mayes flashed his partner a stern look of disappointment, as if he'd caught Mac feeding the liver to the dog. "Mac, you know we work better together on stuff like this. Who knows what we might find up there, and two sets of eyes are better than one. Plus we've got a lot to discuss. Your mom's a grown woman. Can't she drive herself to the doctor, or take a cab?"

Mac couldn't believe what he was doing. It was like an out-of-body experience. Here he was, working on the case of his life, and he was flat out lying to his partner and precinct captain. He was violating every rule in the book, every instinct he learned as a cop. But at that very moment, Mac was more afraid of disappointing Sheyla than facing the Wrath of Mayes. He had no grand plan for her, no probing questions, and no information to confirm. Sheyla wasn't his wife, his mother, or even a good friend. She was a murder suspect, yet Mac was willing to take the risk to see her.

Mac scrambled. "Listen Mayes, Mom's also complaining about dizziness. I can't let her drive alone."

Longley chimed in as well. "Let him go, Mayes. Besides, I think we've got enough to get a search warrant on Damian Puti, and I'll go with Mac to Puti's place. We'll call you right away if we find anything."

"Alright Captain. If you say so."

Before dismissing his detectives, Longley had one more question. "Mac, how did you find out Nadia was at the party?"

"You're not going to believe this, Captain. She told me."

"You're kidding? That woman has balls," said Longley.

"Yes she does, Captain," laughed Mac. "Yes she does."

∽

LONGLEY BEGAN THE PROCESS of obtaining a search warrant. Mayes stomped back to his desk, pulled out his notepad and glared at his scribble. "You sound like you're ready to lock up Osher and Nadia and throw away the key," he argued to Mac, who was concentrating on his Rubik's Cube to avoid eye contact with his seething partner. "I want to remind you that just a few days ago you were ready to slap handcuffs on Paul Osher and his girlfriend. Before you get all carried away, Mac, don't you think we should do a little more homework first, like find a murder weapon? Or the dog? Or maybe find out something simple, like whether or not Nadia or Sheyla is a lefty?"

"I hear you," replied Mac, putting down his toy. "Remember Mayes, I met with Sheyla Samonte, and I don't think she could have done it. You have to trust me on this one. We didn't find her on the surveillance tape, and she doesn't have a motive to kill Michelle Osher."

"I do trust you, Mac, but I haven't looked into her eyes like you have, so I still have my doubts. Osher may have taken good care of her, but she's his mistress, and you and I both know she's still holding onto a few secrets. The fact she doesn't have a solid alibi scares still concerns me."

"Trust me, Taylor," said Mac, who never called his Terminator-shaped partner by his first name. "Sheyla Samonte didn't kill Michelle Osher."

❧

NADIA, OR DAMIAN PUTI, lived in a two-bedroom condo located on Upper Terrace Drive, a prestigious address in Ashbury Heights lined with homes and apartments that overlooked Haight-Ashbury and Golden Gate Park. Mac docked The Sub next to a small park located in the center of a cul-de-sac roundabout, which featured a phallic-shaped stone structure. Filled with weeds, over-grown trees, and cracked concrete, it was easy to be underwhelmed by this piece of San Francisco history. In 1887, a statue of then-mayor Adolph Sutro was erected on top of 570-foot Mt. Olympus, and it served as a beacon to mark what was, at the time, the geographic center of the city. The statue of Mayor Sutro is gone, but not his

name. From the park you could also see San Francisco's 981-foot
Sutro Tower. Now considered a prominent part of the city's skyline,
popular local writer Herb Caen once wrote of the three-pronged
antennae tower, "I keep waiting for it to stalk down the hill and
attack the Golden Gate Bridge."

It was late in the afternoon and Nadia wasn't home, so Mac,
armed with years of experience picking locks, used a nail file to
get inside. A search of her spacious two-bedroom condo, complete with two wood burning fireplaces and a large bearskin rug,
revealed plenty of camera equipment, purses, sexy lingerie, and a
closet full of expensive wigs, but nothing like a date book, calendar, or answering machine that would connect her to either Osher
or the murder. Not even a missing Tea Cup Yorkie wearing a diamond earring.

A neighbor from across the hall poked his head in. "So this is
what his place looks like," he said.

"Do you know who lives here?" asked Longley.

"Yeah. His name is Damian something. Travels a lot, so
I don't see him around much. The guy's a strange bird. He's okay
and all, but he's some kind of crossdresser. Popular too. He's got
guys coming up here all the time, well-dressed corporate types."
Mr. Neighbor took a strong look at Longley. "Hey, haven't I seen
you before? Weren't you just here a couple weeks ago?"

"Must have been somebody else," insisted Longley, who wanted
nothing more at that moment than for Mr. Neighbor to vanish
like a fart in the wind. "Did you happen to see him today?"

"I saw him walking out the door this morning. He was dressed
in a fancy black suit. He said it was made of pure silk, and that he
got it hand tailored in Hong Kong. Whatever. Like anyone gives
a rats ass."

"Did he tell you where he was going?" asked Mac.

"Yeah. He said he was going to a funeral."

CHAPTER THIRTEEN

Tuesday, September 16, 2008 - 6:00 pm

*"Though they are illegal to carry in many parts of the
world, prices for hand-made Balisong switchblades from the
Philippines have skyrocketed on eBay since Michelle Osher's
murder, with some going for as much as $10,000."*

The Los Angeles Times

TURNING THE SHOWER ON as hot as he could stand it, Mac
killed the lights and settled in for a thirty-minute deluge.
Resting his butt on the tile floor, his mind filled with as
much excitement as confusion, Mac tried to picture the evening
ahead. What would they do? What would they talk about? Absent
was the grinding void in his stomach, replaced instead by guilty
anticipation. He was going on a date with a transsexual woman,
something he never would have imagined. Not even in his wildest
dreams. The thought of them together seemed abnormal, risky,
and even dangerous. But like a planet's pull on a neighboring
moon, there was a mysterious force that drew him to her. Mac
couldn't wait to see her.

But why? Why jeopardize his career by lying to Mayes and Longley? Two people from the precinct had already seen Mac and Sheyla together. Why take the risk of being seen with her again? Sheyla had already answered most of his questions. No logic justified seeing her again. Yet Mac was obsessed. He wanted to be with her, to talk to her, to listen and learn more about her. Sheyla was right. She was a puzzle he wanted to solve.

Mac arrived on time. He took a moment to check himself out in the mirrored elevator doors. Black sports coat, matching black jeans, and a white button down shirt. No tie. Nothing special. Just the way he liked to dress. Besides, this wasn't supposed to be a date.

Sheyla had left the front door ajar, and Mac strolled into her apartment. What he saw reminded him more of a museum lobby than a single woman's apartment. An original landscape from Belle Yang graced the foyer. A Cosmopolitan magazine, next to a book about Chinese calligraphy, was on a cut glass coffee table. A ceramic vase from Japan rested on an antique dresser. A reproduction of a nude painting by Renoir stood guard over the dining room. The soulful lyrics of "Something Special" by Tina Turner emanated from the stereo. A diamond-collared black cat, her tummy full after a bowl of milk, was curled up fast asleep on the L-shaped leather sofa.

From a room down the hall came The Voice. "Pour us some champagne, Mac. It's on the kitchen table. I'll be out in a minute." Mac did as he was told, but she never gave him a chance to take a sip.

Sheyla didn't just enter a room. She penetrated it, like a spotlight piercing a moonless sky. Born with glitter in her veins, Sheyla knew how to make an entrance. Wearing a slinky ivory spaghetti strap silk dress with matching high heels, Sheyla looked sleek, modern, and stylish. Diamond chandelier earrings dangled like falling snowflakes. Her brown hair, tipped with provocative highlights, was swept into an elegant updo. A strand of pink pearls added a touch of class. Standing before Mac was more than just a feast for the eyes; Sheyla was the most glamorous woman he had ever seen.

"Well Mr. Fleet," she purred, "don't just stand there with your mouth open. How do I look?"

Mac was speechless. Her aura of chic style mixed with modern sophistication had knocked the wind from his sails. He didn't even realize he was spilling champagne onto her kitchen floor.

"Sheyla...I...I...."

Her hair smelled of lust, and her perfume hinted of sin. Her radiant brown eyes, surrounded by smoky makeup, said she wanted to get the evening started. She leaned in and put her arm inside Mac's. "See, I knew you'd call me Sheyla. Now let's get the hell out of here."

Mac felt as nervous as a teenager on his first blind date. Navigating The Sub through the streets of San Francisco, Mac struggled to keep his eyes on the road. He had chosen an inexpensive Fillmore District bistro, but Sheyla disapproved as soon as she saw it. "Honey, I'm afraid I'm a touch over-dressed for this place. Let's go somewhere else."

"Where else do you suggest?" he asked. "At this hour, we'd be lucky to score a table at In-N-Out Burger."

"You let me worry about that. Follow my directions and I'll tell you how to get there." Once again, Mac did as he was told. He changed coordinates and guided The Sub to 777 Sutter Street, better known as Fleur de Lys.

∽

"I CAN'T AFFORD A place like this. I'm not a C.E.O. I'm a C.O.P."

"Don't worry, sweetie. You're with me." Sheyla put her hand around his neck and kissed him hard, holding the kiss until the valet came knocking. Mac didn't mind the wait.

"Don't you need a line of credit to eat here?" Mac asked while holding her door open.

"Not to worry, baby. Just let me do the talking."

The hostess recognized Sheyla and greeted her as though they were best friends. "My darling Sheyla, what a surprise to see you!" she welcomed with a heavy French accent. "You look amazing."

"Hello Chantal. It's so good to see you too. Allow me to introduce you to my date. His name is Mac Fleet. He's a police detective. I know we don't have a reservation, but I so much wanted to bring him here."

"You're a lucky man to have this woman on your arm, Mr. Fleet," added Chantal, a striking women in her mid-forties.

"Yes I know," answered Mac, peering into the dining room, hoping luck would strike twice and he wouldn't recognize anyone he knew. Then again, at these prices, the chances were slim.

"Sheyla, you know you never have to worry," offered Chantal. "You are always welcome here. Hubert will be so excited to see you."

Fleur de Lys had been a San Francisco institution for years, known for its extravagant décor, romantic ambiance, and a wine list second to none. As the maitre d' showed them to their corner table beneath the richly colored fabric-draped ceiling, every eye in the restaurant was glancing at Mac and his luminous date. The only thing missing was a red carpet.

A tuxedo-clad waiter offered two glasses of champagne. "Good evening, monsieur and mademoiselle. These are compliments of Hubert."

"Of course they are," said Mac. He looked around at the assemblage of elegance and privilege. "I suppose this place would spontaneously combust if I asked for a beer." Sheyla gave Mac a sly kick under the table with one of her Prada heels. He took the champagne.

A tall, willowy, and distinguished-looking man with a long grey ponytail soon appeared at their table. It was the restaurant's owner and chef, Hubert Keller. "Good evening, Mademoiselle Sheyla. It's so wonderful to see you again. I don't know how you do it, but you look lovelier every time I see you." He took her hand and kissed it as though he were cradling a rare jewel.

"Why thank you, Hubert. You look dashing as always."

"You are too kind. And who is this handsome gentleman sharing your company this evening?"

"This is Mac Fleet. He's a police detective." Once again, Sheyla introduced Mac as a cop. Even though she said it with a sense of pride, he made a note to tell her not to give every person they met his resume.

"Mademoiselle Sheyla, I haven't seen you in so long," said Hubert. "I trust I treated you and your lady friends well the last time you graced me with your presence?" Hubert regularly hosted the waitresses from *Pearls of Asia* to dinner at his restaurant. He also liked to gather a group of them together and treat them to a night on the town at some of the finest eateries in the city, a sort of secret society he called 'Reyna's Supper Club.' He enjoyed their company, their flair, and their wicked sense of humor. But what he enjoyed most was their glamour. Like the girls he grew up with in France, the ladies from *Pearls of Asia* knew how to be women.

"How could I forget?" she said. "You always treat us like princesses."

"Because that's what you ladies are. Princesses. By the way, how is Mademoiselle Reyna?"

"She's fine. She missed seeing you last week. You know you're the only reason she likes to work on Sundays. What happened?"

"Chantal wasn't feeling well, and I wanted to care for her." Hubert picked up the menus from the table. "Now let me prepare for you and Monsieur Fleet a fabulous four-course meal, each dish paired with the perfect wine. I love to do this for my favorite customers, and anytime I am blessed to have Mademoiselle Sheyla in my restaurant, I want to do something special for her."

As Hubert walked back to the kitchen, Sheyla reached over and ran her fingers through Mac's hair. "I love a man who takes control," she said, looking into Mac's blue eyes. He knew better, though. When it came to dealing with Sheyla, Mac had about as much control as a cowboy riding a bull.

The champagne was beginning to loosen Mac up, just in time for the first course. "I think I figured out why I was so nervous earlier," he said. "Here I am with this wonderful, beguiling woman, yet I'm the only one who's in on the joke."

"What do you mean by that?" asked Sheyla, pausing her assault on a chilled Dungeness crab salad.

"You know. You. I'm the only one here who knows that you're not really a woman. You're the most dazzling looking person in the restaurant, yet if anyone knew you were a man, they'd be floored."

Sheyla placed her fork on the table and gave Mac a glare that could melt steel. "So I'm a joke, am I? Let me ask you something, Mac. Do I look like a man to you?"

"No. No, of course not. That's not what I meant. I…"

"Do I sound like a man to you?"

"Of course not, but…"

"Then if you ever say that again to me," she said, picking up her butter knife, "I'll take this dull utensil and turn you into a gelding."

"I get the picture." Mac sounded genuinely remorseful, feeling like a dog putting his tail between his legs. "I'm really sorry, Sheyla. Please forgive me. I'm just not used to being with someone like you, that's all."

"Honey," she said, returning to the soft, velvety voice she knew he wanted to hear, "play your cards right, and you and those fabulous dimples of yours will be spending a lot of time with me."

The second course, pan seared foie gras, was now being served. "Mac, its time I ask you a question. Do you have a girlfriend?"

"I prefer not to discuss my personal life."

Sheyla smiled and rested her chin on her hand. "Mac, we have a word in Tagalog called 'charing.' Do you know what it means?"

"I'm afraid I'm a little rusty on my Tagalog. Enlighten me."

"Well, in the Filipino gay community it means something like 'bullshit.' From now on, every time I think you're full of crap, I'm going to shout, 'charing!' So either you answer my question, or I'm going to stand up give this entire room a lesson in Tagalog."

"Well, we can't have that," laughed Mac, sharing an impish smile, "I guess I'll have to tell you the truth."

"I love it when a man tells me the truth. It's so rare." Sheyla reached over the table and placed her hand on top of Mac's. He turned his hand over and was now holding hers. It felt as natural to him as a morning sunrise.

"I'm legally separated, but I'm in the process of getting a divorce. I haven't spoken to my wife since the day she walked out on me."

"That's awful. I'm so sorry, Mac. What happened?"

"We just outgrew each other. She was a fun girl when we first met, but then she got an MBA and became this cold-blooded investment banker. Soon she decided she needed someone in her life she could take to fancy dinner parties who wouldn't embarrass her around her Wall Street friends. In the end our jobs didn't give us time to communicate and work out our problems. The love of my life is my career. I'm loyal to it, and it's loyal to me. When I'm working a case, I work it 24/7. That makes me wary of committing to a relationship."

Silence fell across the table, but not the awkward kind that appears uncomfortable. It was the kind that comes with two people learning about, and learning to respect, one another. Mac squeezed Sheyla's hand and leaned in close to her, "What about you, Sheyla? Have you ever been in love?"

"Never," she said, her eyes looking down at their intertwined hands. "I have a difficult time trusting men. I've spent most of my life with men who cheat on their wives. I want to fall in love, but I don't know whom to trust, or even how to trust. Did I tell you about the time I spent in Thailand?"

"No. Tell me. I want to hear about it."

"After my father kicked me out of the house, I moved to Pattaya, a beach resort on the east coast. The place is full of girls like me, only they're known as 'kathoeys,' or 'ladyboys.' I got a job working as a dancer at a nightclub. It was there that I met a girl named Rose who later became my roommate and best friend. Although I'm not proud of it, I ran into problems paying my share of the rent, and Rose introduced me to prostitution. I hate to admit it, but at first I liked it. I mean, the thought of having a man, paying to be in my company, and wanting to have sex with me, excited me. It validated my dreams of becoming a woman. Then one night a client of ours wanted to have sex with me, but I already had an appointment to meet another customer at his hotel. This guy got really upset, but Rose calmed him down after she told him he could have sex with her instead. So they went back to our place. I don't know what happened, but the next morning I came home and knocked on her bedroom door to see if she wanted to get some coffee. When she didn't answer, I walked into her room and found her lying on the floor, her throat slashed. Oh God, it was awful."

"That must have been terrible."

"It was. But what could I do? Where could I go? My father wouldn't let me come home. Somehow I managed to survive, and a few years later I entered another transsexual beauty pageant, The Queen of the Universe, which is so big in Thailand it's televised to the entire country. I won, and I used the $10,000 first prize to move to San Francisco. Not bad for a poor girl from Cebu, don't you think?"

"You're an incredible person, Sheyla. Not many people could have handled what you've had to endure. I'm sure it takes courage to change your sex, but it takes an iron will to travel the path you've taken."

The waiter brought over the main course; oven roasted venison chops. "Let me ask you a question," began Mac. "How much longer do you want to be a kept woman?"

"How much longer do you want to be a detective?"

"I want to drop dead at my desk."

"Well, believe it or not, I can't stand being someone's mistress."

"I don't believe that," replied Mac. "You have everything you could possibly want: money in the bank, a great place to live, and you get to travel all over the world. How could you give that up?"

"That's just stuff, Mac. Money buys toys and experiences, and I've had my fill of both. But I'd give it all up tomorrow if I could."

"Then tell me, Sheyla. What do you want?"

Sheyla put down her fork and reached for her glass of white wine. "I want a love story. I want to find my soulmate, to be courted, and to be swept up in a tidal wave of romance. I want to be the girl a man looks at from across the room, smiles, and says to his friends, 'that's her.' I'll never forget what Rose once said to me. 'Sex is about shoes and cars, but love is about shooting stars.'"

"Come on, Sheyla. As beautiful as you are, I'm sure you could find someone to settle down with."

"You don't get it, Mac. It's difficult for a woman like me to find true love. Whenever I work at *Pearls of Asia*, men like Paul Osher hit on me all the time. They want to go home with a fantasy, not wake up with reality. They want 'the best of both worlds,' to savor the risk of a sinfully sexual relationship. If they do start to fall for you, they try to keep you a secret, or run away because they don't want anyone close to them to discover what you really are."

"But what about all the glamour, the attention, the way you make men get weak in the knees. How could you give that up?"

"Look, I've been blessed with good looks, but this face and this body aren't going to last forever. What am I going to do when I get older? I can have all the lovers I want right now, but what I really want is a man who will help me walk up the stairs when I'm old, who will take care of me when I'm sick, who will sit next to me on the couch and hold my hand when I'm feeling alone. I want someone to love me for who I am, not what I am."

It was time for dessert. Hubert had prepared a special chocolate soufflé for them to share. Sheyla had become quiet. Mac looked over and saw a tear rolling down her cheek. "Sheyla, are you crying?"

Sheyla reached into her purse for a handkerchief. "I'm sorry, Mac. When I start thinking too much about all this, I get in touch with so many feelings that it's upsetting. I just don't want to live this life anymore. I can't do it."

"Then why don't you just stop? Why don't you get another job, or go back to school?"

"Because I can't just get another job," she said after wiping her eyes, careful not to smear her mascara. "What else could I do? And how could I go back to school? I didn't even graduate from high school."

"You can change, Sheyla. You can turn your life around. You can do anything you want if you put your mind to it. Look at what you've already accomplished."

"You make it sound so easy, Mac. When I was little, I'd lie awake at night and dream about becoming a model, or a famous actress. Being a trans woman, your life isn't easy, and sometimes you have to make difficult choices. I never wanted to be Paul Osher's mistress, but I felt I didn't have any choice. Now it's the only thing I know how to do, and I hate it."

Sheyla's lower lip started to quiver. Mac put his arm around her. She buried her face into his shoulder and cried. He held her tight, and when she stopped, he took her by the chin and kissed her.

"Enough of that," she said, drying her tears. She picked up her wine glass and managed to find her smile. "Grab your glass, Mac. I want to make a toast. But I should warn you. It's a little crude."

"I think we could use something crude right about now."

She held her glass up to his. "Here's to morning sex!"

They laughed and clinked their glasses. Sheyla began to sip, then paused. "And just so you know, I prefer my eggs...like my men...sunny side up."

"Of course you do," he chuckled.

When the check arrived a few minutes later, there was a hand-written note across the front – "My pleasure to have you both as my guests...come again soon, Hubert" – and the total was a bunch of zeros.

Mac folded the bill and shoved it deep into the pocket of his pants. "My kind of place."

⁓

"SHEYLA, YOU TOLD PEOPLE tonight I'm a cop," said Mac while driving back to her apartment. "Be careful who you say that to. I could lose my job over this."

"I'm sorry, baby. It's just that I'm so proud to be with you. You make me feel so safe and secure. Being with you is like being sur-rounded by a warm fluffy blanket. Please don't be upset with me. I promise I won't tell anyone else."

How could he be upset? He enjoyed the evening much more that he thought he would, and he discovered a real chemistry between them. Yet he was as confused as he was excited. Did he want to see her again? Should he see her again? She was beautiful and sexy, but how far could he really go with her?

Sheyla slid down low into the passenger seat and rested her feet on top of the dashboard. Her dress slipped upwards, mak-ing her body looked like one ultra long leg. The passing street-lights reflected off her five-inch stilettos. Mac drove with his left hand on the steering wheel, while the fingers on his right hand began stroking her thighs. He wasn't thinking about his job, and for the first time in months, he wasn't thinking about Denise.

Mac parked in front of Sheyla's building to walk her to her door. He first put his jacket around her shoulders, then his arm around her waist. Sheyla paused in front of the entrance. "I want you to come upstairs," she said. "I don't want to be alone right now."

"Sheyla, I don't think that's a good idea."

"I promise I'll behave myself. You're just so easy to talk to, Mac. I feel like I can tell you anything."

The right thing to do, Mac knew, was to go home and call Mayes to see if anything had happened at Michelle Osher's funeral. There was still a major case that needed to be solved. Yet the moment got the best of him. "Alright Sheyla, but just for a few minutes."

Upstairs in her apartment, Sheyla dimmed the lights and put on "In Your Wildest Dreams" by Tina Turner. She poured two glasses of champagne before joining him on her couch. Like a feline chaperone, her black cat stared at them from across the room. "I'm curious, Mr. Fleet. What does Mac stand for?"

"It's short for Mackey. My mom looks like Stevie Nicks, the lead singer for Fleetwood Mac. They were also her favorite band growing up, so she thought it would be cute to name me after them. No one calls me Mackey except my mom."

"And now me. What does your father call you?"

"He doesn't," replied Mac, looking down at the floor, "and that's all I'm going to say about that."

"Well Mackey, you're an amazing guy. Thank you so much for listening to me. You don't know how much I appreciate you being here with me right now."

"You're a smart girl, Sheyla, and you're a better person than you think you are. You just need to figure out what you want from life, and then go after it."

"Oh really now?" she purred while removing a comb from her hair, releasing a torrent of thick brown locks that cascaded well past her shoulders. "What if I already know what I want?"

She placed her hand on his shirt, and undid one button, then two, until she had undone them all. "Sheyla, you said you'd behave," whispered Mac, who didn't even try to put up a fight. She began kissing his neck. "Sheyla, I can't…"

Sheyla climbed on top of Mac's lap, and straddled her legs over his. Her tongue took a tour of his lips, and then she French kissed him for the very first time. She pressed herself hard against his crotch, grinding her hips like a naughty schoolgirl. She nipped at his earlobes, licked his ears, and ravished him with her perfume. Sheyla then slid off the couch, onto the floor, and got on her knees in front of him. She ran her slender fingers across the soft hair on his chest, and then pinched, kissed, and sucked at his nipples. Her eyes closed and her mouth engaged, her hands approached his lap. She tugged at his black leather belt and released the gold-plated buckle. The next sound Mac heard was a zipper.

Mac's brain told him he shouldn't let her continue, that this wasn't a good idea. He needed to get up and leave, to get the hell out of there. But his body had a better idea. He lifted his hips, ever so slightly, allowing Sheyla to seize his pants and boxers and pull them down to the floor.

"Oh my..." she mused, gazing at his powerful manhood. She took a hold of his thick erectile, and swept her fingers along the formidable shaft. Sheyla then threw her luxurious mane onto Mac's lap, and lowered her head to orally please him.

"No...Sheyla...please...don't...do...that," he murmured. Sheyla alternated between darting her tongue to tease every inch of his phallus, and using her throat to take him all in. She used the polished fingernails of her free hand to lightly tickle and play with his testicles. Mac's moans became louder and lustier with each passing moment. Suddenly, his back stiffened and his legs shook. "Oh my God...oh my God..." His ass flinched and tightened. He felt himself losing control. Sensing that waves of orgasmic sensation were about to sweep over him, Sheyla pulled her head away. "Oh....My...God!" cried Mac, ejaculating high into the air.

Sheyla sat up, beaming, watching him gasp for air. "Well Mackey, I hope you enjoyed that as much as I did."

Mac couldn't speak. Every cell in his body was tingling with pleasure. It wasn't the first blowjob he had ever had, but it was by far the best. "That was incredible," he gasped. "Where did you learn to do that?"

Sheyla crossed her arms and placed them on top of Mac's knees, gazing up at him. "Who better to understand what a man enjoys than someone who used to be a man herself?"

"But wait a second," he protested, brushing Sheyla's hair away from her eyes. "You told me earlier to never refer to you as a man, yet you just did."

"I'm talking about sex, Mackey. I'm equipped like you, but that doesn't make me a man. It's like kissing. I know what feels good because of what feels good to me. Hey, I'm not ashamed to admit it. I like receiving oral sex just as much as you do. Now sit back and relax."

Sheyla rose and sashayed to the bathroom, returning with a warm wet towel to clean him off. Her deft dabs and gentle sweeps felt good against his skin, and her cat-ate-the-canary smile said she was happy to please him.

"Sheyla, this has been the most amazing evening," Mac confessed while putting his clothes back on. "I'd really like to see you again. I'm just not sure I can anytime soon."

Sheyla slipped her arms through the straps of her dress and let it fall down to her waist, exposing her perfectly shaped 36-C's, "Tell you what, Mackey. Whenever you're unsure how you should feel about me, I want you to think of these."

Mac stood in awe, as though Sheyla's breasts were the Eighth and Ninth Wonders of the World.

"I gotta get out of here."

⁓

MAC FELT RELAXED AND exhilarated. He couldn't stop smiling. He lay on the bed and replayed, over and over again, the events of the evening. As he was recalled the look in Sheyla's eyes as she used her fork to place a piece of dessert into his mouth, the hair on the back of his neck stood so straight he'd need a lawnmower to cut it.

Sheyla was left-handed.

CHAPTER FOURTEEN

Wednesday, September 17, 2008 - 7:00 am

"In the above photo, Paul Osher is seen accepting condolences from California Governor Arnold Schwarzenegger at the funeral of his wife, famed anchorwoman Michelle Osher. Standing next to the Governor is Damian Puti, President of ASF International, a software consulting firm based in San Francisco."

Newsweek

MAC DOZED OFF IN the shower. He rolled into bed around midnight but spent the night staring at his ceiling fan. This wasn't the first time Mac had been to this movie. He spent hours watching those same fan blades spin round and round while growing up as a kid, wondering why his dad wouldn't be coming home.

With a tiled wall as a pillow and a hail of water as a blanket, Mac managed to squeeze in a ten-minute snooze in his darkened aquatic man cave. It was a welcomed timeout from the all-night footrace between Sheyla, Osher, and Nadia. When he woke up, he realized his next race was getting his butt into the office. He had to talk to Mayes.

⌒♥

"WHAT DID I MISS?" asked Mac, marching into work and riding the hyper-caffeinated buzz of a triple-shot espresso.

"You mean other than a four hour bumper-to-bumper ride home?" replied Mayes, doing a poor job of masking his frustration after spending the afternoon in Sacramento without his partner. "After you called me from Damian Puti's place, I started looking for a skinny Asian man wearing an expensive black suit. There were only about a million guys matching that description. A photographer finally pointed him out. Puti must know somebody, though. About two thousand people showed up for the funeral, a lot of them red-carpet types. Yet there was Mr. Damian Puti, sitting in the second row of the church behind Paul Osher. He was quite the social butterfly, too. Networking, exchanging business cards, even sharing a conversation with Governor Bench Press. By the way, how's your mom?"

Of all the thoughts that sprinted through his mind last night, updating the fictitious medical condition of Victoria Parker somehow got left off the list. "Mom? Oh...yeah...she's okay. It had something to do with her hot flashes. The doctor gave her a pill and she was back to her old capitalistic-self in a couple of hours. Thanks for asking."

"Glad to hear that. Now come with me, Mr. Bloodshot Eyes. I've arranged for us to have a nice morning chat with your sparring partner, Fernando Mateo. Let's see if a couple days behind bars have loosened his tongue.

⌒♥

"WHERE ARE YOU FROM, Fernando?"

Mayes rolled up his sleeves and stared a hole through Fernando Mateo, waiting for an answer in the windowless interrogation room at the San Francisco County Jail. The bags under Fernando's eyes made a strong case that he hadn't slept. His court appointed attorney, a sniveling Legal Aid rookie fluent in Tagalog who was more afraid of Mayes than his client, sat next to him. Mac stood off in a corner, fighting the urge to catch some z's.

"Man, I'm from Navotas, a fishing village near Manila. Why do you care?"

"I know where that is, Fernando." For years, Mayes traveled to the Philippines with members of his church to help build houses for the poor. Every spring Mayes and a hundred or so adults and teenagers would fly to Manila, then travel by bus for up to twelve hours to remote jungle villages outside the Philippine capital. During the next week they would spend their days under a searing sun pounding nails and pouring cement. At night they would quote the Bible while swatting mosquitoes.

"I've seen those villages, Fernando. The dirt, the poverty, and the hopelessness. Are you sure you want to go back there? Tell me about those knives, or you'll be leaving on the next plane out of the country."

Fernando conferred with his lawyer in Tagalog. *"Seryosa ba s'ya?"* ("Is he serious?")

"Damn straight, I'm serious," yelled Mayes, who was fluent in Tagalog, Spanish, French and Italian. He was getting pretty good at Mandarin, too.

"Okay, man, I'll tell you what you want, but you have to promise me I won't get deported."

"I can assure you, Mr. Mateo," interjected Mac, waking up in time to play the good cop. "that if you cooperate, I'll make sure my partner treats you right."

"Okay, man, here's how it goes down. I go to Oakland and pickup these knives, see. After that I take them to a pier in Hunter's Point, and deliver them to some dude named 'RC.' He then gives me $200. I have no idea what he does with them after that. I swear on my mother's grave, man. That's the truth."

"When were you supposed to meet this 'RC?'" asked Mayes.

"Friday."

"What's his story?"

"I don't know, man. I've never seen him before. I was told to look for a dude with long hair and a nasty scar over his eye."

Mayes pushed away his chair and stood up from the table. "Fernando, you're going to keep that appointment, and my partner and I will be there with you. If everything works out, you won't have to worry about being deported. At least not this time…man."

∽

MAC FELT LIKE SIX-POUNDS of shit in a five-pound bag. Walking back to The Sub with a caffeine-induced headache, the septic combination of guilt and remorse began stirring the acid parked in his stomach. Mayes was striding six steps in front of him, chatting on his phone to confirm an appointment to meet with Jim Grisham. What was he going to say to Mayes? Here he was, Inspector Mac Fleet, working on the biggest case of his life, and he's sharing soufflés and body fluids with a murder suspect. Why was he acting like such a fool? Taking a chance is one thing. Risking everything you've worked for because an attractive woman walks into your life is another. There's a fine line between danger and duty, and Mac had taken an eraser to it.

"Mayes, let's take a walk. We need to talk."

After strolling south on Bryant Street toward Eighth, and managing not to step on two homeless men sleeping on steam grates, Mac opened up to his partner underneath a freeway overpass leading to the Bay Bridge. "I've got good news and bad news, Mayes. Which do you want to hear first?"

Mayes had always been a glass-half-full kind of guy. He always wanted the good news first.

"Sheyla Samonte is left-handed."

Mayes nodded. "OK. Good work, partner. It goes with my theory about 'the other woman.' It means we'll have to look closer at those surveillance tapes, or figure out another way she could have gotten into the building. Hell, maybe Paul Osher and Sheyla Samonte were working together. So what's the bad news?"

"I found out while having dinner with her last night."

Mayes jaw dropped faster than a suicide jumper off the Golden Gate Bridge. "Did I just hear you say you had dinner with a murder suspect last night?"

"I did. We went to Fleur de Lys. The foie gras was fantastic."

Volcanoes don't explode without warning, and neither did the Wrath of Mayes. First he starts breathing heavily through his nose, like a prairie thunderstorm gathering strength. Then his eyes turn red, like a bull readying to mow down tourists on the streets of Pamplona. The muscles of his jaw begin to tighten, and if you listen close enough, you can hear him grind the enamel from his teeth. Then, like swollen rivers, the veins on the side of his head begin to bulge and pulsate. Once the process is complete, the Wrath of Mayes convulses, releasing the pressure built up in one very angry black man.

"You sonofabitch," said Mayes, quiet at first. "You goddamn, sonofabitch," he said again, a touch louder. "You goddamn, no-good, lying-ass, sonofabitch!" This time the cars driving overhead thought they were caught in an earthquake.

"I know Mayes. I know."

"You don't know shit, Mac Fleet," shouted Mayes. The Wrath was in full force. A look of incredulity crossed his face, like a big brother discovering his little brother lied about smoking, drinking, and borrowing the car without permission. All on the same day. "You saw Sheyla Samonte last night? When the hell were you going to tell me?"

"I'm telling you now."

"So that story about your mom being sick was all bullshit," yelled Mayes, his voice loud enough to wake up a nearby drunk curled up on the sidewalk sleeping off last night's dinner. "What the hell were you thinking Mac? What else haven't you told me? What other stories have you been lying to me about?"

"I don't know what's happening to me, Mayes. I was just going to ask Sheyla a few questions, and then she drew me in like a fly to honey. I tried to hold back, but I couldn't help myself. This chick's gotten into my head."

Mayes got within an inch of Mac's face. "It sounds like she's also gotten into your pants. Is that why you think she has nothing to do with Michelle Osher's murder? Which head are you thinking with, Mac? The one above your neck, or the one below your belt? You didn't think it was worth checking her alibi, her phone records, her timeline, nothing? I swear, Mac, I should report you to Longley right now. This is the dumbest thing you've ever done. If you think Internal Affairs roughed you up after Kelso got killed, wait until they hear about this. They'll skin you alive."

"Thanks for the warning."

"Here's another warning, my friend. How do you know this Samonte person isn't setting you up? Of course she's going to say she has no reason to kill Michelle Osher, that all she cared about was her sugar daddy's money. What did you expect her to say? That she loves him, and now that his wife's head was nearly cut off, she hopes to have him to herself someday? Are you that stupid? For all you know she could be luring you into a trap, making you think she's interested in you to keep the heat off of her. Or even worse, Paul Osher. Get a grip, Mac. You're better than this."

Mac backed away from his partner. Mayes was right, but like a cornered animal, Mac had to at least try to defend himself. "I made a mistake, Mayes. No question about it. I'm sorry for lying to you. I thought I'd be able to get away with it, but once I learned she was a lefty, I knew I had to tell you. I still think she's innocent, though I'm not as sure as I was before."

Mayes started to calm down, a hint of rationality returning to his voice. "Even if she were innocent, Mac, can you imagine what would happen if the guys on the force found out you were dating a transsexual woman? San Francisco may be a liberal town, but the police department is more homophobic than a Nebraska prayer group. The guys look up to you, Mac, but they will disown you for this. Not to mention that if Stone ever catches wind of this, you'd better hope the only thing he would do to you is fire you."

"I know, Mayes. You're right. You're always right. Something about Sheyla just got to me. I can't explain it. I knew what I was doing was wrong, but I just couldn't stop myself."

"You couldn't stop yourself?" exclaimed Mayes in disbelief. "Teenage boys have urges, Mac, not hardened detectives. In all the time we've been partners, I've never known you to be anything less than a professional. You love this job too much. Why would you risk losing it for a woman."

"Mayes, I don't know what to say, except that I'll keep it strictly professional with Sheyla from now on. I need you to do me a favor, though. Let's just keep this between you and me. I don't want Longley or Stone to know anything about this. If we end up arresting Sheyla, then fine, I'll come clean and take the bullet."

"Mac, do you realize what you're asking me to do? My obligation as an officer of the court is to report what you've done. Now you're asking me to put my career at risk. I'm not like your buddy Larry Kelso. I've got a family to support; two kids, and another one on the way. I don't know if I can do that."

Mac was pleading. "Mayes, please. We're partners. We're supposed to look out for each other. You know how much I love this job."

Mayes paused and took a deep breath. Like a Kansas tornado, the Wrath of Mayes had blown itself out. His head told him to go to the brass, but his heart said to give his talented partner another chance.

"Ok, Mac, I'll do it. But so help me, if you screw up one more time, I'll go straight to Longley. And if this Samonte woman is involved in any way, I'm going to have to tell Stone what I know."

"Thanks partner. I won't let you down."

"You better not. Now let's go talk to Grisham."

❧

THE TRANSAMERICA PYRAMID IS the tallest and most recognizable skyscraper in San Francisco. Located at the base of Columbus Avenue and Montgomery Street, the building is just a stone's throw from the Financial District, Chinatown, and the city's Italian North Beach neighborhood, where pasta and red wine are two of the four major food groups. The building has two unique design features. The first is the "wings" on the east and west sides of the building, used to accommodate an elevator shaft and a stairwell. The other is the size of the floors. The higher the floor, the smaller the space. The top floor, the forty-eighth, is barely big enough for a half-court basketball game.

Mac and Mayes rode up to the sixth floor, to the offices of the prestigious law firm of Goddard and Goddard, where Jim Grisham was a partner. Fifteen years ago, Goddard and Goddard was located on the twenty-first floor. The firm doubled in size during the next five years and moved down to the twelfth floor. Two years ago, after merging with another firm, Goddard and Goddard moved down to the sixth floor. Unlike most buildings in San Francisco, where the most successful firms moved higher to improve their views of the scenic Bay Area, the more prosperous you were working in the Pyramid, the closer you got to the parking garage.

"Mr. Grisham, what was going on with between your wife and Michelle Osher?" asked Mayes, refusing Grisham's offer to take a seat.

Grisham walked over to a window in his corner office and stared down the steel and concrete canyon better known as Montgomery Street. "What do you think was going on, Inspector?"

"You tell me, Mr. Grisham. Michelle Osher has been renting the same suite at the Fairmont Hotel every Tuesday for the last three years, and those hotel key cards we found in your apartment have your wife's fingerprints all over them. What reason would two women living one floor from each other have to get together at a hotel room one block from their apartments?"

A pained look etched across Grisham's face. "Because they were lovers."

The awkward silence in Grisham's office was punctured by the wailing siren of fire engine rushing through the intersection of Montgomery and Clay.

"They started seeing each other several years ago," continued Grisham, moving from the window to his glass-covered contemporary desk. "It started out very innocently. Paul Osher is a client, and we would get together with the Oshers to play tennis." Grisham pointed to a photo on his wall of Paul Osher and Sonia Grisham. Both were on the same side of the net and dressed in their fashionably correct whites. Sonia was up at the net, holding her racket with both hands, while Osher was returning a serve, smoking his ever-familiar cigar. "We'd have animated discussions over dinner, a bunch of wealthy conservatives working each other into a frenzy. Then Sonia and Michelle started spending time together, just the two of them. They spent hours walking Michelle's dog. They even arranged several 'girls only' trips to the Canyon Ranch spa in Tucson. It was after one of those trips that Sonia told me she had fallen in love with Michelle."

"How did you feel about that, Mr. Grisham?" asked Mac. "That must have been one hell of a shock to your system."

"I was floored. I'll never forget that night. Sonia told me to fix myself a stiff drink and sit down because she had a story she needed to tell me."

"Do you mind sharing it with us?"

Grisham leaned back in his chair, folded his hands behind his head, and put his feet up on his desk. "I might as well. You're going to find out anyway. The first thing you need to know is the Osher's marriage was nothing but a facade. Michelle Osher was gay."

Mac was too flabbergasted to ask a follow up question. Mayes, meanwhile, was unfazed. "You mean it's not legal?" he asked.

"Oh I assure you, Inspector, it's all legal. Michelle thought it wouldn't look right for a former Miss America to come out as a lesbian, so she wanted to get married to maintain her image. The problem was finding the right guy who would go along with her charade. Then she met Paul at a cocktail party, and after too many vodka martinis she spilled the beans on her lifestyle. Paul viewed Michelle's predicament as an opportunity, and he offered to marry her. Their union had all the romance of a corporate merger. It was only after marrying him that she learned about his unique 'hobbies.' Yet they somehow managed to make it work. Throughout their marriage, they've had only one hard and fast rule; that one spouse's behavior doesn't embarrass the other. That's why Michelle rented the room at The Fairmont."

"So Michelle Osher was gay and adopted," said Mayes. "Man, this woman sure liked to keep secrets. We're they planning on getting married, Mr. Grisham? Is that the real reason Michelle Osher changed her mind and became a supporter of gay marriage?"

"I know they talked about it several times. Michelle wanted to leave Paul and marry Sonia, but Sonia would never leave me."

"Why not?"

"Because we love each other. Sonia and I have been married for over thirty years. We have a good marriage. It's just not very traditional, that's all. I never knew Sonia was bisexual, and quite frankly, neither did she. Sometimes you learn things about yourself later in life, but it's no reason to destroy what two people have spent a lifetime building together. Like the Oshers, we figured out a way to make it work."

Mac's mind went numb trying to comprehend the lifestyles of the rich and bizarre. Even Mayes, who was as open-minded as they come, was taken aback by Jim Grisham's revelations. The 1969 free love movie *Bob & Carol & Ted & Alice* seemed like Sesame Street compared to the worlds of Jim and Sonia and Paul and Michelle.

Mayes brought the discussion back to the murder case. "Mr. Grisham, why did your wife leave town after Michelle Osher was murdered?"

"I don't know why. And I also lied to you when I said she went to New York. The truth is I don't know where she is. I went back to sleep after you left Friday morning, and when I woke up around noon, I opened the door of the guest room and discovered Sonia was gone. All she left was a note on the bed saying she needed to leave town and get away for a few days. I haven't heard from her since. You can check our phone records."

"Mr. Grisham, you're an attorney. For God's sake, why would you lie to us about your wife's disappearance?"

"Because she's done this before. Sonia likes to get away when she's under a lot of stress. She's normally not gone this long, however."

"Do you have any idea when she is returning?" asked Mac.

"I don't know. I'm telling you the truth."

Mayes jumped on his phone and informed the F.B.I. of Sonia Grisham's disappearance. Mac took a moment to thumb through his notepad, and then slapped it on his knee in a moment of frustration. "Mr. Grisham, I still don't understand why you denigrated Michelle Osher the morning after her murder."

"Again, I might as well tell you because you'll find out anyway," he answered, his face beginning to flush with rage. "I was angry at Michelle. The Sunday before her murder, Michelle told Sonia she wanted to end their romantic relationship. She said she had met someone else, a much younger woman who worked at the news bureau. Sonia was very upset, as you can imagine. She cried for days. I even stayed home from work last Tuesday. That was the day I saw Michelle in the elevator. I lied when I told you I had invited her to my party. Instead, I confronted her about breaking up with my wife. She said she was sorry, but that she had already moved on." Grisham pounded his fist on his desk. "That bitch! I hate what she did to my wife."

"We need to talk to your wife, Mr. Grisham. Now."

"I understand, Inspector, and I know what you're thinking. Sonia may have been upset with Michelle, but she would never kill her. I can assure you of that."

Mayes pulled a pen from his coat pocket. He had a spark in his eye, the kind of look he gets when knows he's on to something. "A couple more questions, Mr. Grisham. Did you and your wife ever own a dog?"

"No. Never. I can't stand pets."

"What about your wife? Does she like dogs?"

"She loves them. She's like a godmother to Misha. Sonia liked to carry that miniature mutt whenever she and Michelle went on their walks. Sonia would even take care of Misha when the Oshers went out of town. Why do you ask?"

"Just curious," answered Mayes, writing furiously in his notebook.

༄

MAC DROVE THE SUB through the Transamerica garage and waited for a red metal plate, installed after 9/11 and large enough to shield a nuclear bomb, to lower so they could exit the premises. "I can tell you heard something in there, Mayes. What was it?"

"You don't play tennis, do you?"

"No," replied Mac. "You know I don't consider anything a sport if the uniform costs more than the equipment. Why?"

"That picture Grisham pointed out to us? Sonia Grisham was holding her racket with both hands, but her left hand was on the bottom. Only lefties do that. See, I'm getting to be almost as observant as you."

"Okay, Mr. Eagle Eyes. What's with asking Grisham about whether his wife had a thing for dogs?"

"Remember our conversation about what kind of person kills for passion, and I said sometimes it's the other woman?"

"Yeah. So?"

"We may have just found her. And hotel key cards may not be the only souvenirs she collected."

༄

MAC TRIED TO REACH Nadia, or Damian Puti, all day long. A squad car parked outside her apartment on Upper Terrace Drive never saw her return from Sacramento, so Mac stopped by *Pearls of Asia* to find her. Ashley, wearing a deep pink backless sequined cocktail dress that was too short, too tight, and too much, was seated on a bar stool in front of a reservations computer, working the front door as a hostess. She was rubbing her legs together, like two chopsticks ready to attack a plate of chow mien. A long gold necklace with a V-shaped charm gave directions to the diamond stickpin piercing her belly button.

"Well, if it isn't Big Mac," announced Ashley, holding out her hand. "Sheyla told us about your date last night. In case you've forgotten, my name is Ashley."

"Tonight it's Ashley," responded Mac, doing his best to ignore Ashley's dazzling body wrapped inside her even more dazzling outfit. "Last week it was Savannah. How can you keep track of them all?"

"Nadia and I were just having fun. She told me she'd mentioned something to you about the party."

"Of course she did. Doesn't everyone at *Pearls of Asia* know what color underwear everyone else is wearing? Who else is working tonight?"

"Sheyla and Reyna. They're in the dressing room downstairs getting ready. Diamond was on the schedule to work tonight, but she didn't show up. Strange, but no one's seen her since she left for Mexico. She hasn't even bothered to call in. I can't say I'm surprised, though. She's such a tramp."

"I thought she was a diva?"

"She's a diva alright. She's also a 'tramp,' which in our world stands for 'Transsexual American Princess.' I've only been here two weeks, and already I can't stand her."

Mac dispensed with the small talk. "Ashley, I need to ask you a couple questions about the night of Jim Grisham's party. You entered the building a few minutes before midnight with Nadia, and you were seen leaving by yourself about ninety minutes later. What happened? Did they run out of chips and beer?"

Ashley tugged on her dress, trying to ward off a wardrobe mal-function. "That party sucked, big time. I only went because Nadia asked me to go with her at the last second. I had just moved here, you know, and I was hoping to meet some people. It was supposed to be some kind of fundraiser with a bunch of horny old men with lots of spare cash. Nadia introduced me to a few suits she knew, but then this guy flashed a wad of money at her and they disappeared. After some freak offered to fly me to Dubai if I'd play some naked backgammon with him, I knew it was time to leave. Since Nadia was no where to be found, I walked out the door and flagged a cab."

"Do you remember what time Nadia and this stranger took off from the party?"

"I'm not sure. I'd say it was close to one o'clock. I went to this club over in the Castro called Badlands. Ever hear of it?"

"I think my mother has. Look, I need to speak to Nadia. Do you know where I can find her?"

"I have no idea. Why don't you check out her website? Nadia always posts her schedule on there."

"Nadia has a website?"

"Doesn't every pretty girl? She has two, actually. One is for her software company. The other is for her...uhmm... admirers. You should check it out; NaughtyNadia.com. It's so hot."

Mac whipped out his smartphone and moments later he was looking at a picture of a long-legged woman with jet black hair reclining on a leopard print sofa, wearing a dominatrix outfit and holding a whip. After clicking 'yes' to a box asking if he was eighteen years old, he was led to a page filled with a laundry list of options, including a bio, photo gallery, and a menu of "services" with prices ranging from $500 to $25,000. Mac clicked on a link marked "Calendar," and the first line said, "September 17th- 18th... Las Vegas." The next said, "September 19th -24th...San Francisco." Nadia wouldn't be returning from Sin City until the day after tomorrow.

"Nadia takes the term 'working girl' pretty seriously, doesn't she?" asserted Mac.

"Hey, a girl's gotta do what a girl's gotta do. Is there anything else you want from me? My phone number, perhaps?"

"Sure. Tell me about your relationship with Paul Osher."

Ashley's engaging smile turned upside down, replaced by a stoic stare. "Who is he?"

"Do us both a favor, Ashley," replied Mac, moving in so close to her face he could smell the glue on her fake eyelashes. This was a stare down contest he wanted to win. "Save the dumb blonde act for somebody else. Nadia told me she set you two up in L.A. She also told me he paid for those silicone silos sticking out from your chest."

"I've got nothing to say," hissed Ashley, turning her cold, expressionless face to the floor. She looked up again at Mac, returning for round two of the stare down. She wasn't going to give in to him this time, however. After all, this was a woman who walked the minefields of Afghanistan.

Mac decided to go straight for Ashley's proverbial jugular. "Did you know about Paul Osher's relationship with Sheyla?"

Ashley's face turned beet red, matching her pink dress. The scowl she gave Mac rivaled the intensity of The Wrath of Mayes. "Hey look," she said, turning her eyes away from him, "there's an empty seat at the bar." Mac peered through the curtain. There were enough empty barstools for a busload of bachelorettes. "Let me give it to you before someone else shows up."

After showing him to his seat, Ashley blurted, "You know, you're wrong about Paul. He's too classy a guy to go out with someone like Sheyla. Besides, isn't she your girlfriend?"

"Here's a news flash Ashley, or Savannah, or whatever the hell your name is today. You're wrong on both counts. Sheyla's not my girlfriend, and Paul Osher has about as much class as that dress you're wearing."

❧

MAC KNEW *PEARLS OF ASIA* was the last place he should be. Nadia wasn't there, and he had already questioned Ashley, so the right thing to do was to just turn around and leave. Don't be stupid, he thought to himself. Get up and go.

Mac heard footsteps rushing up the stairs from the basement dressing room. Wearing a tank top dress with a matching belt and the standard stilettos, Sheyla ran and nearly tackled him before he could get up from his chair. She gave him a kiss and a hug a *Pearls of Asia* customer would have had to pay a small ransom for.

"Big Mac?" he asked.

"I told the girls we went out for a Happy Meal last night," Sheyla giggled. "Oh don't worry, Mackey. I didn't dish out any details. The girls are just born to gossip, that's all. Besides, they never let the facts get in the way of a good backstabbing." Sheyla stepped back to admire him. "Hey Mackey, you look yummy tonight. I swear I could eat you up right now."

"How about answering a question for me first? Does Ashley know about you and Paul Osher?"

"I don't think so. I know I've never said anything to her about him. She's a terrific dancer, probably the best we've ever had, but she's not the friendliest girl I've ever met. She sort of reminds me of a shark; she eats when she's hungry, and sleeps when she's tired. I'll get to know her better when she's ready to open up. Now, enough about her. Let's talk about me."

"You look great as always," said Mac, "but you look different."

"That's because I'm wearing enough makeup to join the circus. You know, fake eyelashes, heavy rouge, and lots and lots of lipstick. That's what the customers want to see. We're about to start a show."

"That's cool. I wouldn't mind seeing you dance again."

"Well...I wouldn't mind seeing you naked again."

That was the last thing Mac needed to hear. "I'm not so sure I'm ready for that yet."

"You will be." She kissed him and placed something in his hand.

"What are these?"

"They're the keys to my apartment. One of the food runners told me you were here so I brought them up with me. Go there and wait for me. We'll just talk. I promise."

"Sheyla, I can't do this. Plus I know you. You're going to want to do more than just talk."

"Please, Mac. I want to get to know you better. I feel so comfortable with you. Besides, I know you're still looking to find for a few more pieces to my puzzle." Sheyla rubbed her hand along his chest and playfully pinched a nipple. They had only just met each other, and already she knew how to turn him on faster than a flashlight.

Mac took the keys and headed for the door.

CHAPTER FIFTEEN

Wednesday, September 17, 2008 - 11:30 pm

"According to an unnamed blackjack dealer from the Wynn Hotel in Las Vegas, Paul Osher, grieving husband of murdered beauty queen Michelle Osher, celebrated this past New Year's Eve in the high-rollers room with several attractive woman of Asian descent."

TMZ.com

SHEYLA'S WINE CABINET HAD any wine Mac desired, so long as it was red. He opened a bottle of Opus One, a wine he could at least pronounce if not afford. The cigar humidor in her living room rivaled one offered in a high-roller suite in Las Vegas, which included a fine selection of Arturo Fuentes. Mac always wondered what an $80 cigar tasted like. He fired one up and discovered he liked them. So did Sheyla's cat, who followed him around like a KGB spy.

Mac sat down on the leather sofa and turned on her 50-inch flat-screen TV. It was bolted onto the wall like a prized painting from the nearby Museum of Modern Art. Manly intuition took him straight to ESPN. Some former jockstraps in high-definition were discussing the weekend's upcoming slate of NFL games. Sports were fun to Mac, but when it came to Sundays, football was a religion.

Mac took a moment to admire the view of the Bay Bridge, lit up in lights like a movie star. Here he was in a beautiful woman's lavish apartment, smoking an expensive cigar, drinking a glass of vintage wine, and watching ESPN on HD. At that precise moment, everything should have been right with the world.

Instead, he was scared to death.

What was he doing hanging out in a transsexual woman's apartment, acting like an obedient Cocker Spaniel waiting for his master to return home from a long day's work? Why was he indulging himself instead of working to solve the biggest murder case San Francisco had seen in years? What if Mayes was right, that Sheyla's seductive ways were only a means to distract him? Why did just being in her presence cause him to lose all sense of self-control? Over and over, Mac asked himself the same question. What the hell was he doing?

Sheyla's cat joined him on the couch. "How did I get here?" he asked the little black minx. She didn't bother to answer.

On a table next to the sofa were several silver-framed photographs. Most were of Sheyla and her girlfriends taken while they were having fun out on the town. Others were just of Sheyla, wearing exotic costumes or formal gowns while participating in beauty pageants, or sunning herself in a bikini at some far-flung five-star resort. There was even one of her in full scuba gear holding a spear. Over on a bookshelf was an old black and white glossy, like a school photo, of someone who had the same smile and eyes as Sheyla. Perhaps it was her brother. Then Mac remembered she didn't have a brother.

There were no pictures anywhere of Sheyla with Paul Osher. In fact, there didn't appear to be any pictures of Sheyla with any man.

Mac walked into her bedroom, which was dominated by a king-sized four-poster bed. Lacy white curtains were tied across the towering mahogany posts. Fluffy throw pillows were everywhere, enough to cushion an avalanche. The bedspread was a velvety charcoal black, and the sheets were imported red silk. Mac wondered what the walls would say if they could talk.

Another flat panel TV hung on her bedroom wall. He pulled open a set of double doors that led into a huge walk-in closet. On one side were slacks, sweaters, and over a dozen pairs of custom fit jeans. On the other side were cocktail dresses, evening gowns, and silky lingerie. In the middle of the room stood a dresser filled with expensive jewelry and accessories. He opened a drawer and found dozens of silk unmentionables He picked up a bra and looked at the label. He had never heard of La Perla. At the back of the closet was a wall featuring over a hundred pairs of designer shoes. Say whatever you want about Sheyla, thought Mac. This woman knew how to shop.

Mac returned to the living room couch to find a movie. He hit upon "Forrest Gump," one of his favorites. The story of a flawed man, who set his sails to wherever the winds of life would take him, had always fascinated him.

Mac heard the sound of keys at the front door. "I see you've made yourself comfortable," said Sheyla, entering the apartment with her hair tied in a ponytail. She was wearing her standard travel uniform of sweat pants and a t-shirt, accessorized by the Louis Vuitton travel bag she always took to work. She helped herself to Mac's glass of wine, leaving a red lipstick stain on the rim. Then she helped herself to his cigar.

"I love this movie," announced Sheyla, tipping her head back and blowing smoke rings into the air. "I watch it all the time." Sheyla snuggled up next to Mac on the couch. He was excited, nervous, and terrified. He couldn't decide if his next move should be to put his arm around her or arrest her.

"What am I doing here, Sheyla?"

"Relaxing. Now watch the movie for a bit while I take a quick shower. I can't stand coming home and smelling like tuna sashimi."

A howling hair dryer followed a long shower. Mac cranked up the volume, but it didn't matter. Tom Hanks in running shorts just wasn't doing it for him.

Sheyla emerged from the bedroom. Mac wasn't sure whose hips swayed more, Sheyla's or her cat's. Wearing a silk floral robe that stopped just short of her knees, she poured herself a glass of wine and made herself at home on his lap. Her feathery skin was smooth and clean, and her hair smelled like a dozen red roses. Mac took a moment to admire her face. Sheyla wasn't wearing a stitch of makeup. As far as Mac was concerned, she didn't have to.

"Do you like my place?" she asked.

"Where does the maid sleep?" he joked. "This is incredible. I love this television. I could sit here and watch it for hours."

"I should have you over on Sunday. The 49ers are playing the Patriots. The only thing better on Sundays than a three-hour champagne brunch is watching Tom Brady run around in tight pants."

"You like football?" he asked. Mac was stunned. Denise despised sports. She would banish Mac to their bedroom with the 12-inch set he bought for fifty bucks back in college, just so she didn't have to listen to him root for his favorite team.

"Yes. I love watching sports. I enjoy movies, too, especially old ones. I want to be Katherine Hepburn in my next life."

"So let me see if I've got this straight," responded Mac, holding up his hand to count off with his fingers. "You like sports, movies, wine AND cigars?"

"Don't forget I'm gorgeous and have an insatiable appetite for sex."

"How could I forget?" The smile on Mac's face was brighter than the TV screen.

Sheyla slid her hips to one side, causing her robe to ride up her thighs. Mac noticed a small tattoo on her right butt cheek. "What is that?" he asked.

"What's what?"

"The tattoo on your butt. Is it some kind of flower?"

Sheyla stood up, lifting the hem of her robe slightly, letting Mac get an up close and personal view of the work of art inked on her body. "It's a butterfly resting on a leaf. I got it when I was in Thailand. Isn't it beautiful? I made sure its wings were open, ready to fly. It represents me, Mackey. It's a symbol of how far I've come, and how much further I have to go. Becoming a woman was just one step in my journey. I want to get married, have kids, and live a life I can be proud of. I had the artist draw it there because I only like to share it with someone I care about." Sheyla curled up next to him like a cat. "I guess that means you, Mr. Fleet."

"Aren't you more lioness than butterfly?" he asked.

"You're still putting my puzzle pieces together, aren't you?"

"It's what I do."

"Well, the poet Maya Angelou once wrote, 'We delight in the beauty of the butterfly, but rarely admit the changes it goes through to achieve that beauty.' I swear she wrote that line just for me. That's why I chose the butterfly."

"That's beautiful, Sheyla. I mean that. It says a lot about you."

"Speaking of which," she said, closing her robe, "I realize I still don't know anything about you. I'm the one who has been doing all the talking."

"That's because I'm as intriguing as a bowl of cottage cheese."

Sheyla leaned over and softly kissed him on the cheek. "Well, here's another piece for your puzzle, Mackey. I love cottage cheese."

"I'm being honest with you, Sheyla. There's nothing to tell. I'm just a cop who loves his job. Other than that, I'm not that interesting."

Sheyla refilled her glass of Opus One. "Okay, Mackey, then I guess I'll just have to tell you about yourself. First of all, besides being one of the best looking guys I've ever met, you have a great sense of humor, and I love it. It's part of what makes you you. But you're using it to hide something, and it goes beyond breaking up with your wife. Someone, or some thing, has created a pain deep inside your soul that causes you to doubt yourself."

Mac gulped his wine like he was polishing off a glass of grape juice. "Well aren't you a regular Sigmund Freud."

"I'll go even further," she continued, grabbing the bottle to refill his glass. "I'd bet my entire shoe collection that you don't have any tattoos, either. You know why? Because you don't know how to express yourself. That's why you wouldn't talk to me the other night about your father. You're afraid to open up to people, even those who are close to you. You keep things bottled up inside because of some Neanderthal doctrine that says a man shouldn't show weakness. That's bullshit, Mackey. I'm attracted to strong men not because they're macho and tough. I'm attracted to strong men because they're not afraid to be themselves."

"You don't know what you're talking about, Sheyla."

"Charing," she cried, echoing the phrase she taught Mac at Fleur de Lys. Sheyla pointed at the glossy black and white photo on her bookshelf. "Mackey, take a look at that picture. Believe it or not, that's me. Back then I was nothing but a miserable, fourteen-year-old, scared-out-of-my-mind gay boy. I hated my life then, and if I didn't believe in myself I'd be nothing now but a miserable, thirty-year-old, scared-out-of-my-mind gay man. I live my life honestly, warts and all. A lot of transsexuals don't like to display reminders of their past, but I do. My childhood is part of who I am, of who I've become. So many people use the painful experiences of their lives to make excuses, but not me. I'm not afraid of failure or pain, because that's part of what life is all about. The Japanese have a word for it: shoganai. It means shit happens in life, and you can either deal with it and move on or use it as an excuse to do nothing. I've used what's happened to me, both the good and the bad, to create a tailwind to help me grow instead of a headwind to slow me down. I'm proud of who I am, Mackey, and I'm proud to say I'm a transsexual."

Mac sat stupefied and stared at Sheyla. Who was this person, he thought, and how dare she talk to him like that. She barely knew him, for God's sake. But deep down, Mac knew she spoke the truth. Sheyla may not have been formally educated, but she possessed a wisdom that went far beyond a classroom. Unlike himself, Sheyla wasn't afraid to speak the truth, and Mac respected her for it. He moved in close to kiss her when her cat decided to jump between them.

"That was predictable," he quipped. "Who's your roommate?"

"Her name is Esares. Isn't she sweet?"

"What kind of a name is Esares? Is she some kind of Greek goddess?"

Sheyla gave one of her laughs that warmed Mac's heart like a cup of hot chocolate. "No silly, her name stands for the initials S-R-S, which is short for Sexual Reassignment Surgery. That's the procedure a trans woman goes through when she decides to go all the way and get a vagina. Since I'm not planning on going that route, I got a cat and named her Esares. I tell my friends she's the closest I'll ever get to having a pussy."

Mac gave Sheyla a quizzical look. "I thought getting a vagina was the Holy Grail for girls like you. Don't you lay in bed at night dreaming about having a man making love to you? I know I would if I were a woman."

"Of course you would," she chuckled while Esares made herself at home in her lap. "You're a guy, and all you ever think about is getting laid. Having a vagina might make you a female, but it takes more than a hole between your legs to make you a woman. Plus I know plenty of girls who look back and regret having their surgery. Most went to Thailand to get it done, thinking that having a vagina would land them the man of their dreams. The reality is once your penis is gone, you're just like the millions of other women out there dealing with the games you men like to play."

"You just said you wanted to get married. How can you expect to get married if both you and your partner have the same...uh... original equipment? Last time I checked, same-sex marriage is still illegal in most parts of this country."

"Give me a break, Mackey. Fifty years ago it was illegal in most parts of this country for a black man to marry a white woman. It's just a matter of time. Besides, who said marriage had to be between two people who can make a baby? If a couple are in love and want to share their lives together, and are willing to make an emotional and physical commitment to each other, why can't they be like everyone else and make it a legal commitment as well? Not every heterosexual couple who gets married has kids, yet no one from the government knocks on their door telling them they have to return their marriage license."

"I don't understand," said Mac, wearing his confusion on his face. "I thought you wanted to become a complete woman."

"I am a complete woman," she professed, "who happens to love her joy stick as much as you love yours." Sheyla took a hold of Mac's hand and slid it under her robe, flaunting both her building excitement and her decision, for tonight at least, not to wear panties

"Whoa," clamored Mac, pulling back his hand after touching for the first time in his life an erection that wasn't his own.

"Calm down, Mackey," soothed Sheyla. "It's okay. I promise it won't bite." She returned his hand to her lap. This time Mac didn't resist, touching her with less shock and more awe. "Mmmm...you have no idea how good that makes me feel." Sheyla took his hand and wrapped his strong fingers around herself.

"Oh wow," he murmured. Fondling her there, in her most sensitive spot, and watching her lustful reaction, excited Mac, and turned him on more than if he had touched a live wire. Within seconds, the cat was launched into orbit; the pair began necking like two hormonal teenagers on prom night. Mac removed Sheyla's robe, revealing a black see through lace teddy that wasn't meant to stay on. Her breathing turned heavy and heated, compelling

Mac's hands to set off on a search and enjoy mission for her breasts. Sheyla ascended onto his lap, mashing her puffy areolas into his face. Her nipples, made hard by the throes of passion, found their way into Mac's mouth, where he kissed, licked, and bit them ever so lightly. Sheyla leaned her head back and moaned, her luscious brown hair falling like a soft rain onto his thighs.

Clutching her magnificent ass, Mac rose up, lifting Sheyla by her bottom. She wrapped her legs around his waist, and threw her arms around his neck. After another long, wet, and passionate kiss, she took a deep breath and whispered into his ear, "Take me."

Mac carried her into the bedroom and placed her on top of her canopied four-poster bed. Scented candles illuminated every corner of the room. Mac stripped down to his shorts, then circled the bed, stalking Sheyla like a panther approaching its prey. He had never wanted a woman more.

Timeless minutes of amorous foreplay later, Sheyla rolled Mac onto his back. She stared at him for a moment, admiring the prodigious bulge emanating beneath his silky blue boxers. Then she slid her hands along his thighs and pulled them off, exposing his trim and naked body for the very first time. "Incredible," she said under her breath.

Sheyla reached over to a bedside table, opened a drawer, and removed a bottle of lube along with a condom. As usual, Sheyla had taken control. Whatever she was planning to do, Mac thought, was fine with him.

Shela kissed his neck, then his chest, and then flicked her tongue down to his waist. She took his erection into her warm mouth and caressed it like an only child. Without missing a beat, she lubed the index finger on her left hand, and rubbed it around Mac's anus. After rimming the entrance for what seemed like an eternity, Sheyla pushed her finger deep inside him.

Mac took a halting breath. Sheyla wiggled her finger and tickled his prostate, giving him an erotic sensation he never knew existed. Mac was in ecstasy, moaning in delight while Sheyla continued to probe and orally seduce him. No woman had ever done this to him before, and he loved it.

Just as he was about to climax, Sheyla sat up and reached for the condom. After ripping the wrapper off with her teeth, she seductively rolled it onto him. She picked up the bottle of lube and rubbed a handful onto her anus. She then placed more lube in her hand, and lathered it all over Mac's throbbing monument to manliness. "I want you inside me," she begged.

Sheyla got on her hands and knees, and Mac knelt behind her. Using slow and gentle strokes, he began to slide himself inside her. She was tight at first, so he made sure to take his time. Once completely inside, Mac's hips began to thrust, back and forth, back and forth, and Sheyla let out a series of breathless moans and silent screams. Mac went a bit faster, a bit harder, and a bit deeper with each stroke, until he lost himself in the ecstasy of the moment. After endless minutes of pure erotic passion, both lovers climaxed at the same time. Exhausted, they collapsed onto the bed.

Mac stared at the ceiling. He was physically and emotionally drained. He looked over at Sheyla, who looked like she was about to fall asleep.

"Penny for your thoughts?" he asked.

"I was just thinking how happy I am," she said, breaking her silence. "It's wonderful to make love to someone you really care about."

Mac wasn't sure how to respond. He hadn't had sex in nearly a year, and he had just made love in a way he never would have imagined. He started to get up from the bed.

"Where are you going?" she asked, frightened that he was about to leave.

"Do you mind if I take a shower?"

Sheyla told him to go ahead, and that she would keep a spot warm for him under the covers.

Mac turned on the water. Then he turned off the lights.

CHAPTER SIXTEEN

Thursday, September 18, 2008 - 5:00 am

"Photos posted on the celebrity gossip website TMZ.com show Paul Osher and a mysterious Asian model vacationing at the exclusive Four Seasons resort in Maui, where beach attendants spray sunbathing vacationers with Evian water.

US Magazine

AWAKE FOR OVER AN hour, Mac watched the minutes pass by on a digital clock. Sheyla lay next to him, sound asleep, her naked body spooned against his. He needed to get his butt into work, if for no other reason than to prevent Mayes from popping an artery. Yet here he was, laying underneath a white lacy canopy, thinking about his old high school nemesis, Dopey Danny Murphy.

Mac got into a few fights growing up, but there was one he never forgot. He was a scrawny freshman at Mission High School, located two blocks from San Francisco's landmark Mission Dolores. Basketball practice was over, and Mac had his head wrapped in a towel, drying his hair after taking a shower. Then without warning, Dopey Danny Murphy hauled off with a right jab square into Mac's jaw, knocking him to the floor. Mac picked himself up, dusted himself off, and then drilled a right hook to the side of Dopey Danny's head, depositing him into a laundry bin filled with dirty towels and sweaty jock straps. Unlike Ali vs. Frazier, this one didn't go the distance.

The basketball coach grabbed the pint-sized pugilists and hauled them straight to the principal's office. "Alright you knuckleheads," he said, "Let's hear it. What's this all about?"

"During today's scrimmage," explained Dopey Danny, a lump forming on the side of his head, "Mac and I had to guard each other. One time when he was dribbling the ball up the court, he said, 'You can't beat me 'cuz you're gay.' He said it again when he beat me for a rebound. When we were done, Mac wouldn't shake my hand because he said, 'I won't shake hands with a fag.'"

"Is that true, Mac?"

"Um...well...yeah, I guess so," answered Mac, staring down at his Converse Chuck Taylor Hi-tops, "but I was just teasing him. I didn't mean it or anything."

The principal scolded Mac, telling him it wasn't right to tease anyone just because they were different. Their punishment for fighting would be to stay after school helping the janitors clean the toilets for a week. For taunting Dopey Danny, Mac was suspended from two basketball games.

As he sat on a bench outside the principal's office, Mac started to sweat, terrified of what his mom might do to him. He had never been in trouble at school before, except in the third grade, after he put a wad of gum in Jill Malley's hair because he had a crush on her. Mac was a solid student, and he got along with almost everyone. His mother told him never to get physical unless someone was trying to hurt him. His father, on the other hand, would have pinned a medal on him for decking Dopey Danny.

Victoria Parker spoke to the principal before taking her son to the car. She stayed silent as they drove out of the school's parking lot. Once they got a mile or two from the school, she pulled the car over to the curb to give her son a lesson he would never forget.

"Don't ever say anything like that again, Mackey Fleet. Don't even think it. Whether Danny Murphy is gay or not doesn't matter. Frankly, it's none of your damn business. Just because someone is different than you doesn't mean you shouldn't treat him or her with dignity and respect. Do you understand what I'm saying to you, young man?"

"Yes, ma'am," he answered. He knew his mom was right. She was always right.

⁓

AFTER EXPERIENCING ONE OF the most erotic evenings of his life, Mac lay in bed next to his lover and searched for the answer to one simple question. Was he gay?

No matter how much he tried to rationalize, analyze, or scrutinize his behavior last night, questioning his own sexuality had consumed him. He knew he made love to a woman last night, but there was no denying the fact that she had the same anatomy he did. Sheyla had aroused him unlike any woman ever had, yet he couldn't get over the fact that he had touched her "down there." Not only did it not repulse him, he wanted to touch her again. It wasn't because of some inane physical curiosity, but he wanted to please Sheyla, to once again see the rapturous look on her face while he made love to her.

Sheyla woke up as he started to get out of bed. "Good morning, sexy," she yawned while rubbing the sleep from her eyes. The bedspread had been kicked to the bottom of the bed, and pillows were everywhere on the floor. So was a condom wrapper. "Where are you going?"

"I've got to get to work," he huffed.

Sheyla protested, reminding Mac of their toast at Fleur de Lys. "Come on Mackey, stay in bed with me for awhile. I'm not ready to let you go yet."

Mac stood near the bed and started putting on his clothes. He told her he was late, while she pleaded for him to stay.

"Ah, men and their work. Would you mind getting me a glass of water before you leave?"

Mac returned with two glasses of water and sat beside her on the bed. He wanted to talk about last night, because the way he figured it, there was no one else he could talk to. Yet he sat there, silent, searching for the right words to say.

"No, you're not," said Sheyla, finally breaking the silence.

"I'm not what? What are you talking about?"

"You're not gay. I know what you're thinking, Mackey. You made love to me last night, and the look on your face is saying, 'Am I, Mac Fleet, life-long heterosexual male, gay?' Well baby, I'm here to tell you in no uncertain terms, you are NOT gay. In fact, you might be the straightest guy I know."

Her answer did little to quell his concerns; to answer the questions racing through his mind. "Maybe I'm not gay, but it doesn't mean I'm straight either. I don't know what I am. I'm really confused right now."

Sheyla asked Mac to get her robe. She slipped it on and sat straight up on the bed. She took another long drink of water, pulled her fingers through her hair, and then cleared her throat.

"Listen to me, Mac. First of all, there is nothing wrong with being gay. Being gay, straight, bi, green or blue, is just a label some people like to use. What I can tell you is that you cared enough to satisfy me, which in my book makes you a great lover. So let me ask you a question: have you ever been sexually attracted to a man?"

"Never."

"Has a man ever hit on you before?"

"Uh...this is San Francisco."

"And how did that make you feel?"

"I'd rather slit my wrists than have sex with another guy."

"Are you attracted to women?"

Mac smiled at that question. Just looking at Sheyla in her robe, wearing no makeup and her hair a mess, was getting him aroused. "Of course I am."

"Then I have news for you, Mr. Fleet. Gay men want to have sex with other gay men. You just said that having sex with a man repulses you. Then why on earth would you ever think you were gay?"

"Because I just spent the night lying naked next to a person who pees standing up."

Sheyla looked away in reflection before responding. She was facing east, and the morning sun was rising over the Oakland Hills.

"Mackey, I'm going to be honest. I know we just met, but I'm falling for you. I've never felt this way about a man before. But I need to let you in on a little secret if our relationship is going to go much further."

"What's that?"

Sheyla took his hands into hers. "The most important sex organ in the world, the one that gives us the most pleasure, the one that makes us want to cuddle and make morning memories in bed, or the one that wants us to spend the afternoon making love on top of a kitchen table, is not the one between your legs. It's the one between your ears."

Mac leaned against a bedpost. For a woman who hadn't graduated from high school, Sheyla had all the answers. Her words had the same calming effect as those his mother had told him years before. His mom was right then, and Sheyla was right now. For the first time all morning, Mac's mind went calm and his body relaxed. He sat back up and took Sheyla's chin in his hand and looked into her eyes. "That's the best thing you could have said to me." Mac pulled her close and kissed her. Then he got undressed and crawled back into bed, and within moments they began making love again.

Two hours later, after he made her some eggs, sunny side up of course, Mac kissed her goodbye.

༄

MAC COULD FEEL THE Wrath of Mayes before he even walked into the precinct. "Where the hell have you been?" growled Mayes. "Stone's been cooling his heels in Longley's office for almost an hour. Why didn't you answer your phone?"

"I'm sorry Mayes," replied Mac, out of breath after rushing back home to get ready for work. "I slept through my alarm, and I was probably in the shower when you called."

"Whatever. Come on, they're waiting for us."

Captain Longley sat behind his desk, his feet straining to touch the floor. Chief Stone stood over near the far corner of the office, red-faced, with beads of sweat forming on his forehead despite the fog-chilled air blowing in through the open window. Mac and Mayes entered the office. Stone told them to grab a seat.

"I know I don't need to remind you guys that it has been almost a week since Michelle Osher was killed, and not only have my two best detectives not made an arrest, but according to Captain Longley, you don't even have a single credible suspect. Governor Schwarzenegger was all over me yesterday at the funeral, asking when we're going to get this case off the front page. Meanwhile, I've got the press asking me about every insignificant detail, and if I don't give them something, they'll go with whatever rumors and innuendo they've got. And I'm sure you can imagine the new asshole Mayor Newsome likes to give me everyday. You guys are killing me."

Mac could just imagine the pressure Governor Square Jaw and Mayor GQ must have been applying to his boss. "We're doing our best, sir. We've been…"

"Dammit Mac, I don't want to hear you're doing your best. I want a goddamn arrest!"

Mayes interjected, believing he knew exactly what Stone wanted to hear. "Sir, we have several strong leads that will lead to an arrest any day now. We've learned that Michelle Osher was having an affair with another woman, but she disappeared the day after the murder, and her husband doesn't know where she is or when she'll be returning. She has a clear motive, however, because just days before the murder Michelle Osher broke off their relationship."

"Who is this dyke?"

"Sonia Grisham, wife of Jim Grisham, the lawyer who threw the party on the night of the murder. We brought in the FBI to help us find her."

"I don't believe this," cried Stone. "Just what the Republicans in this town needed to hear."

"We've also located a source for the murder weapon, the Balisong switchblade," continued Mayes, "and we've got a sting operation set up for tomorrow. We've also identified Sheyla Samonte, Paul Osher's mistress, as a strong suspect. Thanks to Mac's outstanding surveillance, we've determined that she is indeed left-handed. Plus she doesn't have a credible alibi for the night of the murder."

"So why hasn't she been arrested?"

"Because the evidence is purely circumstantial," added Longley. "To implicate her, we need to find the murder weapon. Otherwise, the District Attorney would have nothing that could stand up in court."

"Screw the murder weapon," screamed Stone. "Let's find something to hang on this Samonte woman, for Christ's sake. I want someone arrested. Now!"

෴

"WHY DID YOU TELL him Sheyla was our strongest suspect?" Mac complained to Mayes after the pair returned to their desks. "Why didn't you tell him about the connection we found between Paul Osher and Damian Puti? Those $10,000 checks he wrote her have to be for something."

"Did you just hear what went on in there? Stone wanted an arrest yesterday," emphasized Mayes, his face flushed with anger.

"We needed to give him something. Be realistic, Mac. We don't know what those checks are for, and we still haven't found a motive for Osher to kill his wife. Sonia Grisham has motive, but who knows when we'll find her. Not to mention, people who live in Nob Hill don't normally carry Balisong switchblades. So let's face it Mac, no matter how you feel about her, Sheyla Samonte is our strongest suspect."

Mac walked around his desk, searching for answers, looking for a reason to prevent a nightmare. "Look, before we do anything, let's ask Osher about those checks he wrote to Nadia, or Damian Puti. There's no better motive in this world than money, and those two are all about the money."

"Alright, partner, I'm with you on that one. But I want you to think about something. Remember when I said whoever killed Michelle Osher was looking for attention, and killed with passion? A murder for hire doesn't fit either of those theories. I've never met Sheyla Samonte, but being someone's mistress falls into that category. I've trusted what you've told me so far about her, but if we can't find Sonia Grisham, then there's a bull's-eye painted on the back of Miss Samonte. If one more piece of evidence points in her direction, such as finding that murder weapon, we'll have no choice but to arrest her."

❧

ON A PICTURE PERFECT September afternoon, Mac and Mayes sat on the hillside overlooking the 18th green at the Olympic Club's Lake Course. The golf course is considered one of the best in the country, and has been the site of several U.S. Opens. The irony with the Lake Course is its name; there's not a drop of water anywhere on the course. Walking up the pristine fairway was Paul Osher. He was arguing with his caddie after knocking his approach shot into a greenside bunker.

"Can you believe this guy?" said Mac. "He buries his wife on Tuesday, and he's playing golf on Thursday. We should arrest him just for being an asshole."

"I remember reading in the paper how he became a member," said Mayes. "The Olympic Club has a ten-year waiting list, but Osher moved to the top when he donated fifty grand to renovate the steam room."

Osher took a mighty swing with his sand wedge and knocked his ball four feet above the hole, leaving himself a slippery downhill putt for par.

"Ten bucks says he three-putts," crowed Mac.

"Twenty says he makes it."

Osher drained the putt.

"I hate him," lamented Mac, reaching for his wallet.

They followed Osher to the clubhouse where he intended to join his foursome for a few post-round beers. As soon as he saw Mac and Mayes, Osher excused himself from his friends. The last thing he wanted was a couple of cops hovering around the venerable Men's Grill.

"I hope you two aren't here to apply for a membership," sneered Osher, as they stood outside the Spanish style clubhouse in the late afternoon sunlight. "Haven't you guys already asked me enough questions?"

"We just need you to fill in a few gaps to your story, Mr. Osher," responded Mac. "Why didn't you tell us you knew the other girls who work at *Pearls of Asia?* From the sound of it, you're there so often you should get frequent flier miles."

"Because you never asked me."

"What about your relationship with Nadia? She says she introduced you to Sheyla and Ashley. We also rechecked your bank records and saw that you've paid her alter ego, Damian Puti, two checks totaling $20,000, including a check for $10,000 the day after your wife was killed." Mac stared at Osher, his face echoing a clear lack of respect. "Can you explain that, Mr. Osher?"

"Yes, I can," he said, taking a step toward Mac. "First of all, Damian Puti is a software consultant, one of the best in the world, and I pay him a handsome retainer to work for me. Second, how stupid do you think I am? Do you honestly think I'd write a personal check for someone to kill my wife? The day after she's murdered? And just for the record, I never realized Damian Puti worked at *Pearls of Asia* until he saw me there one night. What he does with his free time is his business, not mine. Just so long as he does the work I pay him for. Yes, he introduced me to Sheyla a couple years ago, but what has that got to do with anything? As for introducing me to someone named Ashley, I don't know who she is or what the hell you're talking about. Mr. Puti and I travel together a lot on business, and he introduces me to people all the time. So what? You got any other asinine questions you want to ask me, Inspector?"

The tension between the two men was palpable. Mac was letting his feelings for Sheyla affect his objectivity. Osher, on the other hand, was tired of having to explain his lifestyle choices to someone he knew would never understand. This case was starting to get personal.

Mac continued pressing. "Mr. Osher, why did Nadia call you on the night of your wife's murder?"

"You mean Damien? He's starting another project for me and wanted to know when I would be back in town. That's why I paid him the ten grand last Friday."

"Did that project include killing your wife?"

"Go fuck yourself," shouted Osher, sticking his finger into Mac's face. "I'm not saying another word without my lawyer present."

"Alright, we're done here," intervened Mayes, stepping in between the two potential combatants. "Whatever you do, Mr. Osher, don't make any plans to leave town."

༄

EXHAUSTED, MAC TRUDGED HOME, cracked opened a beer, and plopped down in a chair at his mother's kitchen table. He stared out the window, lost in thought while contemplating the electrical

Muni bus cables running above the street. Who killed Michelle Osher? Did Sonia Grisham kill her in a jealous rage? Did Paul Osher hire Nadia to eliminate his wife so he could escape to the increasing demands of his self-indulgent lifestyle? Or did Sheyla Samonte murder the wife of her married lover so she could get her hands on his fortune?

At the same time, Mac was still in the midst of an overwhelming rapture, swept away by his growing affection for Sheyla. Could he really be falling in love with a transsexual murder suspect? Just the thought of it seemed absurd.

Mac could walk into the police precinct and discuss the facts of the Michelle Osher case with any number of people. Finding someone to open up to about his feelings for Sheyla, however, was a little more difficult. There was really no one he could talk to about her, especially someone he could trust. Then he heard a car pull into the garage. Victoria Parker was returning home from the gym. There was someone he could talk to.

"Mackey, what are you doing home?" asked his mother, wearing a green Nike sweat suit, no makeup, and looking at least a decade younger than the age on her drivers license. "Why aren't you out making this city safer for your poor old mother?"

"Poor old mother?" mocked Mac. "This coming from a woman who plays with men like a cat plays with a ball of string. You forget I've seen you and your fellow Cougar Committee members cast your evil spells at places like the Balboa Café. You ladies go through men the way a shredder tears up credit cards. The guys don't stand a chance."

"Are we that bad?" she asked archly. "I certainly hope so. So what's on your mind, Mackey? You've already scratched the label off your beer bottle. That usually means you're doing more than contemplating your navel."

"Let me ask you something, Mom. This case has required me to spend a lot of time at *Pearls of Asia*, and I've gotten to know several of the girls who work there. Watching them in action is like watching the transsexual version of *Sex and the City*. I swear, some of them are funnier than a rubber crutch. What would you think if I ever got involved with one of those girls?"

Victoria Parker joined her son at the kitchen table. "Well, I sure hope you'd introduce me to her. I'm sure she'd have her finger on the pulse of what's fashionable and stylish. I need all the help I can get these days to keep up with what's hot and what's not."

At a time like this, Mac needed more of a mother and less of Victoria Parker. "I'm serious, Mom. I need your advice. I've gotten myself into a situation. What would you think if I went out with a girl who wasn't 'normal?'"

"There's your first problem," she said, rising from the table to fix herself some caffeinated tea. The Asian markets were about to open, and her energy needed some turbo-charging. "You keep thinking of them as not being 'normal.' Take any of those women out of *Pearls of Asia* and you wouldn't have a clue they're transsexual. They are just as normal as you or I, Mackey. What you're really asking is how I'd feel if you started sleeping with one of those girls. And the truth is I could care less. Go knock yourself out. Have fun. What ever you do between the sheets is fine with me so long as it puts a smile on your face. When it comes to sex, all I've ever asked you to do is respect the person you're with. You're my son, and I love you to death, and anything you do that makes you happy is okay by me. Is the sugar bowl over there?"

Mac pushed the sugar toward his mother. "I know, Mom. I guess I'm just nervous about what other people would think if they found out."

What had been a pleasant chat between mother and son suddenly took an incendiary aire. "Mackey Fleet, you should be ashamed of yourself! You're a grown man, thirty-two years old, and I didn't raise you to be a wimp. You've got a mind of your own, and I'd be upset if you started letting other people dictate how you're going to live your life. Respect comes from within, and you have to respect the choices you make in your life, and the people you choose to be with. If you decide you want to date a trans woman, then so be it. If someone has a problem with it, then let it be their problem, not yours."

Mac's phone rang. It was Sheyla. "I've got to take this call, Mom. Thanks for setting me straight. You're right, Mom. You're always right." He scurried down the stairs into his bedroom. "Hello."

"Hey gorgeous, how are you?" Sheyla was scheduled to work tonight, but Reyna had called and asked if they could switch nights. With her evening suddenly free, Sheyla wanted Mac to join her for a casual dinner. Mac declined, telling her the pressure of solving the Osher case required his full attention.

"Oh really now?" teased Sheyla, once again not taking 'no' for an answer. "Now that you've had me in bed, you're too busy for me?"

"Sheyla, you have no idea how much pressure we're under to make an arrest."

After a way-too-long-pause on the phone, Sheyla spoke up. "What if I had some information that could help you?"

That was the last thing Mac expected to hear from her. "Depends. What have you got?"

Sheyla played coy, as always. "I'll tell you over dinner. Meet me in an hour at this fabulous little Mexican place at the corner of California and 19th Street. I hope you like tequila." As always, Sheyla hung up first.

"I'm an idiot."

CHAPTER SEVENTEEN

Thursday, September 18, 2008 - 9:00 pm

"Due to margin calls and a dramatic falloff in commercial real estate activity, Paul Osher is negotiating with a consortium of banks to refinance or sell some of his properties in San Francisco, including several luxury hi-rise apartment buildings."

The Wall Street Journal

SHEYLA DIRECTED MAC TO Tia Margarita, an old-style Mexican restaurant located in Sea Cliff, a quiet neighborhood known for its large houses, ocean views, and never ending fog. Sheyla had picked the non-descript restaurant for two reasons. First, it was far off the beaten path and would allow them to have some privacy. Second, and more important to Sheyla, they made the best margaritas in town. Despite the relative obscurity of the neighborhood, Sheyla decided to make her presence felt by wearing a low-cut red silk blouse topped by a Gucci leather jacket, with black Escada custom fit jeans tucked into a pair of Louis Vuitton leather boots. The only other designer elements at Tia Margarita were the tortilla chips, designed by a guy named Frank.

After ordering a couple of Grand Marnier margaritas, Mac got right down to business. "Okay, Sheyla. Let's hear it. What have you got for me?"

"Okay, Mr. Big Time Detective, I wanted to tell you something about Paul. Did you know he's going broke?"

"Everyone's going broke, aren't they? At least that's what my mom tells me every morning when she opens up her Wall Street Journal. Where did you learn this? Isn't Paul Osher one of the richest guys in town? He's supposed to be a financial legend."

"Oh, please. Paul is barely a legend in his own shower. Anyway, last month we went to Las Vegas, and he said I may need to move to one of his other apartment buildings. The building I live in is his premier property, and he's selling it to pay off the bank. He's leveraged up to his eyeballs, and the financial crisis is crushing him."

Mac took such a huge gulp from his margarita he gave himself a brain freeze. He would never discuss the details of a case with Sheyla, and he wasn't about to now. But she had provided a lead he and Mayes hadn't even considered. He was both pissed at himself and embarrassed. He ordered another margarita.

Sheyla continued. "And did you know he recently bought a huge life insurance policy on his wife, with himself as the beneficiary? Ten million bucks. She was worth more to him dead than alive."

Mac was blown away. "That's a good piece of detective work, Miss Samonte. Let me ask you something. Do you have any proof, or was this just pillow talk?"

"That's your job, Mackey. I'm just the messenger. He told me all this one night when we were at the Wynn Hotel, after I promised him he could strut around our hotel suite wearing my bra and panties. Don't you see how much I care for you? I could have kept Paul's financial problems a secret, but I want you to solve this case and be a big hero. I want you to be happy with me, too."

Sheyla asked for two shots of premium anejo tequila, along with another basket of chips and salsa. She had developed an instant rapport with the bartender, and the two started speaking to each other in Spanish. Mac remembered what Mayes said to him about Sheyla trying to steer the investigation away from her and Paul Osher, but she had just laid down a set a train tracks that led right to Osher's front door. The hour was late, so he'd look into this first thing tomorrow morning. Now was the time to relax. Besides, Sheyla looked so hot she could have set off the sprinkler system.

"Mackey, now that we got the police stuff out of the way, let me ask you a question." Sheyla downed her shot and quickly ordered another round. "If we are together a year from now, would you take me home to meet your mother?"

"Aren't we getting a little ahead of ourselves, Sheyla?" he answered while finishing his margarita, with a pair of tequila shots still waiting for his attention. Trying to keep up with Sheyla at a bar was like bringing a knife to a gunfight.

"I'm just playing with you, Mackey. Just for drill, though, what would your mother say if you told her we couldn't have children?"

"You don't know my mom. They broke the mold when they made her. She'd probably say we should adopt a few kids from Haiti. She's a very cool lady, my mom, though she'll rip your heart out if you're on the other side of a trade with her."

"I love that! I can't wait to meet her. Tell me about your father."

Mac went quiet, his face devoid of emotion. He downed one of the tequila shots. "Like I told you the other night, Sheyla. I don't want to talk about him. As far as I'm concerned, I don't have a father."

"I'm sorry, Mac. I know how you feel." Sheyla polished off her second shot of tequila. "I want to share something with you, something that's taken me years to learn. Remember how I told you my father disowned me the moment I told him I wanted to transition? For years afterward, I was angry with him. I carried around feelings of hostility and bitterness like a hundred-pound backpack. Then one day I realized those feelings of spite and revenge were only hurting me, keeping me from becoming the person I wanted to be. I couldn't control how he felt about me; I could only control how I felt about him. So instead of hating him, or even worse, ignoring him, I decided to forgive him. It was a difficult decision, and I agonized over it, but I'm so glad I did it. An incredible weight was lifted off my shoulders, and I've been so much happier ever since. It was the best decision I ever made."

Mac drank his second tequila shot. Sheyla had taken a shovel to his spirit, and in a few short sentences she had dug her way into his soul. How could this person, this mysterious woman whom he had only met days before, massage the knots of his flaws so easily? Years of repressed anger and guilt began to bubble their way to the surface, penetrating the scabs of scars healed long ago. Feeling weakened and defenseless, Mac tried to shield his emotions by asking her one simple question. "What would you say to your father if you ever saw him again?"

"I'd give him a hug and tell him I love him. Deep down he knows he made a mistake. I'm sure your father feels the same way. But you need to forgive him, Mackey. Forgive him with all your heart and soul and move on with your life. Otherwise you'll never get rid of the pain, and it will hold you down like an anchor on a ship. Someday you'll need to forgive your wife, too, because she's just trying to live her life, a life that you didn't want to be a part of. And somewhere down the road, you'll even find the strength to forgive yourself for Larry Kelso getting shot."

That was it.

Sheyla's digging had found its way to the very core of his being. Mac looked like he had just been punched in the stomach. His skin paled. The look he gave Sheyla was as distant as a desert horizon. "How did you know about Larry Kelso?"

"Simple. I Googled your name, and there it was; a hundred stories about a cop's best friend getting shot on Christmas Day. Remember the first time you knocked on my door and I wouldn't let you in? After you left I decided to check you out. That's why I was late for work that day. I've known the whole time we've been seeing each other. I was just waiting for you to say something, but then I began to realize you don't open up to anyone. You made a mistake, Mackey, plain and simple. It's okay to feel pain, because pain happens when you care. But instead of dwelling on it, do something about it. Learn from it and move on. You think you're a failure because you're not perfect. That's stupid. It doesn't make any sense. You're not a bad person just because life has dealt you a few bad hands. You're just like me, Mac, taking what life has thrown at you and trying to find a way to make the best of it."

Mac reached down and squeezed Sheyla's hand. He could feel himself getting emotional, but it wasn't the tequila that was making his eyes tear up. "I thought you were the puzzle we were trying to solve," he said.

Sheyla put her arm around Mac's neck and pulled him close to her, their foreheads leaning against each other. Mac could feel a few tears starting to fall, his first in over two decades.

"God made a mistake when he made me a boy," she continued. "But I never would have become the person I am today if he hadn't. It took me a long time to realize that, but not only did I forgive Him, I thanked Him. You need to do the same, Mackey. You need to embrace the experiences of your life and grow from them, and not use them as an excuse for being unhappy. You're a good man, Mac Fleet. You've earned the right to be happy."

Like rain falling from a sunny sky, Mac shed tears of relief. For the first time in his life, he had met someone who wanted to help him unwind the bands of doubt and self-loathing that caused him so much angst and misery. He hugged Sheyla and buried his head into her shoulder. She hugged him back, harder than anyone had in years. It was as though she were trying to squeeze the pain and guilt right out of him, replacing it with the belief she had in growth, in passion, and in life.

"I'm glad I met you, Sheyla Samonte," Mac whispered.

"Of course you are," she replied with a smile.

Sheyla grabbed a cocktail napkin to wipe away the tears from his eyes. Then she waved to the bartender. "Another round, por favor."

"Here's to forgiveness," said Mac, holding his third tequila shot of the night, feeling like Mt. Everest had been lifted off his shoulders.

"Here's to staying at my place tonight," answered Sheyla.

༄

SHEYLA LIT CANDLES ALL around her apartment. "Let's Stay Together" by Tina Turner wafted from the stereo. "If you haven't figured it out by now, Tina Turner is my favorite singer."

"I was wondering about that," responded Mac, who was occupied opening up a bottle of champagne. "You got something against music from this decade?"

"No silly. Something about her music just speaks to me; the strength of her voice and the honesty of her lyrics. Whenever my girlfriends come over to drink wine and gossip about men, I put on her hit "What's Love Got To Do With It." Do you know her story? How she left her abusive husband with just 36 cents in her pocket, and she wanted nothing from their divorce except her name? She's a woman who believed in herself and wouldn't give up until she achieved her dreams. I adore her music, and the way she's lived her life has made her my idol."

"That's great," said Mac, pouring two glasses of bubbly. "Let's have a toast to your idol"

"Not so fast," she said. "It's my turn to make the toast. Here's to breaking the rules."

Mac had broken them all, it seemed, and he knew it. Sheyla was like a drug, and he was addicted. "You can say that again."

"I would, except I'm a woman who believes actions speak louder than words. Now you wait right here while I change into something to match my mood."

Mac poured himself another glass of champagne. He sat back and relaxed, expecting Sheyla to return wearing something that would blow his testosterone right off the Richter scale.

Sheyla reappeared, strutting into the room like a cabaret star. To say she met his expectations would be a gross understatement. Wearing a black lacy corset, with matching garter belt, panties and stockings, and a pair of thigh-high stiletto boots, Sheyla was the girl your mother had always warned you about. Times ten.

They sat next to each other on the couch, talked and laughed, and enjoyed their champagne. They flirted like two school kids sitting alone in the back of the bus. Soon they were kissing each other as though it would be for the last time.

Mac placed his hand first on her breasts, and then slid it down to her thighs. Sheyla quivered as he stroked his fingers along her skin, and she moved her leg to give him the freedom she so desperately wanted him to have. Mac slid his hand under her panties, and he touched her in a place that made her stop and catch her breath.

"Will you do something for me?" she asked.

"Whatever you wish."

Sheyla pulled down her panties, revealing herself to him. "Please," she pleaded in her sultry voice, "Do it to me, Mackey. Please. Just do it."

Mac hesitated. Then he took a deep breath, opened his mouth, and extended his tongue to touched her erogenous erectile. He glided it from top to bottom, bottom to top, wondering if what he was doing was right. After circling the tip of her phallus, Sheyla took her hands and placed them on top his head. Then, summoning more courage than he ever thought he had, he placed his lips on the head of her sensuous staff. "Yes...," moaned Sheyla, pushing Mac's head down toward her hairless crotch. Sheyla wanted more, so he gave it to her, taking her all the way into his mouth. She was warmer, stiffer, and smoother than he imagined she would be. He lifted his head up, then down, sweeping his lips along her fountain of joy. Sheyla arched her back, pushing herself deeper into his throat. Her legs started to shake, and her moans became more intense. Mac could barely comprehend what he was doing, but he liked it. He was pleasing her, and that thought alone was turning him on.

Sheyla was ready, and she wanted to make the most of it. Jumping off the couch, she grabbed her lover's hand and escorted him into her bedroom. Sheyla then shoved Mac onto the bed, ripped off their clothes, and ordered him to stay there, flat on his back.

She reached into her nightstand and took out the bottle of lube and a condom. Mac stared at her naked silhouette, illuminated by candlelight, and he could see her roll the condom onto herself. She took a handful of lubrication, coated herself, then spread Mac's legs and applied it around his anus. Mac suspected what might happen next, and it scared him, but he was also curious, and his desire to please her far exceeded his fear of the unknown.

Sheyla got on her knees on top of the bed, and grabbed Mac's ankles, putting one over each shoulder. She then took hold of her potent erection and circled it around his anus. It was a sensation he had never felt before, and it made him wildly nervous and excited. She began to move her hips forward, gently inserting herself into him. Mac felt a sharp pain, and he let out a soft scream. Sheyla pulled back a touch, gave him a moment to relax, then slowly drove herself inside him.

The pain eased, and Mac realized he was sharing his body with his lover. She was inside of him, dominating him, a feeling he never imagined. Sheyla rocked back and forth, back and forth, igniting a rhythmic intercourse that had Mac lusting for more. Soon he was pleading, begging, asking her to go faster, harder, and deeper. Then, in a burst of energy and passion, both lovers climaxed. After she stopped shaking, Sheyla pulled herself out and collapsed on top of Mac, exhausted.

ᘰ

MAC SAT ALONE ON the floor of her shower; the room as dark as night. Against the echo of the falling water, Mac could hear the turning of a knob, followed by the sound of a door being opened and closed. He could feel the lightness of footsteps, and then he heard the click of the shower door. Sheyla stepped inside, and then she sat down between his legs and placed her naked back against his chest. Mac wrapped his arms around her shoulders, his hands caressing her breasts.

CHAPTER EIGHTEEN

Friday, September 19, 2008 - 11:00 am

"San Francisco Mayor Gavin Newsom is pressuring Chief of Police David Stone for a quick resolution of the Michelle Osher murder investigation. The Mayor's office wants the high-profile case to be out of the headlines in time for Newsom's re-election bid in November."

The Los Angles Times

THE GUYS HANGING OUT in the precinct locker room could smell Mac coming from a mile away. In preparation for today's sting operation at Hunters Point, Mac wore his San Francisco 49er pre-game tailgate uniform; dusty blue overalls, mismatched tennis shoes, and a 49er cap reeking of homemade barbeque sauce and stale beer. As he was about to exit the locker room, Mac ran into Keith Nix, a ten-year veteran at the precinct.

"Damn Mac, aren't you getting fired up a little early for Sunday's game? You could have at least washed that nasty outfit of yours. After all, last season did end eight months ago. Save our noses and drop a few quarters at the Laundromat. Otherwise we'll have to hose you down before we let you get near the keg on

Sunday. By the way, I was talking to Jackson a couple days ago, and he said he and his girlfriend saw you at that *Pearls of Asia* place last week, kissing one of the transvestites. What was up with that?"

"She's a transsexual, genius, not a transvestite. Big difference, not that you'd care. Anyway, for the briefest of seconds I became part of the show. It was all in good fun and no one got hurt. Believe it or not, *Pearls of Asia* is relevant to our investigation of the Michelle Osher murder."

"I don't know, Mac. The guys are beginning to talk," cracked Nix. "I just hope you're not turning queer on us or anything."

"Not to worry, Nix. I gotta go. See you Sunday." The guys in the SFPD weren't the most liberal cast of characters in the world, and Mac had told his fair share of gay jokes in the locker room. They just weren't as funny to him anymore.

 ♾

MAC AND MAYES HOPPED into The Sub to pick up Fernando Mateo at the county jail. Mayes, dressed in his usual suit and tie, sat as far away as possible from his malodorous partner. Mac needed to update his partner on the details of last night's conversation with Sheyla without putting himself in harm's way from the Wrath of Mayes. Mac wisely decided that what happened at Sheyla's apartment should stay at Sheyla's apartment.

"Sheyla Samonte contacted me last night and told me Paul Osher is losing his shirt in this financial meltdown, and that he's leveraged worse than a third-world country. Osher also told her he had taken out a $10 million insurance policy on his wife with himself being the beneficiary. I checked it out this morning and she's right. For all we know, he may have had his wife killed for the insurance money."

"Of course she knows about the insurance policy," responded Mayes. "Who do you think is going to benefit from a $10 million payday besides Paul Osher? In my mind this piece of news helps establish a motive for Miss Samonte. I understand that you don't want your girlfriend arrested, but you seem to have lost track of what we need to do. Stone wants an arrest. Period."

"Would you rather arrest the wrong person," replied Mac, "or dig a little deeper and find the real killer? What about Sonia Grisham? Or Damian Puti?"

"The FBI hasn't found the trail of Sonia Grisham, and we don't have enough evidence to arrest Damian Puti," barked Mayes. "Of course I don't want to lock up the wrong person, but if we don't make an arrest soon, we're in big trouble. C'mon, Mac, we both know what's going on here."

Mac did know, and it scared the hell out of him.

∽

THE ODD-COUPLED TWOSOME picked up Fernando Mateo and drove The Sub to the H Street pier in Hunter's Point, an area of drug-infested streets and empty warehouses. Except for a few hungry and noisy seagulls, the area was deserted. Mayes then outlined the sting. Fernando would wait for 'RC' at the end of the pier, while Mac pretended to be a homeless wreck sleeping off a hangover at the pier's entrance. Mayes would wait in The Sub catching the action on tape. When Fernando recognized his mark, he would remove his hat and signal for Mac to start walking toward the end of the long pier, cutting off any means of escape.

At one o'clock, Fernando Mateo saw a tall figure approaching him along the pier, wearing a full-length leather coat, dark oversized sunglasses, and a baseball cap stuffed with black hair. Fernando removed his hat to wipe his brow.

Mac jumped up and galloped toward the end of the pier. Fernando handed the box of Balisong knives to RC, who then gave Fernando a cash-filled envelope. Mac closed in, flashing his badge. "Don't move, RC! Get down on the ground! You're under arrest," he yelled.

RC tried to toss the knives into the water, but Mac grabbed the box before he had a chance. RC hit the ground, and Mayes ran from across the street to cuff him. The next sounds uttered by RC surprised the two hard-boiled detectives.

"I can't go to jail," said a soft voice that sounded more Michael Jackson than Samuel L. Jackson. Mac removed the hat and sunglasses and recognized a large scar over the left eye.

"Reyna?"

"You know who I am?"

"Hell yes," replied Mac, the shock of the moment evident on his face. "You're Reyna. You work at *Pearls of Asia*."

Mac removed his ratty 49er hat. "Oh my gosh. You're Mac Fleet," she declared. "You're Sheyla's boyfriend."

"Say what?" asked Mayes.

"Stay focused, Mayes," snapped Mac. "Okay, Reyna, where does the 'RC' come from?"

"Those are my initials. My name is Reyna Cruz. Please, Mac. Don't arrest me. It's not what it looks like."

Mayes grabbed Reyna's coat with one massive hand and lifted her up like a tackling dummy. "It looks to me like you're pimping illegal switchblades."

"No, that isn't it," she pleaded. "I'm a counselor at a health clinic, not some kind of arms dealer. Have you seen how much these knives are selling for on eBay? I thought it might be a good way to raise money for "Catwalk," my alternative beauty pageant. Please, you have to believe me."

Mayes checked in with the precinct to see if there were any prior arrests of Reyna Cruz. She had been locked up six times in the past for prostitution and drug possession, but her rap sheet had been clean for the past ten years.

"Talk to me, Reyna Cruz," demanded Mayes. "This isn't the first time you've been busted. How do we know you're telling the truth?"

Reyna broke down crying as she tried to explain. "Things were different when I first got to America. I came here with nothing and lived on the streets. I'm not proud of it, but I did what

I had to do to survive. Eventually I got on my feet and found a place to live. Then I started going to night school to become a counselor. I swear to God, I've haven't been in trouble since. Last year, I was attending an AIDS conference in Los Angeles where I met this girl who traded me a half-dozen Balisongs she brought into the country for a bag of hormones. I always carried a Balisong knife for protection when I lived in the Philippines, and I thought it would be smart to have another one. You can keep it in your pocket or your purse without anyone noticing."

"How many of these have you sold?" asked Mac.

"I haven't sold a single one. I decided instead to give them away to the girls at *Pearls of Asia*. Walking back to your car late at night after work, usually alone, can be pretty scary."

Mayes put on his most intimidating scowl. "Alright, Miss Cruz. Here's what we're going to do. We need to account for every knife you've given away. You CANNOT, I repeat, CANNOT speak to anyone until we talk to them first. You got me? If you do, I'm going to put you in jail with a bunch of thugs who'd be delighted to share a cell with a woman like you. Do you get my drift?"

"Yes, sir" she begged, too scared to cry anymore. "I understand. I'm so sorry."

Mac removed Reyna's handcuffs. "You're lucky he likes you," remarked Mac. "Normally he'd break one of your fingers before he said that."

Mac escorted Fernando Mateo back to The Sub, while Mayes grabbed the box of Balisong knives. Before he had gone too far, Mayes asked Reyna a question. "Miss Cruz, by any chance, do you know if any of the girls at *Pearls of Asia* are left-handed?"

"I'm not sure about everyone," she answered, "but I know Sheyla is."

∽

BACK AT THE PRECIENCT, Mac and Mayes discussed what to do next. "It's pretty simple," said Mayes. "We now have probable cause to search *Pearls of Asia*. I say we get a warrant and go straight there and see which one is carrying a Balisong. Then we'll have each one sign the search warrant to see which of them is left-handed. If I'm right, and we can confirm Sheyla Samonte is the only one who meets both criteria, then we'll have no choice but to arrest her."

Mac fired back, still reeking of 49er fumes, "What about my theory, that Osher and Nadia conspired to kill his wife? She admits being at the party, she spoke to Osher only an hour before the murder, and we now know Osher had a financial motive to kill his wife. Ten million bucks pays for a lot of grief counseling."

Mayes walked over and rested his massive posterior on a corner of Mac's desk. "Let me ask you something, Inspector Fleet. Which would you rather tell Stone? That you arrested Sheyla Samonte based on strong circumstantial evidence, or you arrested Paul Osher, who happens to be one of his close personal friends, on a hunch?"

Mac picked up his Rubik's Cube. "Do you want to drive to *Pearls of Asia* or should I?"

⌒

THE TWO DETECTIVES WAITED outside on Howard Street for *Pearls of Asia* to open. Mayes called ahead and learned that Nadia, Sheyla, Diamond, and Reyna were scheduled to work tonight. "We'll go in right after they open," said Mayes. "That way every girl will be upstairs hustling tables. I doubt they carry knives while they're working."

"They don't need to," said Mac, who never bothered to change out of his smelly undercover clothes. "Their tongues are sharper than any knife."

Mayes flashed his badge at Mr. Ponytail, explaining that he was there on police business. Mac followed behind, adding a pair of sunglasses to his disgusting outfit, hoping he wouldn't be recognized. Mr. Ponytail sat Mayes and his grubby companion at a table next to the back stairs, which led down to the girls' dressing room.

After being seated, Mayes pulled out the search warrant and began requesting for the girls to come over to his table.

Reyna was the first to provide her signature. Righty. "Where's the one they call Diamond?" asked Mayes.

"I don't know. She's scheduled to work tonight, but she didn't show up. She's missed her last few shifts, which is strange. No one has seen her since she and a friend went to Mexico earlier this week."

"Would you mind asking the one they call Nadia to come over here?"

Nadia strutted over toward the detectives, wearing more attitude than clothes. "Hello gentlemen. I've been expecting you."

"Really?" asked Mayes. "Why is that?"

"I've got videotape of you guys searching my place. I hope your boss enjoyed going through my panty drawer. What's his name? Oh yes, Longley. He's one of my regulars. He likes his girls to be like his cops; versatile."

"We understand you've been traveling quite a bit," said Mayes, "I guess those $10,000 checks from Paul Osher aren't enough to pay for your lifestyle."

"Honey, between New York, Vegas and Sacramento, in the last week I went to four paydays and a funeral. As for those checks, let's just say Paul thinks I'm a better broker than half the guys who work for him."

Mayes slid the warrant and a pen in front of Nadia. Nadia gave a right-handed signature worthy of John Hancock. Mac's shoulders slumped; his theory for the case just went down the drain.

"Get me Sheyla Samonte," Mayes barked to Nadia. It was an order, not a request.

"I've got to use the head," conveyed Mac, who wanted no part of this exercise. He walked far enough away to be out of Mayes' line of sight, but close enough to see the action. Sheyla came by and nonchalantly signed the warrant. No one was shocked to see her use her left hand. She then proceeded toward the top of the stairway where Mac was standing. He removed his hat and sunglasses and in a hushed tone called out her name.

"Oh my God, Mackey. I barely recognized you." Sheyla wrapped her arms around him and gave him a soft kiss. She didn't seem to notice, or care, that he smelled like a fraternity basement. "You surprised me. What are you doing here, and why are you wearing these awful clothes?"

Mac looked at her with desperate eyes. "Sheyla, do you trust me?"

"Do I trust you?" she asked. "What kind of question is that?"

"Sheyla, something's going down tonight. It's out of control and I can't stop it. I need to know if you trust me?"

Sheyla could tell Mac was serious. "You're scaring me, Mac. Please tell me what this is all about."

"Sheyla, you need to know that no matter what happens tonight, I'm going to make things right. You have to believe me."

"Okay Mac. Okay. Yes, I trust you. Now I need to get ready for a show. Promise you'll wait for me." She blew him a kiss and hurried down the stairs.

"Oh, I promise," he said to himself with a tinge of regret. "I promise."

෴

MAC RETURNED TO HIS table, where Mayes waved the warrant in his face. Nadia, Reyna, and Sheyla had all signed. Sheyla was the only southpaw.

"Well?" asked Mayes.

"I hear you, Mayes, but this isn't right. Besides, we still don't know about the other girls who work here. How come no one has seen Diamond for the past few days? Did she skip town? And what about Ashley? She certainly had the opportunity."

"It doesn't matter, Mac. We're out of time."

In a few minutes the lights dimmed, and Sheyla ascended the stairs to begin her number. Mayes walked over to Nadia and grabbed her by the arm. "Take me to your dressing room."

"Not unless you've got a thousand bucks," she quipped.

The dressing room at *Pearls of Asia* reeked of perfume and hairspray. It's where the girls got ready for work, caught up on the latest gossip, and sometimes did battle. Each girl is assigned a locker where she kept outfits, makeup, and the occasional fifth of vodka. Graffiti on the walls bore more phone numbers than the Yellow pages. Pictures of boyfriends young and not so young were plastered on the locker doors, like fishermen displaying their catch of the day. Diamond posted pictures of herself, although in her absence someone had blackened out her teeth. Mac stood by the door while Mayes began the search.

"Which locker is Sheyla Samonte's?" demanded Mayes.

Nadia pointed to the only locker without pictures or scribble scratched all over it. Mayes walked over with a pair of pocketsize bolt cutters and snapped open the lock. Inside he found several dresses, some shorts, a few t-shirts, and lots makeup. On top of the pile of shoes was her Louis Vuitton travel bag. Mayes took it out and began to sort through the clutter of underwear, gum wrappers, and empty water bottles. After a few seconds, he zipped open an interior pocket and, at the bottom, found what he had been looking for: a Balisong switchblade.

"Paydirt."

Mac stood stone-faced, as rigid as a wooden tobacco store Indian. "Of all the times you were with her," lamented Mayes, "you never once thought to look in her bag. It's pathetic, Mac. It really is."

Sheyla's number was just about to end, and once again the room was in an uproar. The song over, she waved to the crowd and walked off to a standing ovation. As soon as she stepped off the stage, Mayes grabbed Sheyla's arm and showed him her badge.

"Sheyla Samonte, I'm Inspector Taylor Mayes of the San Francisco Police Department. You're under arrest for the murder of Michelle Osher." He pulled her wrists behind her back and handcuffed her. "You have the right to remain silent. Whatever you say…"

"What are you doing?" she protested.

"…can be used against you in a court of law…"

"I didn't kill anyone!"

The room went silent as Mayes finished reading Sheyla her rights. Nadia and Reyna stood in a corner near the back entrance, speechless. Mayes took Sheyla by the arm and led her out of the restaurant. Mac followed behind, his head down, as the three of them walked to The Sub.

∾

SHEYLA SAMONTE WAS TAKEN to the San Francisco County jail to be booked and processed. She was angry and confused. Once before she had experienced the degradation of being arrested for solicitation, and she knew the smartest thing she could do was to keep her mouth shut. Mac remained silent, doing his best not to make eye contact with her.

After being fingerprinted and photographed, Mayes asked Mac what side of the prison they should put her in: male or female. "She's not exactly a woman, and she's not exactly a man. You tell me, Mac, where should we put her for the night?"

"Don't be an asshole, Mayes. If you put her with those animals in the male section, they'll eat her alive. You said yourself she's a woman. Put her in with the female population."

Sheyla was escorted to the women's side of the prison. Still wearing heavy makeup, rivers of mascara streamed down her face. As the door was closing behind her, she turned to Mac, her eyes wide with panic. When he returned the look, the serious expression that had been plastered on his face since the moment of her arrest never wavered.

Except for the wink.

CHAPTER NINETEEN

Saturday, September 20, 2008 - 10:00 am

"Police have announced the arrest of thirty-year-old Sheyla Samonte for the murder of Michelle Osher. Miss Samonte is the rumored mistress of Paul Osher, the victim's wealthy husband. Unconfirmed reports indicate Miss Samonte is employed as a 'gender illusionist' at a popular San Francisco restaurant called 'Pearls of Asia.'"

Associated Press

OZENS OF MEDIA TRUCKS, satellite dishes, and cherry picker vans were stacked outside Police Headquarters like so many egg cartons. Inside, reporters from CNN to the E! Network were crammed into the department's stuffy auditorium for a televised press conference with Police Chief David Stone on the arrest of Sheyla Samonte.

Mayes ran though the hallways looking for Stone. He found him backstage, looking into a mirror while rehearsing his prepared remarks. "Chief Stone, I need to speak to you before you talk to the press. It's very important, sir."

"Dammit, Mayes," said Stone, fussing with his gelled hair that a tornado couldn't have budged. "Can't you see I'm busy?"

"Sir, I need to make you aware of something. It concerns both Mac and me."

"What is it, Mayes? You guys are my all-stars. I'll make sure both get the recognition you deserve."

"That's not it, sir. It's about Inspector Fleet's conduct. Somewhere during the course of our investigation, he became romantically involved with Sheyla Samonte."

Stone stared straight into the mirror, which allowed him to see his face turn red and the veins in his neck began to bulge. "What the hell did you just say?"

"Mac got too close to our suspect, Chief. He also doesn't believe she murdered Michelle Osher. He went along with it only because you put the squeeze on us to make an arrest."

"How long have you known about this, Inspector Mayes? And why the hell have you waited until now to tell me?" Stone's muffled rage could he heard outside by reporters.

"I wanted to, sir, but we're partners, and partners look out for each other. We were hoping that Sheyla Samonte wasn't our suspect and this would all blow over."

"So let me see if I've got this straight. My top team of detectives disagrees about whether or not the person we have in custody actually committed this crime; one of my best officers is jeopardizing the biggest case this city has seen in years, along with his own career, by getting romantically involved with our primary suspect; and you just admitted to the Chief of Police that you withheld evidence of your partner committing a major department violation. Have I missed anything, Inspector Mayes?"

"No, sir."

"Good. Now go find *former* Inspector Mac Fleet and tell him to wait for me in my office.

༄

ATTIRED IN FULL DRESS uniform, Stone stood tall behind a podium as he addressed the scores of reporters. "Ladies and Gentlemen. It is my pleasure to announce that the great men and women of the San Francisco Police Department have made an arrest in the murder of anchorwoman Michelle Osher. The suspect in custody is Sheyla Samonte. She is thirty years old, born in the Philippines, and employed as a waitress at a local restaurant. We are not at liberty to discuss the facts of the case, but we will try to answer as many of your questions as we can."

Copies of the press release were handed out, which included Sheyla's mug shot. It may have been the worst picture ever taken of her. Her face was ashen, swollen, and smeared with heavy makeup.

"Is it true she's a transsexual?" asked a reporter from the *San Francisco Chronicle.*

"We have not ascertained that fact as of yet," answered Stone.

"But she works at *Pearls of Asia.* Wouldn't it make sense?" repeated the newspaper reporter.

"As I just said, right now we do not know that for a fact."

"Is it true she was Paul Osher's mistress?" asked a reporter from CBS news.

"Paul Osher did have a relationship with the suspect. That is all we can tell you."

"Did he give her money?" asked a reporter from *The Wall Street Journal.*

"As I've said, we cannot disclose the facts of this case."

"What motive would Sheyla Samonte have to kill Michelle Osher?" asked a female reporter from *People.*

"We won't discuss a possible motive at this time."

Questions started firing in from all over the room.

"Had the suspect ever met Michelle Osher?"

"How long had she known Paul Osher?"

"Is there one 's' or two in 'transsexual?'"

Sensing the onset of a media feeding frenzy, Stone brought the press conference to a quick conclusion. Within a few short hours,

Sheyla Samonte's picture, and the incredible story of a beautiful transsexual murdering the famous wife of her wealthy lover, was spread to every corner of the planet.

ↄ⌒

"WHAT THE HELL WERE you thinking?" bellowed Stone behind the closed door of his office. Mac knew this moment would arrive, but nothing could have prepared him for the verbal onslaught he was about to take. "Am I to believe what your partner told me, that you're screwing our suspect? Have you lost your fucking mind?"

Throughout his career, Stone had served as a mentor to Mac. Standing before him now, in disgrace, he felt like a son who had just disappointed his father. "I'm sorry, sir. There is no excuse for my behavior. I realize I've failed you."

"I swear Mac, if this case gets thrown out of court because my lead detective acted like a love-starved Casanova, I'll do more than just fire you. I'll have you prosecuted for obstruction and have you thrown in jail."

"Sir, if that's the case, then I'll accept the consequences. But as a sworn officer of the law, it's my duty to tell you I don't believe Sheyla Samonte killed Michelle Osher. I admit I violated department policy, but Sheyla Samonte did not commit this crime. The real killer is still out there."

"Then why did you and Mayes have her arrested?"

Mac's jaw tightened; resolve replaced guilt. "Because that's what you wanted us to do, sir. You made it very clear that we had to pin this crime on someone, or our jobs would be in jeopardy. I'll admit much of the evidence points to her, but it's paper thin and purely circumstantial. We still haven't found Sonia Grisham or a murder weapon. Hell, we still haven't found the damn dog. There are still too many unanswered questions, and I don't think we're doing the best job we can by making a quick arrest just because the media has lit a fire under your ass. I'm sorry for talking to you this way, Chief, but I'm telling you the truth."

Stone had heard enough. He wanted answers, and all he was getting were excuses. "Clean out your desk, Fleet. You've just earned yourself a suspension without pay. Now get the hell out of my office."

༄

MAC GRABBED A CARDBOARD box and began the never-thought-of-process of emptying his desk. All the years of hard work had come down to this. The one thing he loved to do more than anything else in the world was being taken away from him. And he had only himself to blame. Next was the stuff in his locker. Inside the locker room were half a dozen officers in various stages of undress. The roar of testosterone-fueled gossip was silenced the moment he entered the room.

"I can't believe you, Mac," remarked Keith Nix, the officer Mac ran into the day before. "As if sleeping with a murder suspect wasn't bad enough, you had to go fuck around with a tranny. You're pathetic."

"I knew I should have said something to the Captain," added Jackson, who saw Mac that first night at *Pearls of Asia*. "Something about you being there alone, kissing that transvestite. I could tell you were into him. Man, I never would have believed you were gay."

"Guys," responded Mac, trying to stay as calm as possible, "do yourselves a favor and keep your mouths shut. Just let me get my gear and get the hell out of here."

"Guess we won't be seeing you tomorrow, will we?" blathered Nix, getting up into Mac's face and signaling that his presence wasn't wanted at the precinct tailgater. "What's the matter, Mac? Can't you find a real girl to go out with? By the way, Melanie said she saw you out with that tranny last week. You like sucking cocks and having dicks shoved up your ass, don't you, big fella?"

Mac balled his right hand into a fist and let fly with a cross into Nix's jaw. Soon the two were wrestling and punching each other on the floor.

"What's the matter with you guys?" shouted Mayes, racing in to break up the fight. "Let him get his stuff and get out of here. Leave him alone."

Mac dusted himself off, emptied his locker, and left without saying a word. Mayes followed him outside to The Sub.

"Thanks for helping me out there, partner," said Mac. "Or at least you were my partner until a half hour ago."

"I warned you, Mac. You know those guys don't take to kindly to homosexuals, especially when they think they're working next to one."

"I'm not gay!"

"Mac, I don't know, and I don't care. What I do know is that you've lost my trust, and right now your reputation is lower than whale shit. I told you I had to report your behavior to Stone if we arrested Sheyla, and you left me no choice. I'm sorry, Mac. I wish there was something I could do."

"There is something you can do," pleaded Mac. "Help me find the real killer. We both know deep in our guts it's not Sheyla Samonte. It has to be someone else. Please Mayes, will you help me?"

"Sorry, Mac. No can do. I'm already in enough hot water with Stone over not reporting you earlier. If he ever caught wind that I was helping you, he'd fire me on the spot. I've got my wife and kids to think about. I'm sorry, Mac, but you're on your own. You screwed up."

Of course he did, thought Mac. As far as he was concerned, he had failed as a detective. Again.

༄

MAC CLIMBED THE STAIRS in search of his mother. He expected to find her in the dining room office, tabulating her profits from Wall Street's financial bloodletting. Instead the room was silent, the computer turned off, and the chart books stacked under a Lehman Brothers coffee mug. Then he remembered where she'd often go on a sunny September day.

He opened the door to the roof deck. Sitting cross-legged on a lounge chair was Victoria Parker. She had a glass of chardonnay in one hand, a book in the other, sunbathing a body that lied about her age.

"I saw the press conference on TV. Congratulations, Mackey. You arrested Paul Osher's mistress. It's time to celebrate!"

Mac sat down on a thick wooden railing surrounding the roof. He took a look over the edge and noticed The Sub parked in the driveway six stories below. For a moment he wondered if it would cushion his fall. "Mom, I've got good news and bad news. Which do you want first?"

"You know I always want to hear the bad news first. Lay it on me."

"I got suspended from my job."

"Are you kidding? What's the good news?"

"I'll have to get back to you on that." Mac picked up her bottle of wine and took a healthy chug. "There is no doubt in my mind that Sheyla Samonte is innocent. The evidence we have on her is paper-thin. The pieces of the puzzle don't fit, and an arrest wasn't warranted. Stone caved in to media and political pressure and wanted someone, anyone, taken into custody."

"Oh my goodness. Are you serious?"

"Of course I am. And here's the best part. Mayes and I couldn't even agree on whom we should arrest. He was convinced that Sheyla Samonte was our most likely suspect, so we took her in. I told Stone we had the wrong person behind bars."

"Is that why he suspended you, because you and Mayes disagreed?"

Mac took another hit of chilled white wine. "I wish that was the reason."

"Then why, for heaven's sake?"

"Because I'm having an affair with our murder suspect."

❧

MAC AND HIS MOTHER spent the rest of the afternoon discussing the loss of both his job and his lover. Victoria Parker listened and sympathized with her distraught son, but it was also Saturday night, and she wasn't going to let the shock of Mac's suspension get in the way of her having a good time. She was never fond of pity parties anyway. Victoria Parker had stared down adversity in her life by solving her own problems, and she expected her son to do the same.

The Cougar Committee was going salsa dancing, and Victoria Parker felt chic and stylish in a Joseph Domingo cocktail dress with a matching pair of Louboutins she bought earlier that day at Barneys. Wall Street had finished the week in the red, and she wanted to celebrate by finishing her week in purple.

Mac lamented the temporary loss of his paycheck by picking at a pizza and helping himself to a half-empty bottle of pinot noir, which he placed next to an already-empty bottle of merlot. For all the 'friends' he had in the department, he had not received one single call of support. Meanwhile, the pit in his stomach returned after a weeklong hiatus, only this time it had nothing to do with a soon-to-be-ex-wife investment banker, and everything to do with his girlfriend sitting in jail. He agonized over whether or not he should have fought harder for Sheyla and stood up to the pressure Stone had been putting on them. As a boyfriend, he had failed there also.

"Mackey, don't be so hard on yourself," suggested Victoria Parker. "I'm on your side. Nobody has better instincts than you. Stone's a politician. He's kissed more ass than my gay hairdresser. You did cross the line with Sheyla, though, and for that you deserve forty lashes. As for your friends from the precinct, if they're not calling you because you've been with a trans woman, then you might as well tell those jerks to lose your number."

"You're right, Mom. I know you're right, but what am I going to do about Sheyla? Once she's released, how is she ever going to trust me again? I can't explain it, Mom. Something about her made me forget what I was doing and use poor judgment. I acted like a fool."

"Just like every other man who's ever fallen in love," said a wise woman in a gorgeous dress who had broken her fair share of hearts. Victoria Parker helped herself to a glass of pinot noir and sat across the table from her dejected son.

"Mackey, I thought about this while I was getting ready. You once said Sheyla isn't a normal girl. Well, you're wrong. She's as normal as you or me. Think about it. After you told me this afternoon how the case unfolded, I started seeing the girls from *Pearls of Asia* in the roles they fill: Diamond is the Diva; Nadia is the Working Girl; Ashley is The Prodigy; Reyna is the Godmother; and Sheyla is the Beauty Queen. Guess what, Mackey? I just described all the men who worked at my old brokerage firm. You have to forget what's 'normal,' and understand that what happens at *Pearls of Asia* also happens at places like Apple or Google. They're people, Mackey, just like everyone else. They have hopes and dreams they want to pursue, along with bills to pay and families to support. And yes, handsome men like you fall in love with beautiful women like Sheyla. So I've got one question to ask you before I leave here and dance this fabulous fifty-something ass off."

"What's that?"

"What are you willing to do to win your life back?"

CHAPTER TWENTY

Sunday, September 21, 2008 - 6:00 am

*"Sheyla Samonte may not have been the only 'gender illusionist'
bedded by Paul Osher. Another waitress from 'Pearls of Asia,'
who wished to remain anonymous, claimed she once had a year
long affair with the San Francisco tycoon."*

Vanity Fair

MAC'S PHONE JOLTED HIM out of his Napa-induced
coma. The clock on the wall said it was six o'clock in
the morning, but his head begged to differ. At least his
body was clean, thanks to an hour-long midnight shower in the
dark.

"Mac?" asked the female voice on the other end.

"Who is this?"

"It's Reyna. Reyna Cruz, from *Pearls of Asia*. Sheyla gave me
your number. I'm sorry if I woke you up."

Mac didn't mind, but his head did. "It's okay, Reyna. Just don't
talk so loud. What can I do for you?"

"I spoke to Sheyla this morning. She called me right as my
Latin boyfriend was rolling me over to give me 'room service.' Can

you believe the timing of that bitch? Anyway, she told me what you said to her last night. What did you mean when you asked her to trust you?"

Mac hoped sitting up would clear the fog from his head. It didn't. "Because I don't believe Sheyla murdered Michelle Osher. I never have. I'm going to find the real killer and get her out of jail."

Mac stood up and started walking around his room. All it did was remind him of his headache, which at that moment was registering 9.7 on the Richter scale. "The Chief of Police, the Governor, the Mayor, they all wanted us to make an arrest, so we had to peg the murder on someone. Before last night the only evidence we had pointing to Sheyla was that she lacked an alibi and was left handed. Once we found the knife in her purse, it was all over. We had to take her into custody."

"Well..." teased Reyna, sounding surprisingly upbeat, "now that my boyfriend has given me a proper wake up call, why don't you come over to my place. I think I can help you."

Twenty minutes later, The Sub was anchored outside Reyna's house.

∞

"WOW, SHEYLA WAS RIGHT," observed Reyna after sliding into The Sub's passenger seat. "You can have an orgy in this thing. Listen Mac, let's first go to Diamond's apartment. I tried calling her but she doesn't answer. It's really strange. She holds onto her cell phone like a baby holds onto a pacifier."

Reyna pulled out a neatly typed piece of paper. "I've dummied up this petition to give trans people more rights in the workplace. We'll ask Diamond and Ashley to sign it and see which hand they use. If that kind of evidence can work against Sheyla, it can work against anyone else, can't it?"

"No reason why it can't," answered Mac. He looked over at Reyna and noticed the scar over her left eye, which for this morning at least was not covered up by makeup. "Do you mind if I ask how you got that?"

"I usually like to sleep with someone before I tell them, but in your case I'll make an exception. I got it the night I told my father I wanted to transition. He's a general in the Philippine Army, and let's just say he didn't take the news very well. My last memory of him is of his right fist driving into my face. I woke up the next day in a hospital bed. His regiment ring left me with a dozen stitches above my eye. I called my brother, who packed a suitcase for me. Later that day I bought a plane ticket to the United States. I haven't seen my family since."

"I'm sorry," said Mac, shaking his head. "Fathers can be pretty awful sometimes."

Mac docked The Sub at the corner of Fifth and Harrison, across from an all-night donut shop frequented by both cops and crack dealers. Diamond lived in a first floor apartment, and the bars on the windows reminded passersby that this neighborhood wasn't filled with soccer moms and minivans. Mac knocked on the door several times, and then pounded on it with his fist. No answer. Mac wiped away some of the grime between the bars and was able to see into the dim interior of the room. He saw something on the floor and knew right away that Diamond wasn't about to let them in on her own.

"I think that's blood."

Mac kicked in the door, and he and Reyna rushed inside. Lying on top of a neatly made bed, looking as though she was sleeping peacefully, was Diamond. Her arms were stretched out; each wrist had a river of blood streaming from it. On the bedside table was a bloody Balisong knife, just like the one they found in Sheyla's purse.

"Oh no," cried Reyna. "Please Lord, I can't believe she did this to herself!"

Mac pressed his fingers against her neck but couldn't find a pulse. Her body was stone cold. "It's too late. She's gone."

Next to the switchblade was a note, written in an elegant script. It said, "Goodbye, you bitches and whores. My body is tired and worn out, but my beauty still remains. I know only pain and sickness lie ahead for me. Always remember Diamond, because no one shined brighter than me."

Mac snapped open his phone and called 911. The operator put him through to police headquarters. He hoped they didn't know he was suspended. "Dispatch. This is Inspector Fleet. We have an 11-44 dead body. No ambulance needed."

"10-4, Inspector Fleet. We're on it."

Mac hung up and knelt down to console Reyna. After she stopped crying, Mac asked her what the note meant.

"I guess the rumors I heard about her were true. She and another girl, Anna, drove down to Mexico a few days ago to get their hips pumped with silicone. After they got back to San Francisco, Anna started complaining that she was having difficulty breathing and went to the emergency room. She died last night, and the rumor around the trans community is that she had been pumped with industrial-grade silicone some Mexican 'doctor' purchased from a furniture manufacturer. Diamond got pumped with the same stuff, and maybe she thought she was next. She was already sick, although she didn't tell anyone but me. Several years ago Diamond's best friend died from an overdose of hormones that destroyed her liver. She was abusing hormones with her as well, but it just took longer to affect her. Diamond needed a new liver, but because she didn't have health insurance, her name was on the bottom of the donor list. Despite the risks, she still kept taking hormones. That's how much it meant for her to be 'flawless.' I guess she wanted to be remembered that way."

The police and medical examiner arrived, and Mac and Reyna told them what they found. Two hours later, the body was removed on a gurney and the police cleared out, taking the note and knife with them. It was time to make their second stop of the day.

Reyna gave Mac directions to Ashley's temporary hotel room in the Tenderloin. While Mac drove, Reyna stared out the window. "You know what, Mac?" she said after riding along in silence. "They say suicide is the ultimate form of self-absorption, and nobody spent more time thinking about herself than Diamond. I guess I shouldn't be surprised."

༄

MAC PULLED UP IN front of the Roosevelt Hotel. There was a small crowd of sleazy panhandlers huddled out front. Mac couldn't tell if they lived on the street or in the hotel, which was notorious for its filth and squalor.

Reyna led Mac up the stairs. They were soon standing in front of room 408, and Reyna knocked on the door while Mac hid a couple doors down the hallway. Ashley came to the door.

"Reyna! What a surprise," she said, sounding pleased. "What are you doing here?"

"Strictly business, girl. I've been asked by the Mayor's office to get some signatures for an initiative supporting transgender rights in the workplace, so I'm asking everyone I know for help. I realize you're new in town, and I thought you'd want to do all you can. Do you mind signing my petition?"

"I'd be happy to. I love the fact you're so involved, Reyna. I don't know where the trans community would be without someone like you to lead them. You're the best."

Ashley signed the paper. After handing it back, Reyna said in a loud voice, "Ashley, I didn't know you were left-handed."

Mac bolted down the hallway and slammed opened the door, knocking Ashley to the ground. From a far corner of the room, a tiny dog ran out from under the bed, barking furiously and jumping up and down at Mac's feet. The little creature was small enough to fit in his coat pocket. Mac picked up the dog and, sure enough, there was a tiny diamond stud in her right ear. It was Misha, Michelle Osher's missing Teacup Yorkie.

The wind knocked out of her, Ashley got back up and reached into her nearby purse and pulled out the Balisong switchblade Reyna had given her two weeks before on her first night at *Pearls of Asia*. Ashley tried to lunge at him, but not before Reyna tackled her and forced her to the ground, knocking the knife away. Mac picked up the knife and put it in his pocket. Reyna sat on top of Ashley while Mac made a call.

"Dispatch. This is Inspector Fleet calling. Yes, second time today, I know. Listen, I need you to send a car over for an arrest."

༄

LATER THAT DAY, THE reinstated Inspector Mac Fleet was at his desk playing with his Rubik's Cube. After Jim Grisham arrived, Ashley was paraded in front of a mirrored window along with four prostitutes the vice squad had arrested the night before. Grisham took less than two seconds to identify Ashley as the "tall blonde" who had come to his party. "What a shame," lamented Grisham. "I thought she was a model when I first met her. Maybe she should have taken that guy up on his offer to fly her to Dubai."

Ashley was led into the interrogation room, where she began shaking and crying hysterically. The thought of spending the rest of her life in prison terrified her. Left alone in the room, she screamed and pleaded to see Paul Osher, saying that he would make things right. Thirty minutes later, her sobs had settled to shudders.

"Let's get her statement," Mac said to Mayes, peering into the interrogation room through a one-way mirror. Then he remembered how Sheyla had once described Ashley. "Care to join me in the shark tank?"

Ashley spent the next hour telling them her story. She had become friends with Nadia over the Internet while she was still living in Los Angeles. Nadia had arranged for Paul Osher to meet Ashley during one of his periodic visits. He courted her by buying her groceries and sending her flowers, and she immediately became infatuated with him. Over time, Ashley believed Osher's false declarations of his undying love and promises to leave his wife. Growing impatient, she decided the best course of action was to move to San Francisco. Two weeks ago, Ashley surprised Nadia by showing up unannounced at her home, and Nadia got her the audition at *Pearls of Asia*. She was hired right away, and on her first night at work Reyna welcomed Ashley by giving her a Balisong switchblade.

Perhaps because she was now physically closer to him that he wanted her to be, Osher stopped returning Ashley's calls and ignored her text messages. This only made Ashley more intent on getting her way. She believed she was the one for Paul Osher, and she resolved to do whatever it took to have him all to herself.

On the night of the murder, Nadia had asked Ashley to come with her to Jim Grisham's shindig. Nadia had been hired to entertain one of her customers at the party, and he asked Nadia if she could bring along a date for one of his friends.

"The guy who wanted to take me to Dubai told me Michelle Osher lived upstairs, so after I blew him off I went upstairs and knocked on her door. The great Michelle Osher herself answered the door, so I pretended to be a fan of hers and asked if she could give me an autograph. She said she would and invited me in. We talked for a few minutes, and I kept looking around the apartment, thinking how wonderful it would be to live there, to be Mrs. Paul Osher. She was the only person standing between my dream and me. Paul always told me that you had to take risks when you really wanted something. I knew what I had to do.

"She was looking for a pen, so I followed her into the kitchen. I don't know what came over me, but I started to get angry. This woman had everything I wanted. I kept getting madder and madder. So when she had her back turned to me, my instincts from the training I received in the Army kicked in. I pulled out my switchblade, grabbed her around the shoulders and slashed her throat like there was no tomorrow. It all happened to quickly; it was over in the blink of an eye. She fell to the floor, and blood started pouring out of her neck. I felt so relieved. I had done it. Soon, Paul Osher would be mine.

"Then this cute little dog came running out, barking and jumping and sniffing around my shoes. I had always wanted a dog, especially a Teacup Yorkie, but never in my wildest dreams could I afford one. She was darling, and the earring was precious. So I picked her up, hid her under my jacket, and walked out of the building."

Mac looked up from his note taking. "So are you telling us you killed Michelle Osher because you fell in love with her husband?"

"Yes. I love him, and I know he loves me."

Mac shook his head and shrugged his shoulders. "Of course he does."

A knock came from the one-way mirror. Mayes went outside the room and spoke to Captain Longley, who was watching from the other side. Longley told Mayes that Paul Osher had arrived.

"Do us a favor, Captain. Tell Mr. Arrogance he's going to have to wait for us for a change."

Mac waited for his partner to rejoin him before continuing the interrogation. "Ashley, when did you learn that Paul Osher was also seeing Sheyla Samonte?"

Ashley's face turned red. "I only found out when you came to *Pearls of Asia* the other night and told me. I guess I hadn't been there long enough for the girls to let me in on all their dirty little secrets. I felt betrayed by Paul, but I still loved him. It just meant I had one more job to do."

"And what was that?" asked Mac.

"Eliminate Sheyla."

❧

MAC AND MAYES HAD just a few questions for Paul Osher. He was wearing khaki shorts, a green polo shirt, and a green short-sleeved golf sweater. He looked more like a papaya than a golfer. "I was just walking off the eighteenth green at Lake Merced when Stone called. He said you caught the real killer. Claims she loved me and that she killed Michelle just to be closer to me. What a stupid bitch. I hardly knew the girl."

Mac would have none of it. "Why should we believe anything you say, Mr. Osher? You lied to us about your affairs and you lied to us about the checks you wrote to Nadia. Even your marriage was a lie. If we wanted to, we could run you in for obstruction of justice."

"Go ahead and try," Osher said with a smirk. "You guys can't touch me. Stone would never let that happen."

Mac knew Osher was right. "I have just one more question, Mr. Osher. How do you feel now that you've lost the three most important woman in your life?"

"I feel pretty good, actually. Sheyla often told me I was the most desired man in this town, and that all of her girlfriends wanted to go out with me. I'm sure they'll be lining up outside my door in no time. There'll be so many, I may have to ask them to take a number."

Despite overwhelming odds, Mac managed to keep his mouth shut.

∾

THE FOG WAS ROLLING in, and the breeze began to pick up around the plaza in front of the San Francisco County jail. It was early in the evening, and the lights from the nearby skyscrapers started to twinkle.

Sheyla Samonte was released on a $5,000 bail on charges related to possessing the illegal Balisong switchblade. As she tried to hail a cab, a tall, lanky, handsome man with salt and pepper hair approached her carrying a dozen red roses. He gave her a hug and a kiss, and then took by her by the hand and escorted her to a Horizon Blue 1960 Chevrolet Kingswood Estate Cruiser.

"Who put up your bail?" asked Mac.

"Some woman named Victoria Parker. Do you know who she is?"

"Of course I do."

CHAPTER TWENTY-ONE

One Year Later

THE GORGEOUS LADIES STANDING behind the cosmetic counters at Macy's do more than sell bottles of paint and compacts of powder. They sell dreams. Armed with pencils and brushes, makeup consultants are gifted magicians adept at turning ducks into swans. They are the Mistresses of the Makeover.

It was 5:45 on a Sunday afternoon, and Sheyla was ringing up yet another fat sale. She had spent an hour convincing an overweight, middle-aged woman that by purchasing almost a thousand dollars worth of skin-care crèmes, lotions, lipsticks and eye shadows she could be mistaken for Halle Barry. Sheyla Samonte wasn't just good at making a sale; she was outstanding. She could sell sidewalk space to the homeless.

The clock on the wall said the store would be closing in fifteen minutes, while Sheyla's feet said it had been another long weekend. She appreciated the benefits of returning to work at Macy's, but they didn't come close to the benefits she received from Paul Osher. A modest studio in North Beach replaced the fancy hi-rise in South Beach, and the Mercedes Benz was replaced with a Muni bus pass. Life for Sheyla had seen many forks in the road, none more dramatic than the day her mug shot was flashed across the globe. The charges against her may have been dropped, but they were far from forgotten. At this point in her life, there were only two things she could count on: MAC cosmetics, and Mac Fleet.

Sheyla lingered on the corner of Post and Stockton, listening to the bells of the nearby Powell Street cable cars while waiting for Mac to pick her up. She jokingly called the hundred yard stroll from Macy's Geary Street storefront through San Francisco's historic Union Square "The Walk of Shame." She had to traipse past many of her old haunts, including the boutiques of Chanel, Dior, and Gucci, where her credit cards made such an impression the sales clerks knew her by name.

Mac pulled up in The Sub and greeted his girlfriend with a kiss. "Let's grab something to eat," he said. "I'm in the mood for sushi."

"I'm in the mood for a foot rub," complained Sheyla, exhausted after spending the entire weekend on her feet. A Saturday night stint at *Pearls of Asia* had been sandwiched between her regular weekend shifts at Macy's. "I'm beat."

"C'mon, babe. Nothing a couple of drinks and some raw fish won't take care of."

Ten minutes later, they were seated at the dimly lit but sexy bar at Ozumo's, located near the Embarcadero, where a sexy Vietnamese bartender with a mysterious dragon tattoo that ran from her shoulder up to her neck was mixing their favorite cocktail, a "geisha martini." Sheyla said the lychee fruit in the bottom of the glass reminded her of growing up in Cebu. Mac said the drink's twenty-dollar price tag reminded him why he kept working.

"How was work today?" inquired Mac.

"It was okay. Today's drama was limited to where we should have lunch. The girls lobbied for Jollibee, but I just wanted to curl up somewhere and eat in private. They all got glammed up last night and went out to that nightclub, Ruby Skye. The last thing I wanted to do was listen to a bunch of gaggling girls trying to out-brag each other about how every hot looking guy at the club was staring at them, or how so-and-so was about to hook up with Mr. Six Pack Abs until she got clocked. It's always the same old story with them. I just wasn't in the mood to hear their competitive bullshit."

Mac picked away at a bowl of hot edamame, listening to Sheyla with half an ear, while the bulk of his attention was focused on the big screen television broadcasting the hard-hitting Sunday night football game between the Pittsburgh Steelers and Baltimore Ravens. "Keep venting, babe. That's what I'm here for."

"I'm just so tired, Mackey. Two jobs, bills, rent, the girls. I'm just wiped out. I'm beginning to wonder if it's worth it. I live in a crummy little studio, but if I want a bigger place I have to make more money. To make more money, I have to go to school. In order to pay for school, I need more time. I'm frustrated, Mackey. I feel like I'm trapped."

Sheyla was venting like a pot of boiling tea. Miss Vietnamese Bartender asked if they wanted another round, and Mac nodded his head.

"I hear you, sweetheart. It's a dog-eat-dog world out there, and you've got Alpo for underwear." Mac took his eyes off the TV screen to scan the menu. "How about a spider roll?"

Sheyla loved to eat, but the last thing on her mind right now was soft shell crab and avocado. "Hey, are you listening to me? I feel like my life is stuck in the mud. What am I working toward? What do I have to look forward to? I'm starting to freak out here."

"The 49ers are playing the Raiders tomorrow night on Monday Night Football," replied Mac, whose attention was focused more on football and sashimi than Sheyla. "We can look forward to that."

"Dammit, Mac!" shouted Sheyla, slamming her glass down on the bar. "Will you be serious for a moment? This involves us, too. I've been thinking about it for a long time. Where are we going as a couple? We're best friends, and we always have fun when we're together, but what about the future? I love you Mac, and I know you love me too, but the are no goals, no commitment."

"What's the matter with you?" asked Mac. The casual Sunday night dinner he had hoped for had just turned into a scrum. Mac thought he'd been the model boyfriend, calling and texting her often, bringing her flowers, and massaging her aching feet. He had even bought language tapes from Rosetta Stone to learn Tagalog, though the box was still unopened. "Did you take a hormone shot this morning?"

"Look at us, Mac. Whenever we go out, it's always just you and me, or we double date with Reyna and her boyfriend. Whenever we spend the night together, we always stay at my place. You talk about Mayes all the time, yet the only time I met him was when he arrested me. Come to think of it, I've never met any of your friends. What's the deal, Mac? Are you trying to hide me? Are you ashamed to be seen with me?"

Mac held up his empty martini glass and waved it at Miss Vietnamese Bartender. He wasn't going in to battle unarmed. "First of all Sheyla, the reason we stay at your place is because I'm still living with my mother. As for meeting Mayes and my friends, I rarely see them outside of work as it is. But if it will make you happy I'll try to set something up."

Sheyla didn't want to hear Mac's excuses. In fact, she didn't want to hear anything from him at all. "I'm tired of the same old story, Mac. I've been hearing empty promises from guys all my life. That's why I don't trust men. I always make them a priority, yet they always treat me like an option. Deep down Mac, you're afraid. Afraid to tell the world you love me. Afraid to admit that you're in love with a transsexual woman."

Mac looked at his glass and began stabbing a toothpick at the lychee fruit floating at the bottom. The last thing he expected to have tonight was an argument with his girlfriend. All he wanted to do was relax, have a few drinks and watch the game. Sheyla had turned it into a couple's counseling session. "What do you want me to do?" he asked.

"I want you to fight for us, dammit! I want you to believe in us, to believe in our love. Real love means not being afraid, of having the strength to overcome adversity, of wanting someone so bad you'll do whatever it takes to have that person complete your life. I love you, Mackey. I love you so much it hurts. But while you say and do all the right things, you haven't shown me that you're willing to love me completely, that you're willing to risk everything that's important to you just so long as I'm in your life. Remember our first date at Fleur de Lys? You asked me that night what I wanted, and I told you I wanted a love story. Well it's my turn to ask you that question, Mackey. What do you want?"

The Raven's defense had just recovered a Steelers fumble, but Mac wasn't paying attention. Marvin Gaye was wafting over the bar's sound system, but Mac couldn't hear him either. Sheyla had just asked him a question, a question he had asked himself many times during the past twelve months. A question he pondered while spending hours alone in a dark shower, searching for an answer he still hadn't found.

"I don't know."

"That's what I thought you'd say." Sheyla grabbed her purse. She wasn't in the mood to stick around for appetizers. She held out her hand. "Give me back my keys."

"What?"

"You heard me. Give me back my apartment keys. I don't want to see you for a while. I need some time alone. I want to figure out what I'm going to do with the rest of my life."

Mac was speechless. He reached into his pocket and pulled out his key ring. Removing the key to her apartment was like removing a piece of his heart. He placed it in her hand, and then looked at her and saw a single tear trickling down her cheek.

As she headed out the door to catch a cab home, she turned and said to him, "I love you, Mac Fleet, but I'm tired of being braver than the man I love."

Miss Vietnamese Bartender brought over the spider roll. "You screwed up, Mister. Big time."

"Of course I did."

࿐

VICTORIA PARKER HAD PULLED off the financial equivalent of the triple play. Hurricane Lehman Brothers had grown into a Category Five, and she shorted the storm all the way down until the Dow Jones Industrial Average reached 7,000. Soon every market muppet on CNBC was calling for The Great Depression Part II, and she knew what hand to play next: buy here, buy now, and buy often. With the stock market in the midst of the Mother of all Rallies, Victoria Parker saw an opportunity to trade up from her townhouse in Noe Valley for a classic Victorian mansion in tony Pacific Heights. One night an inebriated hedge fund manager, upside down on both his mortgage and his marriage, tried to pick her up at a Marina restaurant appropriately named The Tipsy Pig. She agreed to sleep with him, but only if he'd hit the discount bid she made on his house. By the time the stock market opened the next morning, Victoria Parker was long stocks, a hangover, and a five-thousand-square foot Pacific Heights home located at the corner of Broadway and Baker.

Mac arrived home depressed and found the Cougar Committee in the living room, taking a roll call of chardonnays while discussing the pros and cons of dating men who were born after the Disco Era. Mac grabbed a bottle of Sonoma Anything and headed for the back patio.

Victoria Parker joined her heartbroken son for a glass of wine, and each sat on a reclining lounge chair out on the expansive deck, admiring a spectacular nighttime view of The Palace of Fine Arts. "I guess you won't be staying in North Beach tonight," she said.

"Not tonight, or any other night for that matter." Mac told his mother what happened, how a pleasant Sunday evening turned on a dime into disaster. "I don't understand it, Mom. Sheyla just got pissed, complaining that she's never met Mayes or any of my friends. The last thing she said to me was that she was tired of loving a man who 'wasn't as brave as she was.' I have no idea what she's talking about."

"I know exactly what she's talking about. Fill up your wine glass, Mackey. I'm going to tell you a story."

Victoria Parker kicked off her Manolo Blahniks and took a sip of her wine. "A few months after your father left us for a stripper named Tiffany Dimwit, he came back home and said he wanted for us to get back together. I agreed, only to have him leave me again because Tiffany lost her job and was going through a 'tough time.' I said I understood and foolishly let this go on for a while. It got so bad I could set my watch by him. On Monday morning he would come home and say he wanted to spend the rest of his life with me, and by Friday night he'd leave and tell me he had to go see Tiffany because 'she needed his help.' I was stupid, but I loved him too much to let go of him."

The fog was rolling in through the Golden Gate, and a September night in San Francisco can feel as cold as February in Seattle. Mac got up to retrieve a couple of thick cashmere blankets.

"He later gave me one of those bullshit, 'it's me, not you' excuses. That's when I knew it was over. He was too afraid to make a choice. No matter how much I loved him, I could no longer respect him. If he was too much of a coward to take the life and love I laid out for him, then I no longer wanted him in my life."

"That's a great story Mom, but I don't understand what it has to do with Sheyla. It's not like I cheated on her, or disrespected her in any way. I love her, and I think I've done my best to show it."

Victoria Parker emptied the bottle into her glass. "That's where you're wrong, Mackey. You haven't done enough. Sheyla's special, and she's never had a love story. Sure, men have told her they wanted her, but they liked *what* she was, not *who* she was. Sheyla knows you love her, Mackey. She just doesn't trust your love. You say you aren't cheating on her, but in her mind you are. You have another life completely separate from her. She wants a man to be strong, courageous and brave, just like she was during her transition. She wants a man who not only loves her, but is proud to show the world that he wants to share his life with her."

Mac looked at his mom and flashed her a smile. She was right. She was always right.

"Let me ask you a question, Mom. Have I lost her?"

"No, you haven't. Not yet. But I'm going to ask you the same question I asked you last year after you got suspended from your job."

"What's that?"

"What are you willing to do to win her love back?"

෴

II WAS 5:45 IN THE MORNING, and Victoria Parker was at the bottom of the Lyon Street Steps. Only a climb of two hundred and eighty-eight stairs separated her from her mouse pad, where in forty-five minutes she would be playing video poker with the New York Stock Exchange. The best thing about living at the corner of Broadway and Baker wasn't the incredible views of Sausalito and Tiburon, or the free parking space you could find any hour of the day. It was the hundred-yard stroll to the bike paths and hiking trails of The Presidio, the most beautiful city park in the world.

At 5:49 she stepped into her kitchen, out of breath but not out of shape. Mac was already up, and he greeted her like a six-week old puppy. "Mom, I've got an idea, and I need your help."

෴

AT 2:00, DRESSED IN her bike skivvies, Victoria Parker walked into the living room just as Mac was about to hang up with his partner.

"Thanks, Mayes," he said. "I'll see you dark and early tomorrow. Check with the Pamela and see if you can get a babysitter for Thursday night. It's going to be great."

"Are you ready?" she asked.

"I am. Let's rock."

Mac and Mom wheeled their bikes onto Broadway, and seconds later crossed Lyon Street into The Presidio. Gravity led them down to the Golden Gate Bridge, and a tailwind pushed them across the bridge into Marin County. They peddled hard up the Waldo Grade, and then turned east and rode down the hill toward Sausalito. Thirty minutes after leaving their home, Mac and Victoria Parker were locking their bikes in front of a very special store.

Two hours later, they were back home. Victoria Parker turned on CNBC to get ready to trade in Asia when she heard the following news report:

"Mark Ashley entered San Quentin State Prison this morning to begin serving a life sentence for the murder of Michelle Osher. Ashley's attorneys are still fighting for the transsexual killer to be transferred to a women's correctional facility."

"In related news, Paul Osher married Erica Andrews, a Victoria's Secret model introduced to him by California Gov. Arnold Schwarzenegger. Mr. Osher's best man was Jim Grisham, whose wife Sonia disappeared one year ago and remains missing."

"What a shame," she mused.

෩

MAC DROVE OVER TO OZUMO'S to ask Miss Vietnamese Bartender a question.

"That's an incredible tattoo you have. Where did you get it?" Mac wrote down the name and address.

"Are you also thinking of getting a dragon?" she asked.

"No, ma'am. No dragon for me," answered Mac before closing his notebook. "One more question. What are you doing Thursday night?"

෩

ASK ANY OF THE ladies working at *Pearls of Asia* what their favorite part of the night is, and they'll tell you it's the conclusion of the

Blowout Show. After each girl has done a final number, and Reyna has called them out, there were two things they looked forward to, taking off their shoes, and taking home their tips.

Thursday night had finally arrived. Mac sat in The Sub checking his watch every three and a half seconds. He had wrapped and rewrapped the gauze on his right forearm so often he could do it with his eyes closed. His hand had reached into his left pocket so many times he could have been cited for indecent behavior. Mac had been a cop for over ten years, and the acid roiling in his stomach told him this was the biggest stakeout of his life.

His eyes were focused on the Howard Street entrance to *Pearls of Asia*. He was waiting for a signal, a sign, a beacon of hope. A reason for all the scheming, planning, and praying he had done over the past four days. Then, at the stroke of 10:41, sixty seconds later than scheduled, the silhouetted figure of Reyna Cruz stepped outside the door, and she signaled to Mac by waving a wireless microphone.

The starter's pistol had just gone off.

Mac leaped out of The Sub and jaywalked across Howard Street. Wearing a blue blazer, starched white shirt and navy blue pants, he looked like he had just stepped out of the Preppy Handbook. Mac grabbed the microphone and gave Reyna a kiss on the cheek. She gave him a pinch on his ass. "That's for good luck," she said.

The calendar may have said Thursday, but the energy felt more like a Saturday. Standing on the stage were Nadia and the newest 'Pearls of Asia,' Ericka and Vanessa. Down at the far end of the bar, near the Hot Seat and looking like a figurehead at the bow of a ship, stood Sheyla, looking regal in a blue silk one-sleeve dancer's dress.

Mac climbed the staircase and walked to the middle of the runway. It was rare for a man to be onstage at *Pearls of Asia*. It happened about as often as a solar eclipse. The audience went silent, and Sheyla brought her hands to her mouth in a mix of amazement and confusion.

Mac took a moment to look out into the crowd. Seated directly in front of him, along the leather backrest bench, was Victoria Parker, surrounded by members of the Cougar Committee, dressed to remind men that mothers sometimes do eat their young. To his left, at a table near the entrance, sat Mayes and his lovely wife Pamela, holding hands and enjoying a night away from their now three kids. Chantal and Hubert Keller, who brought several magnificent bottles from the Fleur de Lys wine cellar, joined them. To his right were Captain Steve Longley and Chief of Police David Stone, along with their wives, out of uniform, and judging by the number of empty martini glasses, out of their sobriety zone. Behind him at several tables were over two dozen of Mac's friends, including his 49er tailgate buddies. Sitting in the Hot Seat was Mr. Ponytail, flirting with his newest best friend, Miss Vietnamese Bartender.

Mac threw a wink toward Reyna, who was now standing inside the DJ's booth. She flipped a switch, and a six-foot by six-foot projection screen descended from the ceiling. Then she pushed a few buttons, and the lyrics from "The Best" by Tina Turner began to play.

"I call you, when I need you, my heart's on fire..."

Mac took a deep breath and composed himself. "Ladies and Gentlemen, thank you for joining me on this special evening," he said, standing next to the screen and talking over the music. "One year ago, I walked into *Pearls of Asia* for the very first time, and someone told me this place could change my life. I stand before you tonight to admit they were right. Since that moment I first sat down on the Hot Seat, my life hasn't been the same."

"...give me a lifetime of promises and a world of dreams...speak a language of love like you know what it means..."

"I came here looking for clues, for pieces to a puzzle. I found them, but I also found something else. I found symbols of fortitude, determination and guts. The glamorous women standing before you are more than just sexy and fun. They are also profiles in tenacity and steely resolve. The process of transforming yourself into the person you know you are takes more than just time and money. It takes courage, and these ladies have dug down deep into their souls to find the strength and conviction to change their lives."

"...you're simply the best...better than all the rest...better than anyone...anyone I ever met..."

Mac turned to his left and began walking toward Sheyla. She felt nervous and wanted to run, but the end of the bar cornered her. Escape would have required a four-foot jump to the floor, which is not recommended for someone in five-inch heels. Mac no longer looked at the audience, but instead gazed into the smoky brown eyes of a woman he longed to hold.

"...In your heart I see the start of every night and every day...in your eyes, I get lost, I get washed away...just as long as I'm here in your arms I could be in no better place...you're simply the best..."

"Most people come to *Pearls of Asia* for a good meal and a show," he continued. "The last thing I expected to find was love, but I did. I fell in love with a beautiful woman, who is special in so many ways. I thought I knew how to love her, but it turns out I didn't have a clue. To win her love, to achieve the life I want for us, I needed to tell the world that not only do I love her for her beauty, but for her soul as well...I, too, needed to find the courage to transition."

"...Each time you leave me I start losing control...you're walking away with my heart and my soul...I can feel you even when I'm alone...oh, baby, don't let go..."

As a soulful saxophone welcomed the instrumental portion of the song, images began to flash on the projection screen. First was a photo of Mac and Sheyla, taken at the Ferry Plaza farmers market, where they were buying special dinner groceries to celebrate their one-month anniversary. Then a second photo, taken at their two-month anniversary, of Mac feeding Sheyla a spoonful of their banana split. These were followed by a succession of pictures taken during the year they had shared together; Sheyla brewing morning coffee outside their tent in Yosemite Valley; the two of them on bicycles, posing in front of The Lone Cypress tree near Carmel; Mac and Sheyla enjoying beers at a 49er football game; the two taking a sunset walk on a deserted beach in Big Sur, holding hands. The last photo was taken recently at their one-year anniversary, celebrated over a three-day weekend at a romantic bed and breakfast in Wine Country, with Mac's eyes glistening after Sheyla replaced his Timex with a brand new Burberry watch.

"...Oh, you're the best...better than all the rest...better than anyone...anyone I ever met..."

Sheyla's lower lip began to quiver. Mac started unwinding the gauze on his right forearm. "A wise woman once told me that to become a butterfly, you must be willing to give up being a caterpillar." He pulled back the bandage, revealing a tattoo of a butterfly, with a creative design of "SS," Sheyla's intitials, drawn into its opened wings.

"...I'm stuck on your heart...I hang on every word you say...Oh, tear us apart, no,no...baby, I would rather be dead...OH, YOU'RE THE BEST!"

Sheyla's face dissolved into a torrent of tears. She tried to say something, but Mac wasn't done. He reached into his left pocket and pulled out a handkerchief. He unfolded it and revealed the efforts of the bike ride to Sausalito: a spectacular two-carat diamond ring. He got down on one knee, took her hand in his, and gazed into her eyes.

"Sheyla, will you marry me?"

Managing to speak through the tears, with the room as silent as a tomb, the velvety voice, the one Mac fell in love with only one year ago, gave him the answer he longed to hear. "Yes...yes...Yes Mac Fleet, I will marry you." Sheyla kissed and hugged him before throwing her arms around him and burying her head deep into his shoulder, sobbing.

As they walked off the stage to a standing ovation, Sheyla stared at the dazzling diamond shining from the ring finger of her left hand.

"Mackey, you really do love me, don't you?"

"Of course I do."

11750152R0014

Made in the USA
Lexington, KY
28 October 2011